D1094243

# The Man

## or the

# MONSTER

Qureshi, Aamna, 1999- author.
Man or the monster

2022
33305254902863
ca      08/25/22

ESHI

# The MAN
## or the
# MONSTER

The
Marghazar
Trials

CamCat
Books

CamCat Publishing, LLC
Brentwood, Tennessee 37027
camcatpublishing.com

Hardcover ISBN 9780744305579
Paperback ISBN 9780744305494
Large-Print Paperback ISBN 9780744305661
eBook ISBN 9780744305500
Audiobook ISBN 9780744305609

Library of Congress Control Number: 2022930771

Book and cover design by Maryann Appel

5   3   1   2   4

For Mimi and Papa,
My beloved grandparents.

# THE TRIAL

Durkhanai's gaze met Asfandyar's as he turned to look at her one last time.

There was nothing—no one—in the world but them. In that moment, she saw the unmasked love in his eyes.

She knew the same love was mirrored in hers.

Then he moved across the empty space, toward a door. The door on the right.

Her heart seized, knowing the fate she had ordered him to.

He took one step forward, then another, and the crowd held their breaths, the arena entirely silent in agonizing anticipation.

Asfandyar lifted a hand and gestured to the door. The final decision had been made.

From above, someone worked the mechanism to open the wooden doors.

The heavy lock unlatched, echoing in the silent morning. Slowly, the doors opened to reveal a long, dark tunnel.

Durkhanai curled her hands into fists in her blood-red gharara, trying to stay firm on the fate she had chosen for him, trying not to regret.

From deep within the tunnel, movement could be heard. Across the arena, some people stood from their seats, craning their necks to preemptively catch a glimpse of what would come out.

Durkhanai could see Asfandyar's shoulders were shaking, his hands tight fists at his sides. But he did not move. He stood entirely still, awaiting his fate. His chest rose and fell with short breaths, matching the rhythm of Durkhanai's too-fast heartbeat.

A slanted shadow came into view at the edge of the tunnel, right before the doors, and from the darkness, a pair of eyes shone in the light.

A lion burst forth.

The crowd released a collective gasp. The verdict was in.

Guilty.

There was no time, and all the time in the world. Durkhanai saw the shock in Asfandyar's face.

The lion roared, it's guttural cry rattling every bone in her body. Asfandyar was thrown to the ground. Durkhanai jumped to her feet, her heart seizing.

*No, no, no!*

She couldn't tear her gaze away from Asfandyar. She watched as he rolled out from under the lion, impossibly quick and agile, and Durkhanai knew if anyone could beat the lion, it was Asfi. He had to beat it, he had to.

Or she had sent him to his death.

The instant the door had opened to reveal the lion, Durkhanai understood her mistake: She would rather have him live with another than watch him be torn to shreds.

But it was too late, she had unleashed the lion upon him. But he would be all right, she knew it deep in her bones, he would be all right.

He was the great love of her life, he would be all right. *Please*. He *had* to be all right.

Asfandyar ran from the lion, getting ahead for an instant before the lion leapt. It grabbed him by the torso, claws sinking in deep. Asfandyar's face contorted with pain, and Durkhanai squeezed her hands into fists to stop from crying out as he kicked the lion's face, rolling out of its grip.

But he was growing weak, she could tell, and the lion was too quick. Asfandyar was no match for the lion, after all, and a moment later, the lion sunk its teeth straight into Asfandyar's heart. He cried out in pain, and Durkhanai screamed.

"*No!*"

A thousand faces whipped from the spectacle to stare at her, their faces frozen and stoic. She was making a scene, she was forgetting her place, but she did not care.

"Somebody help him!" she cried, looking at her guards. They would not meet her gaze. "Please! Agha-Jaan, please, stop this," she begged, falling at his feet. He would not look at her.

An iron grip grabbed her arm, pulling her to her feet. Durkhanai looked up to see Dhadi, pushing her back into her chair.

"Sambhallo apne aap ko," she said. "This is no way for a princess to behave."

Durkhanai threw her grandmother's arm off of her, as if about to stand. She would go down there herself, she would . . .

"Janaan," Agha-Jaan said. "Sit."

And she did. She obeyed, locked in place.

In the arena, Asfandyar was dying a slow, painful death, the lion chewing on his leg. A sob rose in Durkhanai's throat, and she looked away. The reprieve lasted only a moment for a hand steered her jaw back to face the arena, its grip lethal.

"Look," the Badshah said. "*Look.*"

The light was leaving Asfandyar's eyes.

"No, *no*," Durkhanai struggled, but the Badshah kept her in place.

"Yes," he said. "See what you have done. This is what happens when you are not careful."

The lion jumped, its paw swiping across Asfandyar's throat. Durkhanai's hand flew to her own neck as blood gushed from Asfandyar's skin. His face was contorted with pain, his eyes rolling back, and she could do nothing but watch.

He tried to run one last time. Her heart soared with futile hope.

But with a final, deafening roar, the lion lunged, suspended in air for a moment, then crashing down onto Asfandyar. They were a blur of limbs and fur; Asfandyar was out of her sight for an instant. Then the lion shifted, and she saw him.

Asfandyar was looking straight at her, but his infinite eyes were empty. For a moment, she did not understand, and then she saw: His head was removed from his body.

He was dead.

Grief cleaved through her, and she swayed. This time, there was no one holding her upright, and she fell back onto her throne, the metal cold beneath her fingertips. She felt everything all at once: the urge to scream; the need to vomit; the desire to sob.

She felt it all so fiercely that somehow none of these actions occurred. She was frozen in place, shocked. The only sign that this was real was her frenzied heart beating against her chest.

The lion did not stop.

Still frozen, Durkhanai watched everything in perfect detail. The lion gnawed on Asfandyar's arm, the same arm that held her so gently mere hours ago. His eyes remained open, the antithesis of the amusement and warmth she had always sought in them. He was surrounded by blood, his body mangled, flesh torn.

Bile rose in Durkhanai's throat.

The people began to leave, the spectacle over, but Durkhanai stayed. She did not notice when her family members had gone, leaving her. This was her fault. So she stayed. When the last rows emptied, the guards returned the lion to its cage, and the world was quiet.

She was alone.

Finally, she lifted herself up and moved. Durkhanai went down to the arena. The stench of blood was heavy in the air, making her sick, but she felt nothing. Nothing at all. Not even as she approached his remains, a mess of tattered clothes and crushed limbs.

She walked as if through a daze until she reached the mouth of the arena. She entered just as he had in those final moments, and as if his ghost possessed her, she turned to face her own throne.

In perfect clarity, she saw her own ghost gesturing to the door that held the lion.

She looked at those doors now, so hideous in their similarity. It was a game, choose a door, choose a fate.

Until she saw the guards carrying away his head.

It was not a game.

Durkhanai fell to the ground near his remains and screamed. They had not taken away the body yet, and it lay beside her, lifeless, limp. She wished she could detach it from her memory of him, pretend it was not his, but she knew his body too well to do so: the veins of his hands; the once elegant neck, now severed.

Blood surrounded the body, merging with the ends of her red gharara, the two indistinguishable as his blood soaked into her clothes, hot and sticky.

She dug her hands into the earth, arching her back and shrieking until she felt the inside of her own throat threatening to tear.

He was gone. She had sent him to the lion. For being a spy, to protect her cousin—all silly reasons now because he was *dead* and there was no reason good enough for that.

She had acted on instinct in that final, fatal moment—doing what her grandparents would have wished, and this was the outcome.

He was dead.

Something vital within her fissured. Durkhanai dragged her hands over her face, dirt and blood streaking her cheeks with the tears, and she tasted the sharp salt of his blood on her tongue.

She vomited, sobbing, feeling like she was dying.

Suddenly, the arena was full again. The spectacle was not over.

Durkhanai rose, turning to see the Badshah on his throne. Disgust was evident in his eyes, his countenance marred with disappointment.

"Don't look at me like that," she whispered. "Please."

"Durkhanai Miangul," he said. "You are held to trial for loving Asfandyar."

She turned to the doors, so hideous in their similarity. And she knew. Behind one stood a man, behind the other stood a monster.

Durkhanai wasn't sure if she was guilty; she wanted to say she was, but if she had loved him, how could she have sent him to his death?

Perhaps the trial could tell her the truth of her heart.

Durkhanai stood and walked to meet her fate. As she reached for the door, a hand clasped over hers from behind, strong and sure. She turned and met Asfandyar's gaze.

"Don't worry, chanda," she whispered. "I will be with you soon."

She opened the door. The last thing she heard was the monster's roar.

# CHAPTER ONE

*D*urkhanai awoke, shrieking.

It was a dream, just a dream, a terrible nightmare in which Asfandyar went to the door she told him to rather than deciding his own fate.

But she could still smell his blood, hear his screams. She could feel the monster's teeth sinking into her own skin.

Durkhanai retched, but only spit and blood from where she had bit her tongue came out. She wanted to sob, but she would not allow herself to. Her heart was buried deep, beneath an ocean and a mountain and a marble house.

She could not hear it beating, could not feel it.

"Shehzadi, do you need assistance?" a maid entered her room, followed by armed guards. Durkhanai shook her head.

A glance to the windows told her it was late at night. She had come straight to bed after the trial, entirely numb, and slept the rest of the evening away in the soft comfort of oblivion.

Until her nightmare, of course.

"Draw me a bath," she commanded. The maid complied. With a wave of her hand, she dismissed the guards. Durkhanai watched them leave, gaze locked on the door. For a moment, she expected someone else to enter in their place but no one did, not her grandparents or Saifullah or Zarmina.

Zarmina would be with Asfandyar.

The thought made her sick. She imagined his fingers in her hair, his lips against her neck the way they had been against her own just two nights ago. It was an unreasonable thing to imagine. Zarmina hated Asfandyar.

Even so, Durkhanai ground her teeth together, simmering in potent jealousy and anger. They were easier emotions to latch onto than the more dangerous feelings lurking beneath.

She had willingly sent him to the lion. But Durkhanai had never considered Asfandyar would not go to the door she chose. When his quick and anxious glance had asked *Which?* she had assumed he would obey her without question.

He had not.

It was why he was still alive. He had opened the door to reveal Zarmina, as shocked as everyone else to discover Asfandyar had been innocent all along.

He hadn't loved the princess.

The trial had proved as much, and the people believed in the trial wholeheartedly. The results were never questioned.

She had made the right choice: Asfandyar was a liar and a spy. He had used her. Her grandparents would have never accepted him.

And yet. She heard the distant sound of her heart beating in its cage.

*You love him.*

It would have been better for him to die at once, and wait for her on the other side.

But he was no longer hers. He belonged to Zarmina, now, and she was glad for it. If it had been anyone else, Durkhanai may have schemed stolen kisses, perhaps content with an illicit affair—but she would not betray her beloved cousin.

Their nikkah, the Islamic wedding ceremony, had occurred right there in the arena, in front of everyone to see. The maulvi had given the khutbah, the lecture, and the papers had been signed. The wedding reception was to commence as soon as Asfandyar's tribe and Wali could come from Jardum.

When the maulvi had asked Asfandyar, "Qabool hai? Do you accept?" a hideous hope had burned within her, the possibility that he might say no, that he might refuse. There would be no wedding without a groom—but he hadn't. He had hesitated, then accepted, his face blank.

The thought had never occurred to her before; whoever was judged innocent was usually so happy to be alive that they consented to the marriage straight away.

Durkhanai had wanted to cry then, witnessing it, but she had not. She had felt Saifullah and Agha-Jaan and Dhadi watching her reaction, so she had shown none. Everyone, including the bride and the groom and the audience, were all stunned into silence during the entire procession.

The law was the law; nobody argued with it.

She had been numb. The moment it was over, she had disappeared.

She hadn't spoken to Zarmina, but she could guess only a fraction of how furious she would be. Her and Saifullah both.

Zarmina had told Durkhanai which door she, the lady, would be behind; thus, the outcome of the trial would make her cousins believe that she had betrayed them, choosing love over blood.

She pushed them from her mind. Asfandyar was harder to keep from her thoughts, and again, guilt and fear rose in her. Guilt for the decision she had made for him; fear of what would have happened had he listened.

Perhaps Asfandyar hadn't seen her gesture, she tried to console herself, or he had misread it—but she knew deep down the perfect clarity that had existed between them in that final, fatal moment.

It was why she had avoided everyone after the tribunal, gone to her room, and slept, warning her guards not to let anybody bother her—though she doubted anyone would try. Her grandparents would let her sulk, at least for the rest of the day; she could feign fatigue, illness maybe.

But come tomorrow, she would need to be the smiling princess once more, planning her beloved cousin's wedding reception, crushing any whispers of rumors that linked her name to Asfandyar's.

While the trial had proved his innocence of loving her, there might still be some lingering suspicions. People would be watching her closely.

He was married now.

*Married.* The thought cut through her like a thousand tiny blades. How ironic and cruel. The one man she wasn't allowed to marry was now married to her best friend, her own blood.

She wanted to sob again, but she bit her lip until it drew blood.

"Shehzadi?" her maid said. "The bath is drawn."

Durkhanai took a deep breath and nodded, unable to speak. Her eyes were blank as her maids helped her undress. She slipped into the tub, hissing as the scalding water touched her skin.

She did not retreat. She submerged herself, and eventually, the pain subsided. Rose petals drifted across her skin as the maids scrubbed her body and massaged her hair with coconut oil.

She was the Shehzadi. It was time she started acting like it.

# CHAPTER TWO
## Asfandyar's Tale

*A*sfandyar wished he could say he was surprised. Yet, he was not.

He knew her, after all, knew of her thorns. He couldn't help his relief when the door opened and the lady walked forth, rather than the lion. Couldn't help his relief, even though he knew what it meant.

That Durkhanai had willingly sent him to the lion. The solace had faded quickly, followed by a thousand warring emotions: betrayal, love, confusion, hatred, pain, loneliness.

When he had turned to look at her one last time after the doors opened to reveal Zarmina emerging from that long, dark hall, Durkhanai's face had been empty.

He loved her.

The truth was when he asked her to run away, he was willing to leave everything behind; to start a new life with her somewhere far away. To abandon his oath to Wakdar and Jardum and spend his days counting the freckles on Durkhanai's nose and cheeks.

He would have done it; he would have been happy.

But she had chosen her people and sentenced him to death when he was willing to make *her* his people, to choose her and choose only her.

He had offered his soul to her, in a cup like wine: She drank from it, growing drunk from its sweetness. Her lips were scarlet red, and he saw it was not his soul but his very life's blood she drank.

She was a monster.

He hated her.

It had been a gamble, either way. Yet Asfandyar was surprised to find his spy in the palace hadn't lied about the doors.

Perhaps the spy had depended on Asfandyar not trusting him and going to the opposite door. It would have been risky to do either, which was why before the trial even began, he had decided to do the opposite of whatever Durkhanai instructed.

Had she sent him to the lady, her love was true, and he would rather die than be with another.

Had she sent him to the lion, he knew anything he felt for her would die instead, and he would rather live and spite her.

And spite her he would. He would finish what he started.

He had let her in close enough to kiss, close enough to kill. She had made her decision—she had picked her side.

They were at war.

This time, he would not lose.

# CHAPTER THREE

*S*leep came to Durkhanai after some time, but did not last. She woke up suffocating.

A hand covered her mouth, and a knife was pressed into her side, but she did not panic.

She knew who it was.

When she met Asfandyar's gaze, the sight seared through her. She lay still beneath him, lips pressed into his palm.

She had made the right choice, she reminded herself. He was a liar and a spy.

He had used her.

His lips distorted into a sharp smile that was both forced and painful.

"Won't you congratulate me?" he said.

Oh, his voice. How she had missed it. Why was it she could not keep her heart buried from him? With one glance, he excavated it from deep within.

Was it really only two nights since they had shared their first kiss? Just one night since he had told her he loved her?

*No.* She would not think of it.

She bit the inside of her mouth; the pain was sharp, but the discomfort helped her quell the emotions rising within her like a tide before they threatened to drown her. The sight of him made her absolutely feral with longing.

There were a thousand and one excuses coming to her mind for why she had chosen to send him to the lion: she had been afraid of her love for him; she was possessive, petulant, and proud; she loved her family more; she cared for her people more. But of course, there were no excuses for what she had done.

*No.* She had made the right choice.

It had been the difference between one impossible big decision or a thousand difficult little decisions; losing him once or over and over again.

It was too late for regret.

"Get up," he snapped, letting her go.

She did, standing in front of him. He removed the blade, but she felt knifed looking at him. It was dawn and he looked like he hadn't slept; she suspected she looked as terrible as he did, despite the bath.

He waited for her to say something.

"You broke my heart," she said, indignant and stubborn and proud.

"And you broke mine." He nearly laughed. "Does that make us even?"

The way he looked at her—she curled her hands into fists, trying to salvage her sanity. But seeing him brought a flood of emotions through her again, strong as a stream, washing over her.

She could bear it no longer. She was unable to build walls around her heart strong enough to withhold him.

Just the sight of him made her foundations shake. Her resolve crumbled, along with her pride.

She broke.

"Please," she croaked, taking a step toward him, but he jolted back, burned. She didn't know what to say, where to begin. She reached for him; he did not reach for her.

He was too far away. Her hands came back empty. She could no longer touch him.

She had lost him—though she supposed he was never hers to begin with.

She thought to lie—to say she had meant to send him to the door on the right all along, that she knew he would go to the opposite door she told him to—but she couldn't lie to him, not now.

Not when he stood before her, face raw with grief. He knew her too well. He knew of her cruelty.

The hideous truth hung between them: That she would sacrifice him to redeem herself before her family and her people. That things would be simpler if he was left out of the equation altogether—thinking it now made her stomach curdle.

How could she have felt that sending him to the lion was the right option, the only option? In that pivotal moment, how could she have felt that was the right decision to make? There had been inexplicable relief when he had gone to the wrong door.

*And now you must suffer the consequences*, a voice in her mind chided her.

"I knew how this story ended," she said, trying to keep her voice calm. He shook his head.

"You made it so," he said. "You could have chosen differently. You are the Shehzadi. You have whatever you wish."

"If only that were true," she whispered.

He stared at her as though he didn't recognize who he saw, and she felt colder than in her loneliest dreams. It made her want to cry, but she would not allow her heart to be broken again and again and again.

"Why did you come here?" she asked, voice hardening. "Should it not be your wife's room you are slipping into for stolen kisses?"

Asfandyar snarled.

His hand came around her throat. She gasped. This close, she could almost taste him. He pushed her against the wall, face filled with hatred.

*Good,* she thought. *Let this end here, tonight.*

He was close enough to kill—close enough to kiss.

Something in his eyes darkened; his grip on her throat loosened until his fingers were soft against her skin. She bared her neck for him, knowing how sweetly she smelled of roses. He ran his thumb over her jugular. She felt a violent twist low in her belly. She desperately clutched the fabric of her shalwar, trying to retain control, though it eluded her. He drew nearer, eyes full of intent, and her lips parted in response, chin tilted up to meet him.

At the last moment, he turned, his cheek brushing hers.

"I hate you," he whispered, and he released her.

She sagged against the cool wall, catching her breath. He stood away from her, back straight.

"I *hate* you," he said. "More so than I have loathed anyone else in my entire existence, more than I have hated your grandmother, who slit the throat of my fiancé in front of me. I detest you more than words can surmount." He stood shaking with rage.

The next time he spoke his voice was raw.

"You broke me."

She felt undone.

"You made me whole again just to shatter me once more into a million pieces, and I will never forgive you."

His eyes shone now with unshed tears, the overwhelming rage turning to pure grief.

"You broke me," he repeated, and the tears fell as he brushed past her, toward the door.

She reached for him, but he grabbed her wrists, stopping her. His grip was lethal.

"You—" His voice broke, his lips quivering. He could not find the words to express how wretched and cruel she was.

A sob rose in her throat.

"I had made you my god," he said. "I put my fate in your hands. And what did you think I deserved? A shredding?" He shook his head. "I was guilty, yes, but my only affront was loving you!" His face hardened, and he released her wrists. "A mistake I will never make again. You're not the girl I loved," he said. "You're a monster."

*No*, she wanted to say, but what was the use now? He was married to her cousin. Their affair would never have worked out anyway.

But she suddenly felt that he was the only person in the world to truly know her, to truly see her, and now that image had been ruined.

If he didn't know who she was in truth, was there anybody left who would? She suddenly felt entirely unknown, unseen, like she was somehow being erased from existence and replaced with the monster he saw her as.

He shook his head. He took a step toward her.

"If you wanted me dead, you should have killed me yourself," he told her, voice low. He unsheathed the blade strapped to his side and offered the hilt to her.

She shook her head, taking a step back, but he crowded her.

"Go ahead," he said, stepping closer. He turned his chin up, exposing his neck to her. Her heart crumbled to dust.

"Asfandyar, please," she whispered, but he would not hear.

"Go on!" he said. "You wanted me dead, didn't you? That would solve all your problems, wouldn't it? Go on, then."

He grabbed her wrist, forced his blade into her hand.

"Stop!" she cried, making to throw the blade from her fist, but he would not let go. Instead, he held her hand up to his throat, where his veins pulsed.

The blade nicked his skin, and a bubble of blood pooled out.

"This is what you wanted, is it not?" he whispered.

"No," she said, tears sliding down her cheeks. "It isn't."

Asfandyar pulled back, disgusted. The blade fell from her hand, clattering against the floor, and she wanted to fall with it.

"Whether you wished it or not, you killed me today, Durkhanai," he said. "How ironic for the lady to rip me to shreds rather than the lion." He smiled a mirthless smile. "I am a walking corpse, and I know nothing but my mission: the promise I made to Wakdar. You will not distract me again."

He choked on his words, turning his back to her.

Turning his back to her so she couldn't see, but she had. She had seen it all: the tears, the grief, everything.

He still loved her. But he hated her more.

"Say your goodbyes," he said. "Your beloved grandparents are as good as dead."

Her heart seized, and with that he was gone.

*He was gone.*

Durkhanai stood alone in the silence, her hands shaking. Her rooms were dark and cold. Mouth dry, she went to her side table to get some water.

She lifted the heavy crystal jug and poured herself a glass, but when she raised it to her lips, she saw her distorted reflection in the glass.

The sight horrified her.

She threw the goblet against the wall, and it shattered with a satisfying crash.

A shard of glass glinted in the moonlight.

She lifted it and, without thinking, dragged it across her palm. The pain came quickly, brutal and bright, and it overwhelmed her.

For a moment, just a moment, she was able to forget Asfandyar's face, and she basked in feeling only the ache of physical pain.

But then the cruelty of what she had done to him came back to her in an astonishing wave, hurting much more than the cut on her hand did.

She cried out, falling to her knees.

Blood spilled from her hand onto the marble floors, a grotesque red against the white.

Finally, she let the tears fall.

# CHAPTER FOUR

"*K*hushamdeed," the Badshah said. "We are so pleased you could join us at this auspicious occasion."

Standing beside her grandfather, Durkhanai smiled at the entering guest, resisting the urge to curl her hands into fists out of frustration at the facade she was forced to don.

She would show no emotions; she would remain the perfect princess, with her perfect king and queen.

She adjusted her crown and straightened her back.

Durkhanai stood between her grandparents, welcoming guests into the hall for a brunch feast. She was adorned in a heavily worked peach sharara and kurta, her sandy brown hair pulled back in a date-tree braid beneath her glimmering crown. Sapphires hung from her ears and adorned her throat, and a similar stone was attached to pearls on a brooch the Badshah wore.

Beside her, the Badshah looked regal as ever, his blue-green eyes shining and alert; he wore a midnight blue sherwani that accented the embroidery on his wife's baby blue gown. The Wali's dark hair was swept into an elegant updo, her face warm.

At the other end of the room, Zarmina stood with Asfandyar, receiving congratulations and smiling sweetly.

Durkhanai did not look at her. Or him. She could not bear to see them together.

She merely smiled sweetly at the guests, the warmth never reaching her eyes as she made small talk and pretended that she had not withered away inside.

Though the trial had proved her innocence of any scandal with Asfandyar—and he was married now—hints of suspicions swirled in her guests' eyes, despite their calm countenances.

It would take some time for the speculations to die down, and what better way to distract the people of her alleged lover than by hosting his wedding?

The reception was in two months, when the Wali of Jardum and Asfandyar's other guests could make their way to Marghazar from Jardum.

Two months. Durkhanai had to hold up this front for two months. The thought alone drew her to madness, but she would bear it. For her people, she would bear anything. And right now, she needed their adoration once more.

"Come, let us congratulate the happy couple," Dhadi said, interrupting Durkhanai's thoughts. The last of the guests had arrived.

"Yes, come," Agha-Jaan said. Durkhanai followed them to the opposite end of the room. Public congratulations were in order. It was already suspicious she had retired so early after the trial. She could not afford any more missteps.

Walking between her grandparents, Durkhanai clenched her left hand into a fist, nails biting into the bandage. The pain was enough to make her dizzy, but it centered her. Better that than to look at Asfandyar's face.

She told herself she would not look at him, she would not glance into those endless eyes, but as she drew nearer and nearer, she could not withhold.

Her eyes were starved of him. She turned her glance to him, and a jolt ran through her body.

She was not the only one who could uphold pretenses.

Asfandyar wore a clean, dark green shalwar kameez suit and a black shawl over one shoulder. His beard was trimmed nicely, his curls smooth beneath his pakol.

He looked nothing like he had earlier this morning, when his face had been feral with love and hatred. Now, he looked every bit a man exonerated.

He smiled at the guests, but there was no warmth in his eyes.

His gaze was cold when he looked at Durkhanai—as if he didn't know her and never had. She looked at him with the same indifference but felt blood wetting the bandage on her hand.

She curled her hand into a fist to stop the bleeding; his gaze flickered down at the movement, but he made no reaction.

He was deadly still.

The hall quieted. Everyone was watching. Waiting.

"Ah, the happy couple!" the Badshah said, greeting them. He placed his hand on Zarmina's head in a sign of affection. Asfandyar lowered his head in respect as Dhadi kissed Zarmina's cheeks.

"Oh, how exciting!" Durkhanai said, taking Zarmina's hands. "My dearest cousin, married to a dear friend." Durkhanai avoided her cousin's gaze. "Though I must say I will be aggrieved to lose you."

The words were shards of glass in her mouth, cutting her tongue. First the bite of losing her beloved, then the bite of having to pretend to be fine—no, to be *overjoyed*. And how Durkhanai hated to be anything other than her true, whole self.

But it was necessary. For the people to believe in her again, it was necessary.

"It seems our darling Shehzadi cannot do without her beloved," Agha-Jaan said.

Asfandyar bristled; Durkhanai stilled. But it was Zarmina Agha-Jaan referred to.

"That will not do," Dhadi said, clucking her tongue. "After the reception, you must stay here, at the palace."

Durkhanai froze. Panic flared through her.

"Oh, how I would love that!" Zarmina said, voice sugared. "I could not bear to be apart from my beloved family."

But Zarmina would not look at Durkhanai. She looked only at Saifullah, who placed a hand on her shoulder.

"Come now, let us eat!" the Badshah announced, and the hall bustled once more with the noise of pushing chairs and chatter and food being served. Durkhanai sat between her grandparents and focused entirely on her food; she could not bear anything more.

Across the great table was a delicious spread: platters of daal kachori and aloo ki tarkari, the lentil filled dough crisp and crunchy with the spiced potato curry; gajar halwa, sweet and warm and drenched in ghee; glasses of yolk-yellow mango lassi, made from the last harvest of the season.

Durkhanai did not touch the lassi. She had an aversion to mangoes now.

There were plates and plates of mithai as well: gulab jamun and barfi and ladoo, the sweets customary for any celebration.

Meticulously chewing a cucumber from the salad, Durkhanai pushed the food around on her plate, mesmerized by the pattern on the porcelain beneath her meal. She looked for cracks and found none. The plate was flawless.

"Durkhanai, janaan," Dhadi said. "Do eat more, chiriya jaise khaati ho."

The words were said casually, but in a tone that was less a suggestion and more a command. Detaching her focus from her food,

Durkhanai looked up to see that people were watching her, their eyes scrutinizing. She could not afford to show them how she was truly feeling.

With renewed energy, Durkhanai ate. The food was thick in her mouth, and she forced herself to swallow, then eat another bite, smiling at anyone she made eye contact with.

She ate until she felt sick, only slowing when Dhadi patted her knee beneath the table. Agha-Jaan was quiet.

She wished Zarmina and Saifullah were sitting with her, as they usually did on occasions such as this. Together, they would make faces at the babies present, making the children laugh. Or she would ask Saifullah what he was up to, and he would explain some complicated trade practices he had recently learned about.

But they were not with her. They sat on the opposite end of the table, Saifullah across from Zarmina, and Asfandyar by her side.

Releasing a short breath at seeing them together, Durkhanai averted her gaze, but she could not help it; she looked upon them once more. They were sitting close together, Zarmina murmuring something under her breath. Asfandyar said something to placate her, and she did not reply.

She was acting demure, which wasn't unexpected for a new bride. Actually, she was blushing prettily and looked quite beautiful in a green ensemble that matched Asfandyar's outfit. Her hair was the same black as his shawl.

They looked good together. With a courteous smile at onlookers, Asfandyar poured Zarmina's chai, stirring in sugar for her.

White-hot jealousy flared through Durkhanai. Her vision blurred, and she clutched her spoon tightly. It clattered against her plate, making noise.

"*Durkhanai,*" Dhadi warned under her breath.

Hand shaking, Durkhanai released the spoon, trying to take measured breaths and calm down. She tried not to look at Asfandyar and

Zarmina, but she could not tear her gaze from them, as if watching some sort of disaster take place. It made her sick, but it was a scab she could not resist picking at.

Durkhanai scrutinized their every interaction. She was not sure which was worse: for him to hate her forever, or for him to move on quickly and fall in love with her cousin.

She did not like either option. She wanted him to be happy, yes, but only if it was with her.

But she could not think such things. She needed to be supportive of her cousin. Zarmina would scorn being wed to Asfandyar, but they all had to work with the hand they were dealt, adapt to the situation they found themselves in.

Even if Durkhanai hated it with every fiber of her being.

She reached for her chai, so the cup could mask the scowl she felt deepening on her face, but when she drank, she burned her tongue.

She swallowed her wince.

After the meal was done, everyone dispersed. Durkhanai hoped to escape unscathed, but on her way out, she passed Zarmina and Saifullah standing by the windows. They stopped talking and stared at her when she neared.

"Salam," she said, trying to force a smile. But the open emotion in her cousins' eyes stopped her in her tracks: They were disgusted with her.

"Are you quite happy now?" Zarmina asked, voice thick.

"W-What?" Durkhanai stammered.

She did as she was told; she had sent him to the lion. Why were they looking at her so?

"You really care more for his life than for your own cousin's welfare?" Saifullah asked.

"No, I—"

"This could have been avoided," Saifullah said. He shook his head, his dark eyes disbelieving.

"I told you," Zarmina said. "I *told* you which door to send him to. Yet you would rather save his life and condemn me to spend the rest of mine as his wife."

"But . . . I did what you asked," Durkhanai said.

"I never knew you to be a liar," Zarmina said, and Durkhanai understood they did not—would not—believe her. Not when the outcome of her action was so evident.

She had misunderstood the emotion in their eyes: it wasn't disgust, it was hatred. They *hated* her.

She was filled with the suffocating feeling of screaming but still not being heard. How could she prove she had chosen them over him? How could she make them see?

They would not believe her.

"Saifullah, please, we cannot be divided, not now," she said. She recalled what Asfandyar had said last night: *your beloved grandparents are as good as dead.* "Something is coming—Asfandyar, he's . . . " She hesitated, not wanting to damn him. But perhaps she could win back her cousins' favor this way. "He's dangerous."

"We *told* you as much, yet did you listen?" Saifullah replied.

"And now I must share a bed with him," Zarmina snapped.

With a final glance of anger, Saifullah retreated, leaving Durkhanai with Zarmina.

Perhaps she could reason with her, make her see. This was her cousin, her best friend, practically her sister. She could come to understand, wouldn't she?

"Zarmina, please," Durkhanai said, voice breaking. She reached for her cousin, but Zarmina pulled away.

"*No,*" she replied, eyes blazing. It was the first time Zarmina had ever been truly angry with Durkhanai, and she couldn't stand the intensity of her gaze.

"How could you condemn me to marry someone when I love another?" Zarmina asked, incredulous. Tears shone in her eyes, and she quickly wiped them away, growing more agitated. Durkhanai was taken aback.

"Love another?" she said. "Who?"

Zarmina's glance flitted across the room, to where a young man stood by an open window, looking miserable.

"*Rashid?*" Durkhanai asked. "How could that be?"

"Why?" Zarmina's brown eyes darkened. "Because he is yours, just as everything is yours? Yours to have, yours to discard, yours to ruin, yours to break. Selfish, *spoiled* . . ."

"What, no—"

"If you must know, I had always thought him sweet," Zarmina said, voice hard. "After you callously rejected him without another thought, I went to see if he was all right. I didn't want our family to lose Naeem-sahib's support because of your frivolity . . . We became friends. He is so kind. I thought, perhaps one day . . ." Her face opened with hope, then shuttered again. "But no longer. This was a flower you cut before it had the chance to bloom."

It worried Durkhanai that so much could have happened without her realizing. What else went on while she was distracted by Asfand-yar?

"I . . . I didn't know." Shock slowed Durkhanai's words. She was disoriented, as if she'd unintentionally fallen asleep and woken to find herself in a different season.

How could she have not noticed such a thing? Along with the disbelief came shame.

"And how could you?" Zarmina snapped. "You only care for yourself."

"No, *no*, that's not true," Durkhanai pleaded, but her cousin would not listen.

Zarmina left without another word, leaving Durkhanai with a tight pain in her chest. She stood in silence for a moment, before she heard another approaching her. It seemed everyone had been waiting for a moment alone with her, after she'd run off to isolation yesterday. How she wished to run off again now.

"Durkhanai, tell me it isn't true," Gulalai said. Her eyes were cold with horror. She leaned on her jeweled cane, a sick look twisting her beautiful features. "Your grandfather truly was behind the attack?"

"What?" Durkhanai said, stilling. "Where did you hear that from?"

"Is it true?"

Durkhanai hesitated, not wanting to lie to a friend, and that was all the answer Gulalai needed. Her eyes filled with tears.

"My father will never walk again because of your family!" Gulalai cried. Durkhanai shushed her, hoping the others would not hear.

"Gulalai, please—"

"I cannot believe it," Gulalai said, shaking her head. "And that you would defend him . . . though I supposed I should not be surprised. Foreign casualties are of no consequence to you, are they?" Her eyes filled with disgust. "Is that why you sent Asfandyar to his death?"

Durkhanai froze. "How did—"

"I watched you," Gulalai said. "I knew you would find out which door held the lady and which held the lion. I saw you gesture to him. When Asfandyar walked to the opposite door, I thought him a fool." She scoffed. "Then I realized we were all fools. To think you loved anyone but yourself."

"Gulalai—" Durkhanai started, but she could not say anything more. Her throat was closing with tears.

Gulalai walked away.

It wasn't true—none of it was true. She had done all this for her country, for her people, for her grandparents and cousins, but they all hated her. They *hated* her.

Aching for a hug, for warmth and love, Durkhanai went to her grandparents. They sat alone at the head of the empty hall, discussing something.

When Durkhanai neared, they quieted.

"Dhadi?" Durkhanai's small voice asked. Her grandmother's green eyes were sharp with anger. Agha-Jaan looked through her.

"Durkhanai, you didn't," Dhadi said, her voice steeped in disappointment.

"What?" Durkhanai replied. She didn't understand. Her mind wasn't working. She couldn't bear any more.

"You knew what was behind each door and sabotaged the trial," Dhadi said, the words more as a fact than a question. Durkhanai stopped breathing. "Saifullah told us. It is because of you poor Zarmina is married to that wretched man."

"No!" she cried, voice high. "It isn't true!"

But she *had* tried to sabotage the tribunal, which her grandfather considered sacred. How could she admit to it? What proved her innocence also proved her guilt.

Her grandparents exchanged a glance, and she couldn't bear for them to be angry with her, too. She opened her mouth, then paused, as gears turned in her head.

Saifullah. . . Saifullah told them.

Why would he have done so?

She thought back to the beginning of all this, to going to Asfandyar's room and finding a hidden box full of letters, letters that informed Asfandyar of the palace's inner workings. She hadn't thought about it then—too overcome with everything—but if she recalled now, there was a reason the handwriting looked so familiar.

It was Saifullah. Dreams were made of stars, and all the stars inside of her had burned out. The night sky of her heart was empty.

How couldn't she have seen it?

Saifullah, distracted. Saifullah, discontent. Saifullah, heading for the passageways and writing letters he would not let her see. Saifullah, waiting for her the moment they took Asfandyar away, when he should have been half a palace away.

But why?

"He's a spy!" Durkhanai cried. "For my—for Wakdar. He's a spy, and he wishes to turn you away from me. Please, you cannot believe him."

The words spilled from her mouth all at once. Her grandparents exchanged a glance, and Durkhanai understood they thought she'd gone mad. They did not believe her.

She wanted to scream—to sob—to cry—to break.

But she would not. She was the daughter of the mountains and river S'vat. She was crown princess of Marghazar, the jewel of the Ranizais tribe and Miangul family. She was to be Badshah one day.

Durkhanai straightened her back and raised her chin.

In that moment, she stitched her bleeding heart together again. She put her heart in a velvet pouch and tied it tight. Then she put the pouch in a wooden box, and the wooden box in a stone crate, and the stone crate in a marble house. And around the marble house, she molded a mountain. And over the mountain, she poured the ocean.

Thus her heart was protected to never be broken again.

The images helped keep her emotions at bay. She would not break.

With a final breath, she took her leave. She did not look back.

In the evening, when the mountains were dark silhouettes against the rose-gold sky, a maid came to tell Durkhanai she was being summoned to her grandfather's rooms. She went and found both her grandparents there, sitting calmly.

"Come," Dhadi said, voice gentle. She sat with Agha-Jaan, steaming cups of tea in front of them. Behind them, in the window, the sun was an orange orb low in the sky, quickly setting.

"Join us," Agha-Jaan said, gesturing to the empty chair between them. Durkhanai sighed, anxiety dissipating, then sat.

No matter how angry they were with her, they loved her. They would not forsake her, as everyone else had.

"Drink," Dhadi said. Everything else could be sorted later. For now, there was only this: Her and her grandparents and their love for one another.

Agha-Jaan poured her tea, and she took a sip. It was scalding and too sweet, but she drank, then drank again. They sat in silence.

Agha-Jaan placed his hand on her head, and the weight of it centered her. When Durkhanai finally stood, her legs felt heavy. She softly lowered to the floor, suddenly drowsy.

"Dhadi," she slurred, eyes closing. Her grandmother's hands were soft in her hair, easing Durkhanai's head onto her lap.

"Shh, janaan," said Dhadi. "Rest, now."

Durkhanai fell asleep without knowing she'd fallen.

# CHAPTER FIVE

When she awoke, Durkhanai's mouth was parched. She pried her eyes open, wiping away dried flakes. Blinking away the drowsiness did not do much to help; she was in a darkened room.

As she took a deep breath, her heart stopped with realization.

She tasted it in the air: the pinewood and mint, and a slight note of salt. Her body, too, felt heavier, not as high up in the mountains. And of course, her surroundings: the small hut, the candlelight, the smell of farmland just outside, and the chorus of goats bleating.

She was no longer home. Or rather—she was finally home.

"You're awake," a voice said, from the end of the room.

"Ammi!" Durkhanai cried. She threw off her covers and ran across the hut, where her grandfather's elder sister sat in a chair. Durkhanai was in Mianathob, the small village in the valley where she had spent the first half of her life.

"I've been waiting for your return, Durre," Bari Ammi said.

A sob rose in Durkhanai's throat upon hearing that name, last used by Asfandyar. She rose and hugged Bari Ammi—it had been so long. Bari Ammi felt so thin in her arms, so much smaller than when she had seen her last. It had been a few years now.

"Oh, Ammi," Durkhanai said, pulling away. She looked at her great-aunt's face, registering the wrinkled brown skin and the beauty mark below her left eye. She had the same blue-green eyes as Agha-Jaan, the same as Durkhanai, too.

Those eyes were filled with such love and sadness now.

"How did I get here?" Durkhanai asked, confused. "When?" She groaned, a headache catching up to her.

"You are here to rest," Bari Ammi said. She sat down in her chair, and Durkhanai gathered at her feet. Ammi's wrinkled hands were soft as she stroked Durkhanai's hair, soft as Dhadi's—and Durkhanai remembered.

She remembered everything. The trial, and everything after. Drinking too-sweet tea and falling asleep. Durkhanai's cheeks suddenly burned with shame; she couldn't bear to look Bari Ammi in the eyes.

What would they have told her?

Shame rose in Durkhanai's chest, but—no. *She put her heart in a velvet pouch . . .*

"You are here to rest," her great aunt repeated.

Bari Ammi rose, and Durkhanai followed her outside. The world was dark and cold, but the sky glittered with thousands of stars. Women gathered around a bonfire in the center of the village, their hands curled around cups of kava or cuddling sleeping children.

The valley was the same as she'd always remembered it: secluded and serene. The village of Mianathob was a small collection of houses by a cerulean lake, surrounded by a silent green valley.

This valley was small and on the opposite side of the populated lands of Marghazar, hidden away. It was why Durkhanai had been sent here after her parent's deaths—so she could be safe.

But that had been a lie, as well, hadn't it? Her father was still alive, and her grandparents had known it then, too.

Had they sent her away because they were afraid Wakdar would come for her?

Durkhanai clenched her hands into fists. *She put the velvet pouch in a wooden box. . .*

"Come, let us drink tea," Bari Ammi said. "You must be hungry."

"Yes," Durkhanai said, following her great-aunt. Bari Ammi handed her a piece of bread and a cup of mint tea. Durkhanai looked at the liquid, biting her lip.

What if Mianathob was just a stop on her journey to somewhere else?

"My brother and his nasty tricks," Bari Ammi said, sensing her hesitation. "But do not worry. I will not replicate them."

"Okay," Durkhanai said. She trusted Bari Ammi. Together, they went to join the others by the fire.

The night was cold and would only grow colder as the days passed. The women's faces glowed golden from the flames, and Durkhanai recalled some of them. Most of the inhabitants of the village were widowed distant relatives, women who had nowhere else to go.

"How good it is to see you again," an older woman said. Her eyes were soft with affection. Durkhanai made her way around the crowd, meeting with them, feeling their hands squeezing hers.

For a moment, she could breathe.

Durkhanai made her way back to Bari Ammi, and they sat together.

She drank her tea.

She slept.

In the morning, she awoke to the crying of roosters.

She groaned, shifting on the charpai. It was a far cry from the four-poster, hand-carved wooden bed and feather-filled mattress she had at the palace. She rose, stretching.

Durkhanai washed and got ready in the plain cotton clothes Bari Ammi had set out for her, then slipped a shawl around her shoulders. She braided her hair as she exited the hut, feeling bare and light without her heavily worked clothes, jewelry, or crown.

There was no room for that here.

Already, the women were at work: milking goats, feeding the cows, collecting eggs. Others were farther away in the fields of crops. It was the harvesting season.

Durkhanai felt a world away from her life, as if she had slipped through time back to the past. Back then, she and the other children would hide and chase one another through the fields, bathe in the ice-cold stream and dare each other to sneak up on the cows or goats.

Durkhanai searched for her old friends, but of course, they were all gone. Married off, sent away. The children here now would not recognize her. In truth, she did not recognize many of the women either. She searched for old faces and saw them missing—they must have passed on.

At least there was one old face still present.

"Is there anything to eat?" Durkhanai asked Bari Ammi. She sat by a large wooden butter churn, turning the cream into ghee.

"Would you like some eggs?" Bari Ammi asked.

"Yes, I would."

"Good." Bari Ammi handed her a basket. "You can collect them."

Durkhanai opened her mouth to protest, but Bari Ammi shook her head.

"You are not a child anymore. There is work to be done."

Bari Ammi was right—she wasn't a child anymore.

She went to collect eggs. The chickens squawked when she approached the barn, running away from her.

The sound echoed through her mind, bringing forth memories of a rain-soaked night with a loi around her shoulders and a man's warm hands around hers.

No. *She put the wooden box in a stone crate. . .*

She shook her head, focusing on the chickens.

After the eggs were collected and breakfast was eaten, Bari Ammi steered Durkhanai toward the stables.

"There's somebody waiting to meet you," she said, and Durkhanai's insides twisted with fear and anticipation as to who could be visiting her. When she left the palace, she'd left everyone in unhappy terms with her: Asfandyar, Saifullah, Zarmina, Gulalai, and her grandparents. But when she entered the stables, her heart stretched with joy.

"Heer!"

She approached the great white horse, and Heer nuzzled against her neck. She inhaled the familiar smell of fire smoke and mountain air, tears welling in her eyes. Heer neighed, and Durkhanai went to find her some apples.

"Let's go for a ride, shall we?"

Durkhanai set off, away from the village and toward the empty meadows. There were no other villages on this side of the mountain, so the lands were clear and empty. The bright greens had turned colder with autumn, the mountains more brown and dark.

A chill ran down her spine from the cold. Winter was coming.

When she returned from her ride, Durkhanai felt euphoric. Like perhaps she had regained some semblance of control over her life. She dismounted Heer and went to retrieve a brush. When she returned to her horse, the euphoria faded.

Heer was nuzzling another horse, one with a black mane and a chestnut coat. Ranjha.

He was her mate, named as such for Heer's affection for him. The two horses were raised together, and Durkhanai had grown up riding both, though she preferred Heer.

The sight of them together brought her back to another night, to another rider.

Sudden anger flashed through her.

"No!" she cried, steering Heer away. "She's mine." She glared at Ranjha, who neighed warily in response, unaccustomed to her fury. "You can't have her! She's mine."

She held Heer's head close, heart feeling frayed. Heer struggled against her, not understanding why Durkhanai would keep her apart from her mate.

Durkhanai did not understand it either, but she held on tight all the same. Tears flooded her eyes.

What was the point of dreaming if all it did was disappoint you?

She had bet on herself and lost; that was what hurt the most. That she had let herself hope, that she had believed in herself, only to be let down.

It was nobody's fault but her own. It was why she never let herself dream unless the odds were in her favor.

What a fool she had been to forget her place, to ask for more than she was allotted, to dream, to hope, to love. What a fool she had been to believe the world would smile on her.

The world was cruel and unflinching—so she would be too.

She would never make a fool of herself again.

# CHAPTER SIX

*O*nce, Durkhanai told Asfandyar she missed Mianathob because of how much simpler things were in the farmlands, and it was true. Life here was more manageable than at court.

Durkhanai was not a princess here, just another village girl.

She rose at dawn and milked the goats, gathered eggs from the chickens, and went to tend the fields of golden wheat. There were no rose water baths or maids to set her clothes for the day. She wore no jewelry, no baubles, except the signet ring on her third finger.

Stripped bare, life was simple.

There was the crisp mountain air in her lungs, the sweet milk on her tongue, a place to lay her head at night. There were the fields, the women, the rivers, the crops, the sunlight, the golden sheen of it all, the stories, the stars.

No one asked her a thing. Here, she was unadulterated and pure. She said nothing.

It was as though she was reborn.

Whenever she thought of Asfandyar, or Saifullah, or Zarmina, or her father, or her grandparents, Durkhanai imagined putting her heart in a velvet pouch, sealing it away, and she could bear to live another day.

She worked, and worked, and worked.

Days passed, shortening as they did. The green leaves changed to red, orange, yellow, curling and wrinkling until they fell softly to the ground. The trees, once full, were now bare. The sky lost some of its brightness, shifting to muted tones of gray and white and ice blue.

A chill seeped into the wind, which howled more fiercely across the fields. The air grew cold and bitter. The crops were harvested and stored for the winter. Autumn was quickly passing.

But she could not forget.

For every time someone called her Durre, she heard the timbre of Asfandyar's voice. For every star in the endless sky, she saw his eyes. For every flame of fire, she felt his hands on hers. For every sip of sweetness, she tasted his mouth.

For every moment she spent forgetting him, another two were dedicated to his remembrance. His name was written on her heart; she tried and tried to scrub the letters away, and while the ink had faded, she was afraid there was an indelible indent left in the skin.

Yet, she would not relent. She would not be weak.

She brushed thoughts of Asfandyar away, telling herself he was nothing to her, he meant nothing; she wished he had listened to her and gone to the lion, she wished he was dead.

She had made the right choice, she reminded herself, clinging to the mantra: *He was a liar and a spy. He had used her. Her grandparents would have never accepted him.*

What she felt for him was no longer a soft, tender thing: It was feral and savage. It clawed at her skin, the thorns cutting deep.

And yet. And yet.

She could not bring herself to mind. She could not.

In the valley, she should have been happy to be home, but she was not. Her grandparents would not visit her, not even when she wrote to them twice. She needed rest, they said. She needed recovery, they promised. She needed to regain her senses, they implied.

The people had been told she was ill, which was why she had been sent away. Perhaps she *was* sick, bedridden with the affliction of love. Perhaps she needed leeches on her skin to suck the venom from her blood.

Her grandparents said they would visit after a month, maybe two, to see how she was faring, but they never did. Durkhanai wrote to Zarmina and Saifullah, as well, once together, then twice separately, but no reply came.

She thought of writing to Gulalai, but if her own family members were not replying, surely, neither would Gulalai. It was Durkhanai's grandparents' fault that Gulalai's father would never walk again, and Durkhanai hid that from Gulalai. Durkhanai was sure Gulalai would never wish to speak with her again.

She missed them, and she missed her people. She wondered how the children of Kajali were doing. They loved to pile the autumn leaves into great heaps and jump into them.

When she returned, would they still love her? Did it appear suspicious to them that she was gone for so long right after the ordeal of the trial? Would they suspect? She did not want to lose their good favor.

Mianathob was nice, and the women were kind, but it was a completely separate entity from Marghazar. Durkhanai felt like she had run away, except she did not get the chance to decide to.

Perhaps she should have gone with Asfandyar when he had asked her to. What would have been different? She would still miss everyone, and they would all still hate her, but at least she would have him. Better than now, for now she had nothing.

Should she have run when she had the choice? Sometimes, in the fields, the cool grass brushing against her bare ankles, she imagined his hand reaching out to hers, beckoning her forward. She always reached for Asfandyar, and he would disappear, a beautiful mirage.

If they had run away together, would she be happier then? Or would she be just as lost as she was now? Would it be like a dream or a nightmare? Would she regret it? Would she be as empty? She was left wondering. And wondering.

She could not even bring herself to write to him. What would she say? Besides, he was married now, to her beloved cousin. There was nothing left to be said. Durkhanai had made her choice; she had to live with it.

And what a choice she had made.

Perhaps she never truly loved him. She was a liar either way. She lied if she said she loved him, for how could she have sent him to the lion? But it was a lie to say she did not love him, too.

So she said nothing.

She stayed silent.

She worked.

The days passed without consequence.

It was the nights that were truly challenging.

She could convince herself not to care, were it not for the dreams.

Some nights, she imagined *she* was being held to trial for not loving Asfandyar. If she was proved innocent, she was rewarded with the man she loved; if she was guilty, she was ravaged by a monster—and the monster was herself.

Eventually, even the dreams ceased.

And she missed him twofold. Every night she closed her eyes, and there was a distant thought that perhaps she would see him again, if only in a dream, even if only in a nightmare, but when she slept, her dreams were empty.

She was empty.

Weeks passed. No one came to visit her, and she stopped waiting. As the weather around her chilled, she felt her heart frosting over.

Faintly, she felt she had rid her system of him. Perhaps she would never feel a thing again.

But then, he came to her, while she was curled up in bed, crying.

She didn't know how he came to be there, just that one moment she was pushing tears back into her eyes, and the next there was a body beside hers. She didn't need to open her eyes to know that it was him.

"Come, sit up," he coaxed, and she did as she was told. He kneaded the tension from her shoulders with the hard curves of his palms.

"What worries you?" he asked. She sighed in response.

"I can't bear it anymore."

"You can," he told her. "And you will."

She turned to look at him and instantly fell into a hug against his chest. She was safe.

They stayed like that for some time. She strained her ear in search of his heartbeat. But he was calm. Sure. Solid.

She pulled back, looked up at him. Gently, his fingers cupped her face like wine—he tipped her chin forward to drink, but paused at the last whisper before skin met skin.

He waited.

And so, soft as sin, she pressed her warm lips against his. He tasted like a thousand stars bursting in her mouth. His fingers murmured across her skin, cold as ice, but everywhere he touched her felt like fire.

She kissed his cold cheek. He tasted like winter: pine-needle and frost, everything that freezes your nose but warms your soul. She was inexplicably warm and closed her eyes in comfort.

Instinctively, she reached for his lips once more—only to find they were not there. He was gone.

When she awoke from the dream, she felt unaligned. As though her soul had been roughly shoved back into her body. She was paralyzed, as she was when she awoke from nightmares, her body frozen with fear—yet this was the opposite, for when she awoke, her reality was the nightmare.

Slowly, the ice burned away. The pain was sudden and swift, knocking the breath from her lungs. Durkhanai began to cry. She loved him. The realization struck her.

She loved him.

And there was nothing to be done.

"What is it, janaan?" Bari Ammi asked, brushing her hand across Durkhanai's cheek.

"I love him," she blurted in response. "I love him. I love him."

Bari Ammi stilled. There was no room for misunderstanding. She knew right away who it was that Durkhanai spoke of. Durkhanai sat up in her bed, and Bari Ammi braced her shoulders, giving the younger girl a shake.

"You cannot," Ammi said. "He is married, to your dearest Zarmina."

"I love him," Durkhanai whispered, cheeks wet with tears. "I love him."

"Are you quite sure it is love, chiriya?" Bari Ammi asked, voice gentle. "Perhaps it is infatuation."

But Durkhanai was sure.

What was love? How could she describe what she felt to somebody who wouldn't understand? Their love was the extra sweetness in life: the soft sunrises, the sugar in her tea, the splendid sunsets—beginnings and endings and everything in between.

"I love him," she murmured. "I love him."

It was everything at once: pyaar, ishq, mohabbat. She loved him. Durkhanai felt an ember blazing inside of her, coming to life.

"Bari Ammi," she said, meeting the older woman's eyes. Durkhanai grasped her hands, and Bari Ammi flinched at the emotion in Durkhanai's eyes but did not pull away.

"There is madness in your eyes," Ammi said. "A madness I know well. I have seen it in my dear brother's eyes too often."

"I am his blood, am I not?" Durkhanai asked.

"Tell me," Bari Ammi said. "Tell me how this came to be."

Durkhanai did.

"I hated him when I first met him."

She told the old woman about their first meeting, how infuriating he had been; then of their reluctant alliance and how that gave way to friendship; the attraction that lived between them, like a live wire. How he challenged her and believed in her and made her laugh and made her smile.

"Then there was this mess with another boy, Rashid," she continued. She spoke of petty jealousies and silliness and finally, succumbing to her emotions.

The feeling of flying.

She left out their kiss because she did not wish to scandalize the old woman.

It was improper, she knew that, but she did not regret it.

"Then he was to leave," she said. "I almost let him without saying goodbye. I tried to push him away because it hurt too much to have him so near."

Durkhanai told Bari Ammi then of how she couldn't let him go, how she wrote to him and found other letters, uncovering his betrayal, that he was a spy for Wakdar and had only been using her.

The pain of that, though, was not worse than the pain of his trial, not worse than the pain that came with the regret of her decision to send him to the lion.

"He hates me now," she finished. "And I love him."

Ammi sat quietly, taking in the story. Durkhanai was surprised to see that Bari Ammi was not scandalized or taken aback; she did not lecture Durkhanai or chide her behavior. Instead, she hummed to herself, as if she understood.

"I have heard a story like this before," Bari Ammi said. "Of young lovers and a trial. It did not end well." Hearing that, Durkhanai began to cry. Bari Ammi wiped her tears. "There is still hope."

"Now what is to be done?" Durkhanai asked.

"We wait," Bari Ammi said.

A crow cried in the distance.

# CHAPTER SEVEN
## Nazo's Tale

*I*t had been decades since Nazo Miangul visited Mianathob. Yet, when she saw the village approaching from her horse, she was filled with that familiar dread, freezing around her heart, as though her ribs had turned into an ice cage.

It had been her prison for a year, that awful year after Yaqut's trial. Her last year of freedom, before she was married off to her husband.

Nazo rode past the lake, its waters still clear. She was close enough to see the mountain peaks and the clouds in the still water, yet far enough to avoid her reflection. She was afraid she would see the young fool she once was shown back to her, rather than the woman she had become.

She was here with a purpose.

She would not fail.

Decades ago, after Ghazan lost his family to the war against the Lugham Empire, he sent his mother and sister away to Mianathob to be safe. It was where he hid his most precious of precious things, a gilded aviary for the birds of his heart.

When Nazo fell in love, she was sent away to this same village. And now, Durkhanai was here, for the same reason, for the same damning sin.

Nazo saw her niece, then, in the field of wheat. She immediately recognized the despair of heartbreak written on Durkhanai's face. Though the shining sun turned her skin golden, her once vibrant blue-green eyes had lost their luster, like marbles buried beneath layers of dust. She seemed to be reaching for something, perhaps someone.

"Durkhanai!" Nazo called, dismounting from her horse. The girl froze, then thawed, and ran toward her. Nazo opened her arms and welcomed Durkhanai into a hug.

When she pulled away, Durkhanai clasped her hands.

"Come, we must sit," her niece said, making to lead her back to the village. But Nazo would not have Bari Ammi's prying ears listening in. Her phuppo may have been old, but she still had sharp ears.

"Come," Nazo said, leading her to a tangle of emptying trees. They sat on the ridges of the trunk. She pulled her shawl tight around her shoulders as a gust of wind rustled through the air, and a flurry of aged leaves fell from above them.

Durkhanai shivered, but made no move to warm herself. How it pained Nazo to see her beloved Durkhanai so. Durkhanai had always burned bright, but now, she hardly flickered. It was what losing love did, was what it had done to Nazo all those years ago. It was as though no time had passed at all, and Nazo stood staring at herself. They had an uncanny resemblance, after all. Durkhanai was all Wakdar, and growing up, people had always said Nazo and her brother could have been twins, despite the five years that separated them.

"Oh, janaan, you think I do not understand you, but I do. We are so alike, you and I," Nazo said. She lifted Durkhanai's face to meet her gaze.

"We are?" her niece asked.

"Yes, we are," Nazo said. "I understand you as no one else will. The man I loved had also been put to trial, so many years ago."

"Tell me," Durkhanai said, voice desperate. "Tell me the story."

Nazo smiled. With Durkhanai sitting by her feet, begging for a story, she did not see the eighteen-year-old who could determine the fate of a nation—she saw a child, begging for more than was allotted to her.

"Once upon a time, in a very olden time, there lived a semi-barbaric king," Nazo began. She ran her hand along the stories woven into the tapestry of her youth, her fingers catching at old threads. She pulled, and the memories unfurled.

Nazo, twenty years old, practicing archery in the woods.

She missed her mark—again. She notched another arrow into the bow, took aim, and missed again.

"Your elbow," a deep voice said. Nazo startled. She had thought herself alone in the woods. It was Yaqut—her eldest brother Wakdar's best friend.

He was a few years older than her, and as he approached, she saw that he had a kind, pretty face.

Too pretty a face for an accomplished general: smooth and free of scars, with kind hazel eyes, and deep-set dimples that showed even when he was not smiling.

Nazo scowled as he plucked her arrow from the floor. The entire reason she had retreated to the woods was so no one would witness her struggle.

"Would you like some aid?" he asked, voice gentle. Nazo ignored him, instead taking her stance. The arrow sailed and miserably missed its mark yet again.

Scowling, Nazo took out another arrow.

"Are you sure?" he asked. She gripped the arrow tight, felt it splinter beneath her palm. Yaqut chuckled.

"I am the best archer in Marghazar," he said. This got a reaction out of her.

"No, you aren't," Nazo said reflexively. "Wakdar is."

Yaqut shook his head. "He is the best swordsman, yes, but I am the best archer."

He neared and plucked the bow from her hands, then reached into the pack on her back to pluck out an arrow.

Without taking his gaze off of her, he notched an arrow into her bow and let go: It soared through the air and struck a pheasant, which fell to the ground.

Nazo nearly smiled, then, impressed.

"Show me," she ordered. Yaqut smiled, coming to stand beside her.

"Take your stance," he said. She did, and Yaqut tsked. "The angle must be like so."

Fingers skimmed across her skin, and she shivered, despite the summer heat. He guided her into an appropriate stance.

"Let go," he whispered. She did and the arrow sailed into the tree trunk. A bit higher than she'd have liked, but still better than before.

Nazo turned to look at him, really look at him, and only then did she smile.

"It's strange," Nazo said, regarding him closely. "I've known you my entire life, yet I've never really *known* you."

"I do hope we can remedy that now," he said.

And they had.

"We became acquainted, more and more. It was the wonder of discovery, like stumbling upon an unvisited land and every inch you see, you adore even more. We fell in love," Nazo said, and at this, a soft smile did make an appearance on her face.

"What happened?" Durkhanai asked, her voice filled with dread.

"He was put to trial," Nazo said, and the smile was gone. "For colluding with the Lugham Empire. It was said they paid him to lose certain battles, which allowed the Lugham Empire to advance."

Nazo had not been given a chance to speak with him before they had locked him away, but she had known it wasn't true, had known he was innocent. Love without intuition was not love at all, and she had believed in him.

"I fought the Badshah, of course, told him to hold off the trial. It was well within his power to do so, but he would not," Nazo said, and she could tell from the growing tears in Durkhanai's eyes that she knew far too well how such a scene would have played out. "The Wali claimed he had committed kala jadoo—sorcery—on me to turn my heart against my family. They would not cancel the trial."

How the Badshah could not bear to see his daughter adore another man more than she did him. How he positively writhed at the concept.

Nothing had changed in the decades since then: Still he could not bear to see his beloved granddaughter in the same situation. The same granddaughter who wept now.

"Forgive me," she said, wiping her eyes. "I can't seem to stop crying."

Nazo set her jaw. She had long since stopped crying; Durkhanai would too.

"When Yaqut was ordered to trial, I begged to be the lady," Nazo said. The memories still burned her tongue; how naive she had been, so full of love and hope, thinking the stars would smile upon her.

Though her parents had refused, at first, to allow Nazo to be the lady, she had convinced them. She had said if they truly believed Yaqut was guilty, her parents did not need to worry at the possibility of her marrying him; if he was guilty, like they believed, he would be torn to shreds. Yet, if he was innocent like *she* believed, then they should be glad to marry her off to someone so highly regarded.

Her parents had agreed.

Too quickly, Nazo could look back and realize now, but then she had been too naive to see clearly.

She had dressed in the red wedding lengha she had always dreamed of wearing. In the lady's suite, she sat patiently, nerves skittering through her, but she had full faith in his innocence, in their love. She had the maids apply her mehndi, hiding his name in the patterns on her skin. They set her dupatta and crown and jewels, and she waited, eager to marry the love of her life.

All the nastiness would be behind them in a few hours: She would have her love, and all would be right in the world.

She had waited, and waited. As the hours had passed, she had prayed, despite her confidence in him. She prayed and prayed—but it did not matter. The matter had already been decided.

When they had come for her, it had not been to lead her to the chamber behind the door.

"When I entered the arena, Yaqut was dead," Nazo said. "Ripped to shreds by the lion."

Nazo's hand curled around her throat; she felt the phantom echo of the bloodcurdling scream she had released that day, the pure pain and rage of it.

It still reverberated through her.

It would not be silenced until she had her vengeance.

Something in Wakdar broke that day, witnessing his best friend slaughtered. He had not believed it, either. While he let it go, Nazo had looked into the matter and slowly came to the conclusion that the trial was rigged.

Nazo found out that Yaqut knew the Badshah wished to create an alliance with the Kebzu Kingdom. Yaqut, who had seen too many of his men die fighting the Kebzus, refused this alliance. When the Badshah had insisted, Yaqut threatened to alert the public, and thus to silence him, he had been killed.

By then, it was too late for Nazo.

She'd been sent to Mianathob and married off immediately after. She'd moved, and the twins had been born. Soon after, Wakdar had

Durkhanai, and once his heir was sired, he ran. Though miles apart, neither Nazo nor Wakdar ever forgot the injustice that had been done to their beloved Yaqut. They still had not forgotten.

The scars scorned love left behind did not scrub away easily.

There was work to be done. Then, they would know peace.

"I am not telling you this so that I may earn your sympathy," Nazo continued, as the wind quieted around them, "but so that you may understand." She paused. "Your father loves you dearly, as do I, and as do Zarmina and Saifullah."

"How are they?" Durkhanai asked. "Zarmina was so terribly angry with me the last I saw her. Saifullah, too, though I should have been angry with him. He was the informant Asfandyar colluded with in the palace."

"They are angry, yes, but they love you still," Nazo replied. "You must know that and hold onto it. You are our family, and we cannot stay angry with our family for long. Saifullah knew this, which is why he did what he had to. You can be cross with him for it, but he did what was best for his people and his blood, just as you must." Nazo paused. "Durkhanai, you have no idea of what is coming, which is why you must understand what I am telling you."

"Kya, Phuppo?" Durkhanai asked. "What is it I must understand?"

"I was denied my love," Nazo said, eyes hard, "but I will not let you suffer the same fate. He can be yours—you can have everything you ever wished. Your crown, your people, your love. Me, and Zarmina, and Saifullah, and Asfandyar, and your father. All of it."

Durkhanai's eyes widened, and she neared her aunt, listening close.

"Kaise?" she asked, voice soft and desperate. "Phuppo, how?"

"It is simple, janaan," Nazo said, tucking a strand of hair behind her niece's ear. "You must denounce the Badshah and welcome your father home."

Durkhanai pulled away as if scalded.

Nazo saw herself in Durkhanai. As a girl, she too had been fiercely loyal to the Badshah and the Wali. Had worshiped them. Taken their every word as law.

Until, of course, she fell in love.

"I know it is against what you believe," Nazo said, voice coaxing. "But it is what must be done. After your grandfather upheld an alliance with Marghazar's enemies, after your grandmother killed your sister, after they put your lover to trial—after all they have done, they cannot rule." She paused. "Don't you wish to know your father, chiriya? He has longed for you all these years. He has waited to return home to you."

Durkhanai's bottom lip trembled, but she lifted her chin. "I won't," she said, voice strong despite the fractured despair written on her face. "I will not do it."

"Durkhanai—" Nazo began again, trying to sustain her patience.

She hated to admit it, but they needed Durkhanai.

Even disgraced by the affair with Asfandyar, Durkhanai was still the beloved princess, and Wakdar wished to reign with Durkhanai as his successor.

To take the throne, remarry, and sire another heir now would be too much. Especially as long as Durkhanai lived.

But Durkhanai shook her head. Her eyes filled with tears, and she closed them, a breath deflating her chest as she shook her head once more.

Nazo said one last thing before leaving.

"It is time to choose your fate."

# CHAPTER EIGHT

Durkhanai still had not recovered a week after her aunt's visit. She replayed the words in her mind all day, arranged the clouds into scenes that played out in front of her, and yet, she could not grasp the true meaning.

It wasn't that she did not believe Nazo Phuppo—it was that she did not know how to process such truths, or how ironically history repeated itself, again and again, and with such brutal accuracy.

She sat on the sharp grass, staring into the sky. Autumn was leaving to welcome the frigid cold of winter, and the first snow was soon approaching. She could taste it in the air, so brisk it burned as it entered her lungs.

Distantly, Durkhanai wondered why her grandparents had not rigged Asfandyar's trial. But after Wakdar had found out about Yaqut's trial, they had lost him, so perhaps they had not wished to risk the same mistake with her.

And they hadn't lost her, despite everything they had done.

She didn't know why she couldn't bring herself to hate them, even when she tried to.

She did not know how to act. She had chosen her fate once before and was still reeling from the consequences. She did not know if she had it in her to choose again.

Durkhanai pulled a flower from the earth, twirling it between her fingers as she walked toward the thin stream that cut through the ground. She plucked the petals from the stem, dropping them into the stream as she did, and watched them get carried away by the current. Some way along the stream, the water was cut by a large stone, and some of the petals went one way, while the others went another.

This choice was a double-edged blade: Either way she got cut.

"Durkhanai!" Bari Ammi called. She turned, dropping the stem. Bari Ammi approached, out of breath. "There is someone here to see you. Come at once."

Durkhanai took the older woman's hand and was led back to the village. Ammi's hand fidgeted in hers. Was Ammi nervous? But when Durkhanai analyzed the older woman's face, it was composed.

Who could be visiting her now? Perhaps Nazo Phuppo, hoping to persuade her again. She knew it would not be either of her cousins; they must hate her still.

She was not prepared for the sight of her grandparents.

They looked as regal as ever, only slightly mussed from the travel. They stood by the charpai, candlelight flickering across their features. Agha-Jaan's face looked twice as severe in the harsh light, Dhadi's straight posture twice as daunting. Durkhanai paused in the doorway, Bari Ammi going ahead of her.

"Baji," Agha-Jaan said, regarding his sister. Ammi lowered her head in respect and squeezed her little brother's shoulders.

"Come, Durkhanai," Bari Ammi said, looking at her with something in her eyes Durkhanai could not understand. It was like Ammi was trying to tell her something.

Durkhanai was frozen: She did not know how to act, or how they would react. She hadn't seen them in two months now. The sight of them now brought tears to her eyes.

Were they still angry with her?

But then Dhadi smiled, and Agha-Jaan's eyes—she could see that they loved her.

"Jaani," Dhadi said, opening her arms. Instinctively, Durkhanai ran to her, burying herself into her grandmother's arms. She felt, somehow, that in the past few weeks, she had been stripped away of everything she had ever been, and now all that remained was a child, searching for love.

"How are you, chiriya?" Agha-Jaan asked, hugging her next. She held him tight.

"I missed you," she said, offering her bravest smile. *I miss everything.*

"We missed you, too," Agha-Jaan said, beard wrinkling beneath his smile.

"We were so sorry to have you sent away, but you must see it was necessary," Dhadi said. "You understand, don't you?"

"Yes," Durkhanai said. "I understand."

They merely thought they were doing what was right. Perhaps they did know more than her, perhaps even the Kebzu alliance had some hidden wisdom, perhaps all of this was right and she was wrong.

She couldn't tell, she didn't know, she hadn't decided yet. She had avoided thinking for weeks now, and wanted to avoid it a little longer for fear of what she would find buried deep within her mind.

They sat, and Bari Ammi left to make chai. When it was ready, she brought the chai in little matke, which gave the chai a special wood smoked flavor due to the clay. Durkhanai sipped her chai, wincing as she burned her tongue. Agha-Jaan smiled.

"How are wedding preparations coming along?" Durkhanai asked, tone casual. She fiddled with her shalwar a moment, then smoothed her hands and straightened.

"They are coming along, slowly but surely," Dhadi said. "I've already decided which jewelry I can part with—not my own wedding sets, of course, for both of those I have saved for you, meri jaan." It was custom for mothers to pass on their jewelry to their daughters. "But the one your grandfather gifted me on our tenth anniversary will do—the rubies are so lovely. Besides, she does have Nazo's old sets to wear as well, so Zarmina really cannot complain."

"Oh, I do love that set," Durkhanai said with an empty smile.

"As for the dress, the artisans are nearly done with the work on the lengha, and the dupatta is completed. We decided on a gold tissue dupatta with heavy dabka kaam . . ."

It was all a facade, this frivolity. An opulent distraction, so people would not see the ugliness hidden beneath glittering clothes and shining jewels. So they would not suspect this marriage was anything other than one of divinity and happiness.

They made no mention as to whether they were taking her back with them. Durkhanai assumed it depended on her behavior.

Which was precisely why she smiled and ate her food and held her grandfather's hand and laughed. Yes, it was natural to do so, and yes she loved them still, but the act was not entirely free of pretense.

"Has Safed-Mahal been fortified to accept the baraat?" Durkhanai asked, voice gentle. The wedding-party would be made entirely of foreigners. It would be a first, since the people of Safed-Mahal did not marry outside of the mountain. "Perhaps the wedding should take place in Zarmina's home of Dirgara, just like when Nazo Phuppo was married. Didn't all the wedding events take place in her husband's home? I doubt anyone would question it."

Agha-Jaan smiled. "That's my Shehzadi," he said. "Always looking out for her people. Yes, the mountain has been secured. The baraat is hardly eighty people, besides. We could allow them so much. It is our beloved Zarmina's wedding, after all. We cannot have the people believing us stingy. And as for the matter of doing it in Dirgara, we did not even consider it. This union is born of the trial, and the trial is *our* custom."

Durkhanai wished to warn them further. Her grandparents were proud and secure in the knowledge of their safety, thus brushing her off.

But they did not know, could not know, about Wakdar, about Nazo Phuppo's visit. And Durkhanai didn't know enough to warn them about it, nor did she wish them to believe her mad.

She needed them to think she was entirely recovered, that she was fit to go home, or she might be stuck here in Mianathob forever.

She would not ask them to confirm the veracity of Nazo's tale, nor would she conjecture as to what was coming.

Durkhanai smiled, despite the creeping feeling growing inside of her. She offered her grandparents a plate of almond biscuits.

"Here, have some. And how is Zarmina?" Durkhanai asked. She did not ask about Saifullah, afraid her grandparents would recall the last thing she had said about him, that he was a spy for Wakdar. "Is she adjusting?" She tried to mask her curiosity with cousinly concern.

But Dhadi saw right through her.

"The happy couple is good at putting up pretenses, if that is what you wish to know," Dhadi said. Durkhanai stilled, not daring to ask more, yet desperate to hear more. "Do not worry. When a suitable time has passed, we will get rid of the boy."

Durkhanai stilled, heart beating fast. Blood rushed in her ears like a river and she was drowning beneath its current.

After what Nazo Phuppo had told her, she should not have been surprised, yet she still was.

She did not know why she could not bring herself to hate her grandparents, why she could not bring herself to betray them as Nazo Phuppo had urged her. She wanted too much—she wanted every-thing: to love Asfandyar and to love her grandparents, both. Yet each kept plotting against the other.

"We cannot be rid of him soon enough," Agha-Jaan said.

"Though not too soon, or the people will be suspicious," Dhadi reminded him. "We cannot have the people thinking the Badshah is interfering with the tribunal results." She paused, gauging Durkhanai's reaction, which was calculatedly empty. "Perhaps when they are on their honeymoon, there will be a terrible accident."

Durkhanai wanted to scream, to fight, but she made no move.

She could not show them that she cared for him as it would only give them more cause to kill him. She needed them to believe she was recovered from him.

"Perhaps Zarmina will fall into a stream and Asfandyar will die saving her—there, we shall make him a hero, won't that make you happy?" Dhadi asked, tucking a curl behind her granddaughter's ear.

"You indulge me." Durkhanai said. She forced a smile. "That ending will suffice us all very well."

"Yes, I believe so," Agha-Jaan said.

Durkhanai took a breath. "May I return for the wedding?" she asked gently, a child once more asking for permission and gifts. "Zarmina must be needing a friend. And I'd hate to miss the festivities."

Dhadi regarded her closely. Durkhanai warmed her gaze, molding her expression into as normal a one as she could. With bated breath, she waited as her grandmother analyzed her, staring deep into her eyes. Durkhanai did not look away.

"Yes, it does seem you are much improved," Dhadi finally said, lifting a hand to caress Durkhanai's cheek. She leaned into her grandmother's hand, smiling against her palm.

"I feel wonderful," Durkhanai agreed.

"I do believe you have rid your system of him," Dhadi said. "Were we not right to send you here?"

"Yes, Dhadi," Durkhanai said. "You were right."

But she knew the truth inside of her.

She loved him.

Which was why she needed to leave this village now and return to him, even if just to warn him. He could still run, could still save himself.

"You may return home," Dhadi said.

Durkhanai smiled, releasing a breath. She was going home; she passed the test.

But now that the prospect was here, the path entirely clear, Durkhanai was afraid. To face . . . everyone. Who would she be? It was time to choose her fate, and she was frightened to take even one step.

"We will send for you in a week," Dhadi said. "Pack your things, and if you wish to return then, you may."

Another choice. She was not obligated to go . . . Things were so much simpler here.

"And do wear something warm," Agha-Jaan said. "The snow season is nearly upon us."

It was a few days' travel, which meant she would arrive the day of the reception. While they may have been convinced she was recovered, they still did not trust what she would do when she returned. Perhaps she did not trust herself either.

Shortly after, her grandparents left her to return home. They had traveled far just to visit for a few hours in order to see her state for themselves to discern the truth.

Bari Ammi entered the hut, fidgeting with the end of her dupatta.

"How did it go?" she asked, voice wary. So Agha-Jaan had not told her.

"I may return home," Durkhanai said, emotionless. "They will have him killed."

With a shaky breath, Ammi came and sat beside Durkhanai, taking her hands in hers.

"It is good you may return," she said. "I am sorry I did not say anything to your grandfather myself in your defense, but you must understand if I had, he would have kept you here."

"Why?"

"I was tasked with monitoring you these past weeks, to ensure you would forget Asfandyar. If I had urged my brother to let you return home, he would have suspected foul play and kept you here longer, if not forever. Just like he has kept me here."

Durkhanai looked into Bari Ammi's aging eyes, the wrinkles folding her brown skin.

"You did not wish to stay here?" she asked. Bari Ammi shook her head.

"Do not fret for me now. I made my peace with it, long ago, but you must not. Your wings have not yet been clipped; you can still fly. You must." Ammi squeezed her hands. "You are different. Nazo, too, was sent here, and she remained for a year before she was married off to another. She accepted her fate, just as I did, because she had nothing else to fight for. But you—" Her eyes lit with fierce determination. "—*you* can still fight. There is hope for you, yet."

"But how?"

"Mohabbat, true love, is rare and beautiful and does not bloom often, but when it does, you must do everything in your power to ensure it thrives and flourishes and lives. You told me Asfandyar hates you, but I do not believe this is your end. Your love can still be saved, which is why you must go."

"I'm afraid," said Durkhanai.

"Be brave, Durkhanai. Dare to love."

Bari Ammi stood and leaned in to kiss Durkhanai on the forehead, then left her.

Releasing a long breath, Durkhanai curled into a ball on her charpai; she felt so tired these days, as if she could no longer bear the weight of her own skull. She pulled her shawl close. It was getting colder and colder. Her heart ached.

The flickering flame of a candle danced before her eyes, and she reached out to feel it's warmth, but it was too far away. She turned, looking up at the ceiling and its uneven pattern. She sighed, sinking deeper and deeper.

She lay wrapped in the fabric of old dreams which still kept her warm, wrapped in the idea of him. She stared at the shadows, and the world stripped away until she felt his phantom fingers brushing her cheek, his lips kissing her neck, that sweet, slow smile spreading across his face.

A tear trailed down her cheek.

Hours passed, and her tears had dried. Her skin was stiff, for she had not wiped them away, merely let them fall. She had not moved— did not move until Bari Ammi sat beside her, shifting the charpai.

Bari Ammi brushed a finger against Durkhanai's face, trying to coax her up and out of bed. Durkhanai did not meet her gaze. She was fixated on the ceiling.

"Kahan gum ho?" Ammi asked. "Where are you?"

There was nothing left but the truth.

"With him," Durkhanai whispered.

Bari Ammi nodded once.

"Then go."

# CHAPTER NINE

As the time grew nearer to leave, Durkhanai found herself more and more afraid. She had never been so fearful before, and it unnerved her to feel it now. A part of her did not want to leave Mianathob or the comforts and simplicity the village held.

She prepared for the journey, as it was all she could do. Even Heer was restless to go home, and Durkhanai assuaged her with a sugar cube, brushing her hair.

She was thinking of him, always thinking of him. She would see him again soon, making it to the palace just in time for the wedding. She did not know how to feel.

Would he still be angry? Of course he would. He hated her, and she deserved it, but he loved her, too, she knew that much.

Was it foolish to hope that love would conquer all?

She had spent so much time with him in her mind she nearly felt he might forgo his hatred for her, that despite the distance and the betrayal served by her hand, they would still be close.

She would tell him stories, he would look at her with those eyes that saw everything, she would run her hands through his curls, he would kiss her neck, and all would be as it should.

A fantasy, of course, but all she had were her thoughts: She could at least conjure up a fairytale for herself to believe in. She was so far away from the princess she once was, from the future queen, and was now simply a broken-hearted fool.

The loss of that princess, that queen, was just as keenly felt as the loss of her love.

Releasing a sigh, she petted Heer's head, running her fingers across the horse's mane, the both of them breathing in tandem. Above them, the sky was gray and still without the movement of clouds. As if all the world was on pause.

Suddenly, she heard a cry.

She turned, a gust of wind upending her hair. A company of soldiers on horses infiltrated the village, coming from all sides.

Her heartbeat pounded against her chest, startling her. In a swift motion, acting on instinct, she mounted Heer and kicked.

"Ammi!" Durkhanai screamed. Heer shot forward, cutting through the company, but there were too many soldiers. About twenty men on horses with swords.

The women weren't armed and were severely outnumbered, but they were Marghazari women, after all. They grabbed the scythes from the fields and warded off the soldiers as best as they could.

But it was too late.

The horsemen rounded up the women, crowding them together with uniform precision. They were clearly from an army, not merely somebody's personal guard, but Durkhanai could not recognize where they were from, who could have sent them.

Durkhanai did not fight when she saw how the men held their bows and arrows notched at the women's throats. All eyes were on her, as if waiting to see her reaction.

She would not jeopardize the villagers.

With a glare, Durkhanai settled Heer, calming her, and glared at the soldiers. As she did, her mind rifled through possibilities as to who could have sent them.

Not the Lugham Empire, not the Kebzu Kingdom. Not any of the other zillas. They wouldn't dare. And who had known of this palace?

It was a secret, the trail leading to it guarded for decades by her immediate family. Not even her extended cousins knew of it. . .

Then she realized. And her breathing stopped.

It was Wakdar's army.

# CHAPTER TEN

*T*he women of Mianathob were cornered.

A soldier came forward on a horse, another horse riding alongside him. He must have been the general: his uniform was more elaborate than the others. He dismounted quickly and pointed to the secondary horse. Durkhanai raised a brow.

"I don't think so," she replied, though she did not know what choice she had. The soldier made an exasperated sound, as if he knew she was out of options as well. His mustache twitching, he glanced at his companions. They lifted their swords to the women's throats. The general looked at her again. Raised a brow to match hers.

Dismounting, Durkhanai held up her hands, as if in surrender. "Let's be civilized, please," she said. Releasing a measured breath, she looked around for something to do, strategies flitting through her mind.

Before she had the chance to seize one and think it through, hands gripped her waist and an arm wrapped around her torso, lifting her into the air. She was seated on the horse, sidesaddle, without another word.

The general mounted his own horse as two other soldiers came to flank her sides, guarding her. While she preferred riding astride, when she made to adjust, the general tsked.

"No funny business, please, Shehzadi," he said, voice gruff. He gave a pointed glance to the soldiers who held the village women. Durkhanai narrowed her eyes.

The general clicked his tongue, and they rode forward. Behind her, the soldiers slowly released the women and mounted their own horses, trailing behind. Durkhanai looked over her shoulder, eyes meeting Bari Ammi's.

"It's okay," Durkhanai mouthed, telling Bari Ammi that she would be all right and not to do anything rash in the meanwhile. Bari Ammi nodded, eyes hard.

She rode on.

"Dear Papa has not come to fetch me himself?" Durkhanai asked. She had to admit she was a little offended. The soldiers gave her no response. The general was ahead of her, but he did not turn either.

Durkhanai gripped the horse's hairs, trying to commandeer it, but the horse merely neighed, not budging.

Durkhanai bit back a groan. Her body jostled back and forth as the horse trodded along. She wasn't used to riding sidesaddle through terrain like this: She only rode sidesaddle when she was wearing a lengha or other clothing that wouldn't allow her to ride astride. She felt unbalanced, as if she could fall off the horse. . .

An idea clicked in her mind. They could take her, but she would not go without causing some chaos first.

She faced forward, toward the soldier on her left. He did not look at her.

Taking a deep breath, she leaned back—and kicked her legs out with all her strength. The consequence was immediate: The soldier on the left fell off his horse, while the soldier on her right threw out his arms to keep her from falling.

Realizing what she'd done, the soldier holding her released her, and the muscles in her core screamed as she righted herself. The soldiers behind were thrown into a commotion as they avoided the felled soldier.

The general turned around and glared. She smiled.

With a motion of his head, the general communicated to another soldier. Her horse stopped, and the soldier came to sit behind her.

She scoffed at the impertinence. She hadn't ridden with anyone except Agha-Jaan, and even that was only when she was a little girl. She bristled as the soldier adjusted behind her, his arms locking around her.

"Don't touch me, and get the hell off my horse," she seethed.

"You've lost the privilege of riding on your own," the general snapped in return. She made to elbow the soldier's chest, but his arms locked her in place. Durkhanai scowled.

For a few moments, she remained mollified. She felt the soldier ease behind her, his grip not so tight, though she could still scarcely move her arms.

No matter.

She dropped her head forward, as if she'd fallen asleep, eyes closed. As the soldier drew near to check on her, she whipped her head back.

His nose cracked against her skull. Blood dripped down her back.

"*Kuti!*" he snarled, hands coming up to hold his now broken nose. As he did, she reached behind and pushed him off *her* horse. He swore again, and the other soldiers came round, blocking her path. The general stopped in front of her.

He withdrew his sword, pointed it at her. She extended her throat for him, a sweet smile spreading over her mouth. They wouldn't hurt her. Father dearest must have given them strict instructions.

She held her hands up in innocence.

"Are you quite done?" the general asked, voice exasperated.

"Now that you ask, I am thirsty," she said. The general snapped his fingers, and a skin of water materialized in front of her. She drank, then dabbed at her mouth with her dupatta. "And I will ride alone."

"Anything more, Shehzadi?" The general asked, voice ironic.

She shook her head, which was starting to hurt.

"Ride on!" the general called once more. Durkhanai settled into her saddle, bracing for the rest of the journey

She heard the soldiers muttering to themselves, annoyed. Satisfied, she nearly smirked to herself. She couldn't do much, but she could at least be a nuisance.

They reached the camp quickly after that. It was a short distance from Mianathob, but while the village lay by the lake and meadows, the camp was set up around the bend of the mountain.

It was a small camp, about double the size of the company that had been sent to retrieve her. Durkhanai wondered just what Wakdar was getting at if *this* was the group he was traveling with.

When they grew nearer, Durkhanai saw the valley. She stilled.

There was an army, setting up camp. They must have stopped to rest while Wakdar and a small company traveled up the mountain to retrieve her, though he himself did not come to Mianathob; it looked as if he had only sent a third of his company to get her.

The other two-thirds were in the camp, and the rest of his army waited in the valley below. Waited to go straight to Safed-Mahal.

Durkhanai memorized the details as much as she could, trying to surmount numbers and horses and cannons. But she was quickly steered away from the sight, led toward the cluster of tents.

The rest of the soldiers left to their own business, leaving her with the general. He escorted her to a large tent in the center of the camp.

Durkhanai dismounted the horse. Anger beat through her veins, overwhelming her with the sudden influx of feeling. She did not wait to be prompted into the tent; she pushed the curtains aside and marched in past the soldiers.

Lamplight illuminated the tent, which was modest with a washing basin, a charpai, and a table covered with papers. At the head of the table stood a man.

He looked up as she entered. Durkhanai fixed him with her deadliest glare.

He smiled, and she froze, stopping in her tracks. She stood rooted in place, as if thrown into history.

Durkhanai had seen portraits of Agha-Jaan when he was young, seen portraits of him in his middle age. There had been none of Wakdar—they had said the sight made them too sad, but now she realized that had been a lie, too.

He looked exactly like Agha-Jaan, two decades younger.

The same blue-green eyes, the same hefty build, those striking features and the honey-colored hair now streaked with gray that tinged his neatly trimmed beard, as well. He looked nothing like Dhadi, with her dark brown hair and softer features, just as Durkhanai herself looked nothing like Dhadi. He looked just like Agha-Jaan, he looked just like Nazo Phuppo.

And he looked just like her.

She saw it in the shape of his nose, the arch of his brows, even the curl of his lips. And she filled at once with belonging and then intensified hatred.

It was one thing to know her father was alive, existing somewhere outside of her world. It was another thing entirely to see him standing before her, his features giving no doubt that he was hers and she was his.

"I must confess, I was disappointed to find you were out hiding," Wakdar said, breaking the silence. His voice was deep and foreign.

She held on to how foreign it sounded. This man may have been her father, but she knew nothing of him.

Durkhanai made no response, though his statement was surely meant to rile her. He must have heard of her from Nazo, who had kept in touch with him all these years.

"My brave daughter, as I have heard from dear Nazo," he confirmed, following her thoughts. He paused. "She does love you so, even when you act the fool for Ghazan and Bazira."

Durkhanai balked. No one called her grandparents by their names. He took another step toward her, hands behind his back. He smiled, clearly enjoying himself, his voice sugar sweet.

"Now, won't you come home?" he asked gently, coaxing as . . . well, as a father to his petulant daughter. She lifted her jaw.

"You know nothing of the word," she said. "Though your ignorance is expected. Mianathob is home."

"No, it isn't," he said. "Your home is Safed-Mahal. Just as mine is. You are my daughter, whether you accept it or not. It is my blood that runs through your veins. You cannot run, nor can you hide from that." Durkhanai's heart quickened with the words, a strange dread entering her. What he said was true; no matter how she resisted, he was her father, and she was his daughter. Nothing could change that.

He reached out a hand. "Shall we not go home together?"

Horribly, her bottom lip trembled with emotion.

She spit at him.

"You're a coward," she snapped. Since she'd found out he was alive, Durkhanai hadn't even considered what she would say to her father once she saw him—she hadn't allowed herself to think of it. But now that he stood before her, the words bubbled up. "You abandoned your family," she seethed. "Your child, your wife—my mother is *dead* because of you! I grew up without parents because you were weak. You lacked the courage to face your fate. You ran."

Wakdar took her words within his stride, his smile not faltering. "Aren't you doing the same now?" he asked, voice tauntingly gentle. Anger flared within her—then she realized. He was right.

She had been asleep these past two months. She had been running and hiding and avoiding it all.

She made a decision right then. She would not be a coward.

No matter what happened, she would not be her father's daughter. She would not let his blood rule her.

She hoped she was strong enough to fight it. That her struggle would not be futile.

Durkhanai straightened her back, raised her chin. She was the daughter of the mountains and river S'vat. She was a princess to this valley and the purest tribe.

It was time she went home.

But how? What did Wakdar want from her? Surely he had not captured her for this lovely reunion.

"You did not deny the claim," Durkhanai said, steadying the emotion from her voice. She did not need to clarify. A shadow crossed over Wakdar's face. He leaned back on his table, regarding her.

"I did not," he replied, emotion entering his voice. "I am the reason your mother is dead, though the blame is not mine to bear."

"And what is that to mean?" she asked, circling the tent, taking quiet inventory. "She killed herself because you left."

At the entrance, she saw the feet of about four soldiers, standing guard. That would not do.

"Is that what they told you?" he asked, surprised. He scoffed bitterly, and a chill ran down her spine, seeping in from outside the tent. "When the simple truth is they killed her."

"Please," she scoffed, rolling her eyes. As she did, her gaze caught at the space where the tent's cloth joined behind Wakdar's table. That could do . . .

"Nazo found the evidence herself," Wakdar said. "A poisoned naan, half-eaten."

"That does not refute the claim that she committed suicide," Durkhanai countered.

"Doesn't it?" Wakdar tsked. "You're disappointing me, Durkhanai. I thought you were more than just a pretty little princess." She bristled, despite herself. He smiled, his words finding their mark. "Why would your dear mother go through the trouble of kneading poison into dough, then baking it in naan? When she could simply drink it and fall soundly to sleep?"

Durkhanai furrowed her brows. It did make sense. Her breathing grew shallow. Wind brushed against the tent, sending distorted shadows across Wakdar's face.

"Your beloved grandparents even tried to have me killed," he continued. "The moment I left Safed-Mahal, I was attacked by three assassins, their faces cloaked. While they were covered in black, they had palace swords."

"If Agha-Jaan and Dhadi wanted you dead, you would not be standing here," Durkhanai said. "Perhaps it was a warning."

Wakdar shook his head at her innocence, at her naivety. "Perhaps. Though it would have saved them lots of trouble if I had died that night."

She didn't believe it, but something did not fit, something did not make sense. Wakdar on one side, her grandparents on the other. Something was missing.

"And what of the murder of your sister, Naina?" he asked. "What of that?"

Durkhanai faltered. This, she had no response to.

"You look nothing like her, though she had my eyes, as well. More green than blue, hers were, in the most stunning way. She was all effortless, simple beauty, just like her mother, not as coarse or striking as you and I," he said, pressing into her vanity. "You would have liked her, you know," Wakdar continued. "Everyone did. Particularly Asfandyar. His love for her was unlike anything I'd ever seen. Truly astonishing. My dear Naina was the love of his life, you see."

Durkhanai's hand curled into a fist, jealousy burning through her.

"Poor Asfi." He tsked. "How is our dearest friend? Married now, I hear? He has had such struggles with love, the poor boy, so I am glad to see him settled and happy." Durkhanai said nothing. "Though not too happy, one can assume, since the reception has not yet happened. It is the wedding night where things truly become fun."

Durkhanai blinked at him, refusing to allow her envy to show.

"I am sure you have ample knowledge," she replied instead, voice sharp. "With so much interest in wedding nights, I wonder why you have not married again. Third time's the charm, is it not? Though perhaps with two wives and a daughter dead you do not wish to tempt fate further by plaguing innocent women."

The smile dropped from his face. Satisfaction coursed through her. The tent was silent for a beat, and she glanced around indifferently, though really she was looking for a weapon.

Her eyes glazed over his helmet and sword. That would not do; she was not trained. But there was not much else save for papers and a pitcher of water.

Perhaps . . .

"You have seen my army, I presume?" Wakdar asked, changing tactics. "I have heard you are a devoted Shehzadi. Surely you wish to avoid war?"

She narrowed her eyes. She did not wish to concede, her pride bristling, but if he could give her a solution to avoid this war and save countless bloodshed. . .

"Yes," she said, voice even. "What do you suggest?"

"I am on my way to lay siege to the capital, to return home," Wakdar said. "With Marghazar's resources thinned by the wars with the Lugham Empire, my conquest will be swift and brutal." His voice was matter-of-fact; he was not trying to intimidate or threaten her, merely make her understand. "Countless lives will be lost on either side . . . "

His voice trailed off. He looked at her expectantly.

"I assume you wish me to say 'unless?' now?"

"*Unless* you join me," he said. "You are my daughter, my blood and heir. The people love you. We can dispose of your grandparents quickly, and no lives need be lost."

Nazo had said the same. Durkhanai could not consider it: Her mind was a tangled mess of thoughts, so she reached only for instinct, for core-deep truths she had known her entire life—for feelings of duty, for the love of her grandparents, for her devotion to her people.

"I won't," she said through clenched teeth. "I will protect my people."

"You don't know who your people are," he replied easily. "You don't even know yourself." He came near, and she recoiled. "Dear Durkhanai, my daughter. Let me guide you. Follow your blood. Do you not wish to be a family? Join me, and you will once more have the love of your cousins and aunt. You will have a father. You can have everything—or nothing. Surely you must know your grandparents cannot live forever. Once they have gone, you will be alone."

Pain filled her chest at the thought. She could not even consider it. He drew even closer, eyes softening, but Durkhanai was clever enough to see he was more interested in the political gain he would have by earning her favor than in soft feelings of family.

That was enough.

"I will never join you," she snapped. And then she attacked.

# CHAPTER ELEVEN

Durkhanai punched him square in the jaw.

Her knuckles split with pain, and she winced. She wasn't strong enough for a punch to do much damage. It did succeed in stunning him, however, giving her a moment of time, and she rushed behind him, grabbing his helmet.

She lifted the helmet and slammed it across his skull with all the strength and fury and grief she held. He buckled, and she struck again, in the same spot, then again, one last time for good measure.

Holding her breath, she waited. Would it be enough? She had never been trained to fight, and here was a full grown soldier.

But then his knees gave out. She rushed forward to grab him, slowly easing him to the ground without a sound so as not to alert the soldiers outside. Blood wet his hair, and there was a cut across his jaw from her ring.

Once he was on the ground, she headed to the back of the tent. Along the way, she picked up his sword. It was heavier than she expected it to be, but it might come in handy. At the very least, it would irritate him; men were very attached to their swords.

Heart beating fast, Durkhanai slipped out the back of the tent. The sky was darkening; the sun had set. Clinging to the shadows, she searched the camp. There were groups of people sitting around a bonfire, eating and drinking cups of steaming tea. In the distance, some men were praying maghrib, the sunset prayer.

She didn't have much time. Wakdar might not be out for long.

She scanned her surroundings, searching for a path out. The tangle of trees, the open field, the dip and rise of the mountain.

She saw it.

Now she needed a horse. There was one ambling by the creek, drinking water. Heart beating fast, Durkhanai made her move.

She slipped out of the shadow of the tent and ducked behind another. Voices filled her ears: The tent wasn't empty. She waited a moment, then moved again. And again. Until the horse was within reach.

She clucked her tongue gently, to get the horse's attention. It looked up at her, and she said a quick prayer, hoping she could succeed. *Ya Allah.*

"Ao," she said to the horse, voice honey sweet. "Come."

She clucked her tongue again, and the horse took a step forward, then stopped. The rest she had to do on her own.

She took a deep breath and leaped from the shadows.

"Hey!" someone cried.

There wasn't a moment to hesitate. Durkhanai ran to the horse and mounted, then kicked it into motion. A dozen heads swiveled to look at her, half of them already running toward her.

"Yah!" she cried, and this time, the horse listened. With a loud neigh, it bolted, and she steered it forward. The sound of swords unsheathing filled her ears, and she unsheathed her own. Holding the reins with one hand, she slashed her sword blindly with the other as her horse cut through the crowd.

The sword was heavy, and she maneuvered it awkwardly with both hands, but it was enough to ward off some of the soldiers. She swung haphazardly again, through the last push of the crowd, and it caught.

The sword slipped from her grasp, but it was no matter now. The road ahead of her was clear.

"Chalo, chalo!" she said, urging her horse forward. "Come on!"

The horse ran, and the wind whipped against her cheeks, frigid and harsh. The sound of the horse's hooves matched the quick beat of her heart as they flew forward.

As she exited the camp, there was an itch at the back of her head. She braced for the sound of horses behind her, of soldiers chasing after her. But she heard nothing.

Wind whipping through her hair, she turned to look over her shoulder.

Just as Wakdar emerged from his tent. His gaze caught hers, and a chill ran down her spine. He smiled at her. The message was clear.

He had let her go.

# CHAPTER TWELVE

*D*urkhanai rode back to Mianathob, not looking back.

She had a feeling no one would be coming after her. Is this what Wakdar had wanted all along? To frighten her, send her scurrying home in fear to warn her grandparents at the last moment?

She felt her control slipping from her fingers, a thousand pieces moving in directions she couldn't follow.

When she neared the village, it was empty and silent, eerily so. Night had fallen, and not a single torch was lit.

Just as she entered, the women emerged. They were prepared for a fight, armed with scythes and cooking knives and bottles of rancid smelling liquid meant to momentarily blind people.

"Shehzadi!"

"She's back!"

Durkhanai dismounted the horse in a fluid movement. She stood steady on her feet despite her sore legs and searched for Bari Ammi. Torches were lit, and firelight illuminated the women's faces.

"Is everyone all right?" she asked, checking to see if anyone had been harmed. No one was hurt.

"Durre!" a voice called. She turned to find Bari Ammi approaching, Heer's reins in her hands. Durkhanai ran and hugged the older woman, breathless for a moment as emotions overcame her.

Heer was already packed with her things and food for the journey. There was no time to wait for the guards from the palace to come and retrieve her. Time was of the absolute essence.

Bari Ammi took her shawl off and wrapped it around Durkhanai's shoulders, squeezing her shoulders once.

"It'll be all right," the older woman promised. She pressed a kiss to Durkhanai's forehead. "It is time for you to go home." Bari Ammi gazed into her eyes. "And remember, *be brave*."

Ammi grabbed a large cloak and fastened it atop the shawl: The night had brought with it a deadly chill, and Durkhanai had far to go. Someone handed Durkhanai her riding boots, as well, and then there was nothing left to be done but to leave.

Durkhanai mounted Heer, then held out her hand. Bari Ammi squeezed it, and tears blurred Durkhanai's vision for a moment.

"I'll send for you all," she said. Mianathob had been compromised. "Soon."

"Don't worry about us," Ammi insisted. "They aren't here for us; I doubt they will come again." Durkhanai nodded, but she could not help but fret. "You have a battle ahead of you," Ammi said. "Be safe. Now go. Allah de havale, go."

She did.

Heer rode like hell.

The wind whipped across Durkhanai's cheeks, ice-cold and furious, but she was never more glad for it. She felt she'd suddenly woken up, and there was much to be done. Her head throbbed from where she had hit the soldier, and her knuckles hurt from punching Wakdar.

Everything was sore—but she was alive, and she was going home.

Despite the head start she had, she raced back to the capital, riding Heer as fast as she could. One traveler would be faster than Wakdar's army, and while he had to use the valley, and the canons would slow him down, she could cut through the woods and take the quickest route back.

The problem was that she hadn't traveled this path in some time, now. It was the darkest of night, and as she maneuvered through the tangle of trees, fear awakened in her. The night would be long, and despite the shining half-moon above them, it was getting difficult to see.

She was exhausted; Heer was, too.

They stopped for the night.

Not in the woods, for Durkhanai feared what animals roamed, but not entirely in the open, either. She found a dip in the terrain to make her camp, where the trees weren't so thick, so that she could see the moon and the stars.

While fear arrested Durkhanai's senses, she could not dwell on it for the adrenaline that thrummed through her, and the importance of her task.

She needed to return to her people, ensure that they would be safe from this army. She had to protect them, no matter what.

Durkhanai ate, then settled against Heer, covering them both with her cloak. They warmed one another.

The next morning, she awoke for fajr. She and Heer set out before dawn and watched the sun tint the sky as they rode: purple, pink, yellow, white.

As they reached the middle of the journey, Durkhanai found herself faltering. While it was easy to maneuver the area close to Mianathob, and she would recognize the lands near Safed-Mahal, this in-between land was foreign to her.

Luckily, Heer was not so hesitant.

All those years traveling back and forth when she used to live in Mianathob must have been ingrained in the horse. Slowly, Durkhanai recognized the turning of the scenery that pointed toward home, and so did Heer.

By the third morning, Durkhanai saw her marble palace glistening in the sun like a pearl embedded into the shell of her mountain.

She was almost home.

"Chalo," she told Heer, nudging her forward. "Last push."

They were both exhausted and hungry and sore, but she couldn't stop, not now that she was so close.

They made their way down the mountain, across the valley, avoiding villages as they did. While Durkhanai wished to stop and speak with her people—see how they were doing, see that they still loved her—there was no time to stop. They would have too many questions for her, besides.

Surprisingly, the valley was full of troops from the other zillas. They must have been the armies the Badshah had previously bargained for with the ambassadors.

The sight of them made her uneasy, but there was no time to dwell on it. Besides, they would soon be leaving for the front against the Lugham Empire, so they would not linger here long.

Finally, she reached the gates of Safed-Mahal.

While Safed-Mahal was the name of the capital city, it was also what the people referred to the entire mountain as. This was the legendary jewel that blocked passage to foreigners, and just as anyone else would be, she was barred from entering.

From here, nobody could enter; nobody could leave. It was how they kept their land and their people pure. Only those from their own tribes were allowed in. For a moment, the ghost of her sister, Naina, lingered beside her.

This was where she had died.

She had come here, those few years ago, with her beloved by her side and hope in her heart. She had believed she would be able to reunite her family, believed they could all exist together.

Deep down, Durkhanai desperately hoped for the same, but she knew enough to understand it could never be. She would need to salvage what she could, and mourn the rest. But that would not stop her from trying.

The base of the mountain was protected by large boulders, a natural barrier. There was only one way through, and it was blocked by heavy iron gates; she could not even see past them. From above, guards watched from towers, looking below.

She removed her cloak, showing her face.

Even dirty and tired, she was instantly recognizable. Guards scurried from their posts, and after a few moments, a small door opened beside the gates.

"Shehzadi!" the guard cried, lowering his head in respect. She dismounted Heer and strode forward, through the door and into the watch tower's base.

"Let me bring you something to drink," a guard said. "And something warm to wear."

Durkhanai held up a hand. "There is no need. Please tend to my horse and take me to speak to your commanding officer."

The guard acquiesced, taking the reins from her. Heer was passed on to another, who brought her toward the door leading out on the other side.

"This way, Shehzadi," the first guard said to her, leading her to the flight of stairs. She followed him until they reached the watch tower's apex. The commanding officer rose when he saw who entered. She was glad to recognize him.

"General Rizvi, how good to see you," she said, nodding at him. He lowered his head in respect. He was an older man with a harsh but kind face.

"Shehzadi, what brings you here?" he replied. "A squadron of soldiers left yesterday to retrieve you."

"There is an army headed by Wakdar coming to lay siege upon Safed-Mahal," Durkhanai said. "I must hurry to the palace at once to warn my grandparents. I expect he will arrive in the next day or so."

"An army, led by Wakdar?" he repeated. "Shehzadi, you seem to be in a shock. Why don't you sit down for a moment and I will call for some tea—"

"I don't *need* to sit," she snapped, lifting her chin. "What I *need* is a competent general. You have been tasked with overseeing these gates, have you not?"

General Rizvi swallowed. "Yes, Shehzadi," he answered reluctantly.

"As I thought," she continued. "So surely the news of an *army* swiftly approaching should concern you more than whether I have had my morning's tea or not."

"Shehzadi, forgive my impertinence," he replied. "But how did you come across such information? What exactly happened? You speak of your father, though he died the night you were born."

"Your request is denied. I do not need to explain myself to you," Durkhanai said through clenched teeth.

He should not have been questioning her. There was no time to explain. She needed to get home. But she needed to make sure the gates were adequately fortified, first.

"But as it seems you will not be forced to action without a story," she said, releasing a measured breath. "I will tell you one. Wakdar, obviously alive, infiltrated the village I was in and kidnapped me. He then took me to his camp, where I saw about thirty companies of foot soldiers and five companies of cavalry. They also have canons, by which I am sure they wish to tear down the boulders and these gates. He warned me of his plans to lay siege to the capital. I escaped and came straight here to tell you that you must prepare."

"But Wakdar—" the general began, dumbfounded.

"Is dead, yes, I know," she replied, rolling her eyes. "Evidently not."

As she spoke, she walked over to General Rizvi's desk, looking at the files there. The gates were from where each battalion of Safed-Mahal soldiers left for battle, whether it be to the eastern front against the Lugham Empire or the northern front to the Kebzu Kingdom.

"Are there any squadrons scheduled to be leaving Safed-Mahal in the next few days?" she asked, rifling through the papers.

"Yes. There is a battalion meant to leave later today for the eastern front," General Rizvi replied.

"No longer," Durkhanai said. "No soldiers are to leave these gates. We need every man and woman on hand to face this army when it comes. For those who have already been dispatched, send messengers to call them back."

She considered sending troops to the path Wakdar would be taking, the secret route from Mianathob to Safed-Mahal, but it was too late to send all their forces there and risk slaughter while leaving the capital unmanned. No, it was best to fortify the mountain and wait for him to come here.

"But—"

"Shukria, General Rizvi," Durkhanai said, approaching him with a sweet smile. She placed an appreciative hand on his arm. "I will remember your courage and loyalty during this egregious event. I will be sure to mention it to the Badshah, who I am sure will be equally grateful."

She met his gaze. He hesitated a moment, and she waited, her gaze unwavering, not allowing her expression to show even an inch of the doubt she felt—until he spoke.

"I am at your service, Shehzadi," he said, lowering his head in respect.

"Shukria, General," she said, nodding once. "I will be taking my leave now."

"I will get guards to escort you," he said. With a quick motion, guards materialized, and Durkhanai was led back down the flight of stairs. They opened the door, and she was met with the familiar sight of her mountain. High above, she caught a glimpse of the marble palace, glistening.

Durkhanai took a breath, inhaling deeply the scent of pine needles and petrichor. The air was brisk and light.

"We will take the back passage," Durkhanai told the guards tasked with escorting her home. There were four of them, and while she would have preferred only one so the other three could stay back and fortify the gates, she knew it would be a waste of time arguing with General Rizvi over this.

They began their journey, taking a secret route to get to the palace quickly. It bypassed the main trails and was out of sight of the villages. With a start, Durkhanai realized Wakdar would know about this trail, and she wondered if she should order the guards to fortify this path.

But even if he broke through the gates, he would not use this route to access the palace: It was quick but made only for a small group of people.

Wakdar would know the route, but he would not attempt to attack the palace with only a handful of soldiers.

The terrain was relentless and difficult to maneuver unless one was familiar with the contours of the land.

Luckily, she was.

Night fell as she made her way back. The trail led to the back gardens of the palace, then took her straight to the edge of the stables.

She brushed off the head stable boy's surprise and questions, letting the guards who had escorted her explain as much as was necessary: that she was back and she needed to speak to her grandparents immediately.

They did not ask more.

"I'll see you soon," she whispered to Heer, nuzzling her nose against the horse's.

Walking to the palace doors, she took a deep breath. The sight of the entrance felt right; she knew bone deep that she was where she was meant to be. She pushed open the doors.

She inhaled the scent of roses. She was home.

# CHAPTER THIRTEEN

*D*urkhanai took a step forward, then stopped. The guards shadowed her movements and stopped with her. She turned to the one on her right.

"That will be all," she said, voice dismissive. The guards exchanged a wary glance.

"We are to escort you safely to your room," the one on the left, with the mustache, said. She smiled at him, lips saccharine. She turned and faced them both.

"Shukria, but that is not necessary," she said, taking a step forward. The guards took a hesitant step forward as well. "This is *my* palace. I know perfectly well how to get around."

"Nonetheless, we must accompany you to safety," the other guard replied. Durkhanai stopped in her tracks, eyes cut into slits.

"I suggest you focus less on escorting me to my own room and more on protecting this mountain from an impending siege," she snapped.

"But, Shehzadi——"

She held up her hand, and the guard stopped.

"If made to choose between the war and me, the war is the better option," she said, voice deadly. "Trust me."

She glared. The guards lowered their heads, and left without another word to fortify the borders.

Releasing a measured breath through her nose, Durkhanai stretched her neck. She pressed her cold fingers to her throat, where her pulse beat erratically against her palm.

There was a long way to go. She marched toward her grandparents' rooms, intent on alerting them at once. They might have been asleep already, but she would wake them.

But as she passed through the halls of the marble palace, her feet slowed of their own volition, and her gaze caught at an empty room.

Her urgency swayed.

She entered the room, a shiver running down her spine from the cold. In the center of the room hung a jhula from the ceiling.

The seat was hand carved with floral motifs and large enough to seat two, perhaps even three. The chains holding the swing up were entwined with leaves and flowers, giving the effect of twisted branches.

There were no roses, now, no candles either. Even the chains were cold to the touch. But when Durkhanai ran the fingers of her left hand against the chains, a chill ran through her, sparking memories as it did, igniting within her the last time she had been here, and with whom.

She did not sit. Instead, she closed her eyes, her right hand still pressed against her throat. She heard the echo of a laugh in her memories, and she felt as if she'd been pierced by something sharp. She could nearly feel the weight of his arm in hers, his hand on her leg.

She opened her eyes. Melancholy spread through her, pressing down on her chest as heavy as two hands pushing the blood from her heart's vessels.

Silent so as not to disturb the memories in the room, Durkhanai exited. She began walking to her grandparents' rooms, then stopped.

She stood in the center of the hall, her mind taking a moment to catch up with her body.

If she went to warn her grandparents now, they would surely have Asfandyar arrested for collusion, and hanged. They didn't need evidence, just a good reason to have him killed. This would save them the scheming of his demise on his honeymoon.

Durkhanai's heart beat frantically against her chest, and much as she willed her feet to move, they were rooted in the spot. Hesitantly, she looked over her shoulder. The hall was empty and quiet, silent and still. Cold reverberated through the marble floors.

*He was a liar and a spy. He had used her.*

She took a step forward.

*She put her heart in a velvet pouch and tied it tight.*

Another step.

*He was a liar and a spy. He had used her. . .*

She stopped.

What she had done was wrong, too.

Two months without him had been brutal, but the knowledge of his existence had still warmed her. Now, standing in the same building as him, the warmth was spreading through her as the sun softened dawn. She could not imagine him dead—could not imagine a world without him—as she had intended, at the trial.

She had been *wrong*.

Durkhanai turned around. And ran.

Her khussay slapped against the marble floors as she ran, past confused guards and maids who gave her second glances, and she didn't care. She knew Asfandyar was working with Wakdar, that surely he had a hand in all this, the coming siege, and she was a fool to do what she was going to do.

But she would do it anyway.

She would warn him. Give him time to escape. Give him life after trying to take it.

Slowly down to a quick walk, Durkhanai caught her breath. As she maneuvered through the halls, she calculated her time. She had at least a day before Wakdar would arrive. An hour detour would not change much, in the grand scheme of things.

She would allow herself this. She had become illiterate in her love: She could read nothing but her desire for him.

She ducked through to the passageways. She knew the way by heart. Had it not haunted her, all these months away from him? Had she not imagined herself going to him?

She stopped before his door. Would he be there? Would he be alone?

Somehow, she knew he would. She knew with clarity, the way one does in dreams, without reason, yet without doubt, either. Love without intuition was not love at all.

She waited by the door, heart beating fast, much too fast. She was afraid. Tears flooded her eyes. She was so afraid. Bari Ammi's voice sounded in her head: *be brave.*

She brushed the tears away and opened the door.

His room was dark, but she saw him immediately. He was asleep, lying on his side. His back was to her.

Holding her breath, careful not to make any noise, she walked around his bed to face him. Seeing him cut open the scar of her heart: It was a fresh wound, sharp and painful.

Tears welled in her eyes, blurring the sight of him, and she blinked them away, gaze hungry. How she had pictured him again and again, yet the truth of him surpassed her imaginings: the blood and bone of him, right before her.

Those devastating eyelashes, the indent in his cheek where a dimple would appear. Soft curls, a little longer than before, and a strong jaw.

Durkhanai came closer as if drawn by a magnetic pull. He did not stir. She crouched down in front of him. The floor was ice beneath her knees, but she was inflamed by the sight of him.

Her heart beat so fast she thought her ribcage would crack like glass on the slow journey to shattering into a thousand mutilated fragments.

She lifted a shaking hand. With a deep breath, she reached for him. Then stopped. Her hand hovered midair. She wouldn't be able to bear seeing the hatred in his eyes.

But she had to.

Swallowing hard, she touched his arm gently.

"Asfi," she whispered. He stirred. "Asfi."

"Durre?" he murmured. Her breath hitched.

"It's me."

"Chanda," he sighed. His hand closed around hers, and she expected him to discard her, but he held onto her, taking her hand. His eyes were still closed, and she took the opportunity to stare at him without his searing gaze staring back.

"You're so far away," he said. He held her hand to his heart, and she felt it's steady rhythm beneath her fingertips. "Come, be near me."

She did not protest. He shifted, making room for her, and she crawled beside him, exchanging the cool marble floor for the warmth of his body. Releasing a long sigh, she nestled into the soft bed, facing him. She was exhausted from the journey.

"Aren't you angry with me?" she whispered. He looked at her from beneath hooded eyes.

"No, Durre, not angry," he said, his arm coming around her waist. "Just sad. Though I cannot blame you entirely, for I am not proud of all that I have done, either."

"But—" she began, then stopped as her voice broke.

"Main tera, main tera," he promised. "No matter how we have hurt each other, I'm yours."

And he pressed his lips to hers. She closed her eyes, melting against him. He tasted like the best dream made real, his kiss so sweet and tender, she lost herself.

"You taste like starlight," he whispered against her mouth. He deepened the kiss, and something stirred within her.

"Asfi," she gasped, pulling away. "You must listen to me now."

She got out of bed and stood in front of him, holding a hand to her chest, trying to catch her breath. He shifted to sit up as well, then reached for her, eyes sleepy.

"Must you go?" he asked, taking hold of her stray hand.

"Asfi, please——"

"Don't," he said. "Aaj jane ki zidd na karo." He pressed a kiss to her palm. "How I wish this wasn't a dream."

"It isn't," she whispered, but she could no longer tell. She could not tell because it tasted like one, like perfection. Perhaps it truly was a dream, she thought to herself, as Asfandyar pulled her back to bed, back into his arms.

He could dream a little longer, and so could she. She was tired, she was so tired.

She curled against him. Her breathing steadied. His eyes closed once more, and her own eyelids began fluttering in response.

Sleep spread through her, overtaking her toes and traveling up. Her eyes closed, fully, her breathing slowing, slower, slower. . .

*No.* She could not sleep.

She jerked awake and leapt off the bed. She slipped her feet out of her khussay and pressed them into the cold marble floors, wincing as she did so, but it did the trick. She was awake.

This wasn't a dream.

This was real.

She slapped him.

Asfandyar jolted, confused, then was suddenly very, very awake. The love on his face was replaced by hatred once more.

"What are you doing here?" he asked, voice hard as he stood. She had to look up to meet his gaze, and in that moment, she realized precisely how wrong she had been.

In that moment, that final, fateful moment, she had acted on instinct, making the decision her grandparents would have wanted her to make.

She had been a coward.

She should have fought for her and Asfandyar to be together, rather than admitting defeat and sending him to the lion.

And now he hated her.

This was the price she had to pay. It was her own doing.

"I came to warn you," she said, voice flat. "You must leave." He narrowed his eyes at her. "Wakdar is coming." He hardly reacted, which meant he must have known. "I saw him," she added quietly. "I expect he will be here in a day."

"No," Asfandyar said, finally speaking. "He will be here in three days."

"He may be expediting that journey," she said. "Which is why I am telling you. Either way, you must leave. Once my grandparents learn of his intended siege, they will not hesitate to kill you. You must go."

Having warned him, she tore her gaze away from him. Ya Allah, she loved him. Where could she put what she felt for him? It was getting too heavy to carry.

Looking away did not help. Her eyes were starved of him already. She looked again. This time, *he* looked away.

"Don't look at me like that," he said, voice hard. "You summon something sinful within me."

"You must leave," she said. "Now."

"And why would I do something so foolish as to believe you?" he asked, stepping closer. "Why would I trust you?"

His eyes were blazing. Her breath caught.

"I—" she started. "I sent you to your death once. I wish only to settle the score now." She swallowed, cleared her throat. "If you stay in the palace, you will surely die. I do not wish that."

He laughed, quick and hard. "You believe saving my life now will absolve you from what you tried to send me to?"

She looked away again.

This time, he seized her shoulders.

"No, *look at me*," he growled. She did. His face was raw with emotion.

"Leave," she whispered. It was all she could manage to say. He shook his head.

"You are worse than the war," he said. "I used to have nightmares of bloodstained soldiers and the clashing of swords." He swallowed. "Now, you visit my dreams, your savage little teeth trailing across my skin. At first, it is the best of dreams, for I believe them to be kisses. I realize too late your teeth are those of a lion—a monster. How you slaughter me with a kiss."

"I—" Her voice broke. "I'm *sorry*. I wish I could take it back."

Tears welled in her eyes, and this time she let them, hoping he could see she meant it, that she was not playing a trick on him.

And somehow, he did.

Slowly, the anger receded from his face, and she was glad to see it go until it was replaced by something deeper, something truer: sadness. She did not know which broke her heart more.

They watched each other, neither knowing what was left to say.

"Did you ever love me, in truth?" she finally asked, voice small. She needed to know. They might never see each other again; this was the time to ask.

She no longer felt betrayed by his spying and lying. She knew that the moments they had spent together had not been entirely false; he had still been honest about himself, because it had cost nothing to his plan.

"For what it's worth, I felt awful about it once I knew you, but I could not back out," he said, voice hoarse. "I owed as much to Naina and to Wakdar." He paused. "So yes, I did . . . " He swallowed. "I do."

Running a hand through his hair, he opened his mouth as if to speak, then stopped. A muscle ticked in his jaw. Then he said, "Did you ever love me?"

That he even had to ask.

"For what it's worth, I am sorry for sending you to the lion," she replied. "And yes, I did . . . I do."

They stared at one another, but they did not touch, hands still tangled in the stars between them. They both had done terrible things: him spying and colluding to collapse her country, her sending him to death.

But they loved each other still.

In another lifetime, they could marry and live in the valleys under a thousand and one stars, but in this lifetime, they couldn't: They were tied to their people and their pasts and their families and their histories.

They were on opposite sides of a war, bound by duty. Him to his vengeance for Naina, her to her family.

And yet . . .

"You must leave, Asfandyar," she said, voice soft. "If you stay, you'll die."

"This does not make us even," he whispered. She knew that. They could never be even.

"Go," she said. "*Go.*"

Tearing his gaze from her, he reached behind his wardrobe and pulled out a bag, already packed. There was a bag of dried food with it, along with a skin of water. He moved toward the passageway door, and she held her breath.

This was goodbye.

Her heart cried out, wishing to stop him, but she did not.

He paused in his tracks and turned to her. A thousand emotions warred on his face.

"Oh, Durkhanai," he whispered. "My delicate and deadly Durkhanai."

His eyes burned into hers. Dropping his bag, he bridged the space between them in two steps and pressed a searing kiss to her lips. She did not even have time to react, then it was over.

She was already starved for more. He leaned his forehead against hers, and she closed her eyes, listening to his voice, just his voice.

"I will see you in the war," he said, voice rough. "When there will be no lady and no lion to decide our fate."

# CHAPTER FOURTEEN

*A*fter he'd gone, Durkhanai touched a hand to his pillow. It was still warm.

She lingered until the fabric was cold once more.

Straightening her shoulders, she exited. There was work to be done. She had dallied enough.

She went straight to her grandparents' rooms.

The guards let her through, and then she stood just outside the doors. Durkhanai paused, mustering her courage, trying to keep her turbulent emotions contained. She could not appear as unhinged as she felt. With a deep breath, Durkhanai pushed open the doors.

And there sat her grandparents, poised and regal as ever, drinking kava. They were not in their night clothes, as she had expected. Almost as if they had been waiting for her.

"Durkhanai, what a welcome surprise," Dhadi said, though she was not surprised in the least. Durkhanai expected someone had run from the gates to inform them. "What a fuss you've caused, chiriya."

"Agha-Jaan, Dhadi, there is an army heading straight for Safed-Mahal and Wakdar is leading it," she said, breathless. Agha-Jaan looked at her with warm eyes.

"Yes, a messenger from the gates just left," Dhadi said.

"Come, sit," Agha-Jaan said, tone soothing. "You've had quite the journey."

He gestured to the third chair, the one between them, and she sat, fidgeting with her hands in her lap.

"Agha-Jaan, you must prepare for a siege," she said, mind moving quickly through the preparations that must be made. "Who knows how long it might last. The merchants from the valley should be called back at once, and food stored, and warm clothing inventoried, what with the first snow quickly arriving—"

"Don't worry about all that." Agha-Jaan said. "His attempted siege will fail and be over scarcely after it has begun."

Durkhanai blinked, startled by his calm tone. She looked closely at her grandparents' faces and realized that they were not worried, not in the slightest. Her body chilled with dread.

"Agha-Jaan, you didn't see his army," she said, throat tightening. "*I* did. They will use their canons to break through the boulders and take down the gates."

"They won't," Agha-Jaan said, shaking his head.

"But—"

"We'll have to cancel the wedding," Dhadi said, interrupting. It was as if she had been waiting for an excuse to cancel. "And after all the preparations were done, too . . . say Durkhanai, you really don't wish to marry Rashid? I am sure he will still have you."

Durkhanai's mouth dropped open. Here she was warning them of an impending siege, and all Dhadi was worried about was weddings?

Dhadi waved a hand at her open mouth. "No, you're right, of course," she continued. "We would need much more time to make this wedding suitable to your tastes, dear Shehzadi."

"Did you even hear what I said?" Durkhanai asked, dumbfounded. "You should be worrying about fortifying the gates and protecting the mountain!"

Dhadi exchanged a glance with her husband.

"Jaani, don't you worry about that," Agha-Jaan said. "The mountain is well protected."

"At least we may expedite our plans to be rid of the boy," Dhadi said, sipping her tea. Durkhanai's heart writhed at the sight of her casual calculation. "We'll have him arrested at once for collusion and he'll be hanged, and what a clean ending that will be. Even Zarmina will be spared having to be properly married to him."

Durkhanai's eyes hardened, and Dhadi watched carefully as they did. At the very least, Durkhanai had been right about that. She was glad to have seen him before coming here.

"But you've already warned him, haven't you," Dhadi said, once again unsurprised. Durkhanai met her eyes. Her grandmother released a soft sound of disappointment, then resumed drinking her tea.

Something stirred deep within Durkhanai, an indignation she could not ignore. She resisted the urge to stand and yell, instead forcing her tone to remain level.

"I love him," she said simply. Her grandmother opened her mouth to speak, but Durkhanai lifted a hand. "*No*. Listen to me. The day of the trial, I sent him to the lion. He went to the wrong door, and I thank Allah for it every day." She lifted her shoulders, helpless. "I love him."

She hadn't expected to fall so terribly in love. It was not a fall so much as a plunge, and she could not understand how it had occurred. She thought she had everything, yet quickly she came to realize that *he* was everything.

"He is a spy. He used you and lied to you," Dhadi said.

This was true, but it was not the whole reason her grandparents had not accepted him.

Everyone was aware that judgment based on race was wrong, yet still some did not persist from their hidden prejudices; her grandparents were no different.

"I don't care," Durkhanai said. "You are being unkind."

"Are we?" Dhadi asked, voice amused. "Have we not accepted him as Zarmina's husband?"

"Only because you wish to kill him!"

Agha-Jaan shook his head, not meeting her eyes. She could not bear his disappointment, and it hurt her to see the dismay on his countenance, but she would no longer be a coward just to spare their feelings.

"You're being a fool," he said.

"I am a fool for him," she replied, and while once she would have balked at making such a statement, she said it now with simple truth. She was done hiding her feelings. "When this war is over, I will have him."

*If he will have me.*

"Dear Nazo wished for the same," Dhadi said, eyes sharp. "Surely you see how that turned out for her. History has a funny way of repeating itself, in matters such as these. You cannot run from such a fate."

Which was precisely what Durkhanai was afraid of. She did not wish to be like Nazo.

"I will not have the same ending she did," Durkhanai swore, as if saying the words out loud might make them true. "I won't." With nothing left to say, she stood. "Shabba khair," she said. "I will see you in the morning."

She left. They did not stop her.

Durkhanai wanted nothing more than to go to her room and sleep, but there was something she needed to do before then. She went to the guests' wing of the palace, where Asfandyar's room had been, and as expected, there was an entire group of guards up and down the hall. Surely to watch his every move and ensure he did nothing he should not have.

When she approached, the guards turned to look at her, straightening ever so slightly.

"He is gone," Durkhanai announced. "You are needed elsewhere. Go to the mountain's gates and prepare for a siege."

The guards looked at one another, confused.

"Pardon us, Shehzadi, but is Bajwa-sahib aware of this?" one guard asked. Bajwa-sahib was in charge of the palace's guards.

"He is aware," Durkhanai lied. "I have come here to personally give you these orders while he attends to a different matter. You are no longer needed here and are instead needed at the gates."

The guards exchanged another glance, confused. When one opened his mouth to speak, Durkhanai held up a hand. She was too tired to be patient.

"You are all leaving the palace now," she said, eyes sharp. "Whether it is with or without your uniform is up to you."

The guard closed his mouth. There were no questions after that. They began marching out.

"And inform General Rizvi I will be checking in with him tomorrow morning," Durkhanai said.

They left her. She was alone.

Finally, she returned to her rooms. Zarmina and Saifullah must have been asleep by then, and she did not wish to disturb them. She did not know if they were still angry with her. They had never replied to the letters she had sent from Mianathob.

She did not have the energy to face them just yet. Especially if they would only reiterate what Wakdar and Nazo had said to her.

She called the maids for a rose-bath and some food. As she sunk into the sweet, scalding waters, some of the tension eased from her body. The masala chai, though too heavy with turmeric, warmed her insides, and the fresh keema-naan helped the ache in her stomach.

The maids scrubbed her body clean, then massaged her stiff limbs. She had lost some weight from working in Mianathob, but her body was still soft and heavily cushioned. She had missed these delights, to be sure, and was much obliged for the coconut-oil scalp massage she received.

By the time she made it to her plush bed, she was already half-asleep. Despite the ominous feeling spreading through her chest, she fell asleep quickly, just as her cheek met the soft silk of her pillow.

That was when she saw him.

Asfandyar, his back to her. They were in the woods, in the dead of night. There were no stars above them, just a harsh crescent moon stamped into the sky like a scythe.

"Asfi?" she asked, voice quiet. She reached for him. He turned at the sound of her voice, and she jumped back, startled. His mouth was covered in blood: It ran down his chin and throat in rivulets. He was eating something straight from his hands, something beating and alive.

It was her heart.

She pressed a hand to her chest, and just as she did, the scene switched. When she pulled her hand out, a heart pulsed against her palm.

"No," she cried, shaking her head, but her hands brought the vessel into her mouth, and she bit deep, the salted taste of blood filling her mouth and spilling across her lips. Asfandyar lay motionless on the floor, wrapped in white, wrapped in his funeral shroud.

"No!" she screamed.

She woke up with her mouth open, but no noise came. Her body was paralyzed, and slowly, her limbs reawakened. She leaned over her bed and retched, but nothing came out.

It was a nightmare. Just a nightmare.

Durkhanai tried to go back to sleep, but she knew with clarity that there would be no rest until she had set things right with Asfandyar once more.

# CHAPTER FIFTEEN

*O*ut of habit, Durkhanai woke up early. Just as the roosters crowed and dawn spilled across the horizon.

There was much to do anyway.

The maids helped her to dress, and while it was strange to be back, it felt right. She had allowed herself to wallow whilst in Mianathob, and she would allow it no longer. Her people needed her. And she would be there for them.

Durkhanai dressed in a velvet shalwar and embroidered kurta, the maids twisting her hair into elaborate braids. Finally, they set her dupatta across her head, and above it, a smaller crown. While it was extravagant as compared to what she had worn for the past two months in the village, it was not so ornate to limit her movement. She needed easy motion.

And warmth. She slipped a shahtoosh shawl around her shoulders. It was colder in Safed-Mahal than it had been in Mianathob, and she hoped for snow to come early, if only to delay Wakdar's troops.

"Please bring me breakfast to my rooms," Durkhanai told her maids. She considered going to see Zarmina and Saifullah, but she did not want to waste time arguing with them. Perhaps after she had accomplished her tasks for the day, she would seek them out.

She went to her writing desk, and pulled out parchments of her letterhead. There was work to be done, and she didn't want to see anyone just yet. As she sat drinking chai and munching on toast, Durkhanai wrote out orders for General Rizvi to follow. She told him to call the merchants back from the valley where they had gone for trade. While foreigners were not allowed entrance to Safed-Mahal, they were allowed in the valley below, where merchants from the mountain would routinely go for trade.

The valley was not populated much beyond a handful of villages, and Durkhanai wondered if she should alert them of the impending army. It would only create panic, and there was not much to be done for them, she finally decided, so it was best not to. Besides, those were the people of S'vat, and Wakdar would not hurt them, would he? They were the people of the very throne and crown he coveted.

But Durkhanai had an uneasy feeling all the same.

Durkhanai also instructed General Rizvi to purchase extra supplies from the valley. When Wakdar's army came, the gates would be closed entirely, and they needed to prepare. While the villagers from the valley would be free to travel, everyone would be locked in on Safed-Mahal.

Along with those instructions, Durkhanai advised General Rizvi to adequately spread his troops out and prepare for battle should the gates fall. She hoped he had done this already, after her warning yesterday, but she would like an update all the same.

When these papers and instructions were through, the morning had passed by in a cold, white haze. The sun was shrouded by clouds, and the entire mountain was heavy with fog. Durkhanai could scarcely see ten feet in front of her.

"Send these to General Rizvi, immediately," Durkhanai ordered a messenger. He took the papers from her hand, running off with haste. She hoped it was not too late and that all of these tasks could be accomplished today.

Feeling frayed, Durkhanai set on a walk. She meandered down the mountain, observing the rattling of bare branches, the frozen little streams hidden in nooks and crevices of the land.

Durkhanai went to Kajali, her favorite village. She ached to see her people, though she felt trepidation to do so.

How would they react to her? She had been absent these past two months, and while it was said she was ill, she did not know if the people believed it.

When Durkhanai entered the village, everyone was busy with their day-to-day tasks, bustling about. With a deep breath, Durkhanai walked forward, and as she did, a young man looked up, meeting her gaze.

"Shehzadi," he said, so startled he dropped the chicken's egg he was holding. It splattered across the floor, and time slowed in the village as everyone turned to look at her, quiet and assessing. She stopped in her tracks, blood rushing in her ears, frightened they would forsake her.

"Shehzadi!" a little girl cried. "You're back!"

She ran and tackled Durkhanai in a hug, clinging to her legs. The silence broke, and her people rushed toward her, smiles on their faces.

"You've gotten so thin," an old lady said, inspecting Durkhanai's face. "Let me make you meethi tikkiyan."

"She does not need sweet cookies," her husband argued. "Let me make her broth! I've just slaughtered chicken this morning."

"We missed you," the little girl hugging Durkhanai said, looking up at her with wide, innocent eyes.

"I—I missed you, too," Durkhanai managed to say, her voice tight as she looked around and saw the same love in the other villagers' gazes.

She did not have a lot of time, for she had to return to the palace and continue preparations for the siege, but she went and met with the villagers, as many as she could. Durkhanai threw stones with the children, then leapt into piles of leftover leaves and smiled as they played.

She went to where the women were hanging laundry to dry and helped them, chatting and gossiping and covering her mouth as she laughed. One woman introduced Durkhanai to her new daughter-in-law, who had just arrived from a neighboring village, and a younger woman showed Durkhanai her newest born child.

She went to where the men were tending to their animals and helped feed the chickens, impressed by the size of the goats and cows. She joined the men as they gathered around a small fire and exchanged songs, their melodious voices rich in the morning air.

"I will visit again, soon," she promised as she was leaving, her stomach full from soup and sweets and chai, and her heart filled with love.

Previously, she had felt she was entirely alone, without her friends or cousins or family, who all wanted nothing to do with her unless it served their own purposes. But the people loved her as she was, and she realized that as long as she wore the crown, she would never be alone, for she had them.

But she had to be worthy of such a crown, she knew that. Motivation flared within her.

As Durkhanai walked through the marble halls back to her room, her mind flitted through other preparations that needed to be done, especially concerning what would happen should the gates truly fall.

It had never happened, not since they were built centuries ago. The mountain of Safed-Mahal had always been fiercely protected for the vast treasures it held: the jewels and rich natural resources.

With a sigh, Durkhanai realized Saifullah would probably know what else to do.

He always was good with planning and preparing.

Almost too good, she thought bitterly. After all, he had been the one feeding Asfandyar information about her all that time. Secretly working with Wakdar.

Durkhanai stopped.

Speaking of Saifullah, where was he? She had meant to look for him and Zarmina this morning, but had gone to visit Kajali instead.

She looked for them, but had a feeling she would not find them. If they were in the palace, surely they would have crossed paths by now, or they themselves would have sought her out after finding that she had returned.

Despite her suspicion that her cousins would not be in the palace, she was still surprised when she did not find them. Both of their rooms were tidy, and most of their belongings remained, but it looked as if no one had been there for a day or so.

Had they escaped to go to be with Wakdar?

And where was Nazo Phuppo? She expected she would have made the journey to the palace by now. Surely, they should have all been here for Zarmina's wedding reception.

Her uncles, Zmarack Chacha and Suweil Chacha, were at the palace for that very occasion, as were most of her cousins and other relatives.

The wedding was called off this morning when it was announced Asfandyar was wanted for colluding with the enemy—perhaps they had left, then?

But where had they gone? Surely they would not fight against their grandparents . . .

Durkhanai didn't know what to think.

"Shehzadi, how are you?" a voice asked.

Durkhanai saw it was the maulvi, the religious leader at court. He was an old man with all-white details: a long, white beard, starched white shalwar kameez, crisp white kufi. His fingers absentmindedly ran over a tasbeeh.

"Salam, Maulvi-Sahib," Durkhanai said. "I am well, and yourself? What brings you to the palace?"

"Quite well, quite well," he replied. "I was just on my way to the southern tower. The Badshah has reason to believe that treasonous man will be captured soon."

Durkhanai stilled. The southern tower was where executions took place. There was a small masjid up there, for the accused to make their last prayers, before they were pushed off the steep cliff to fall to their death. The accused in question was Asfandyar. Unable to stop herself, her mind conjured up the image of him, arms tied behind his back, murmuring his final prayers, before catapulting down, down, down to splatter across the rocks.

She straightened her body to bite back a shudder.

"Yes, I am sure the guards will capture him soon," Durkhanai said, mouth tight. "If you will excuse me."

She hastily walked away, but the image of Asfandyar falling to his death lingered in her mind, Asfandyar in white, in his funeral shroud, just like in her dream. The slow, grotesque spread of blood, the red consuming the white. And it was these thoughts she was lost in when she quite literally ran into someone.

"Oh, I'm so—" she began, then stopped when she saw who it was.

It was Gulalai. Durkhanai blinked.

Gulalai reared back, leaning on her jeweled cane. Shock registered on her face, then immediately morphed to anger.

"You!"

Durkhanai's heart sank. She recalled their last conversation, how angry Gulalai had been.

It seemed she was still angry now.

"Gulalai—"

"Where have you *been*?" Gulalai interrupted. Her face was still scrunched in anger, but there was something else more, another emotion Durkhanai couldn't decipher.

"Wh-What?" Durkhanai asked. She took a step back, confused.

"I said, where. Have you. Been."

"I was . . . in a village with my great-aunt . . . "

"And you didn't think to write, not even once?" Gulalai asked. "One day you are here, being frustratingly proud and stubborn, and the next you are simply gone, without so much as a goodbye, and everyone says you have fallen deathly ill."

"To write?" Durkhanai repeated. "But I thought you were angry . . . "

"I was angry!" Gulalai said. "I am still! But that doesn't mean I wasn't worried, as well. You didn't write once to tell me of your health." She pouted. Durkhanai realized what the emotion was: concern. "What a wretched friend you are."

"We are still friends?"

Gulalai made an irritated sound. "Unfortunately, my heart cannot be rid of you so easily."

"Oh, Gulalai!" Durkhanai threw her arms around Gulalai in an encompassing hug. All was not lost!

"Goodness," Gulalai said, releasing a little laugh. "What a display of emotion."

"But we are still friends?" Durkhanai asked again. Gulalai rolled her eyes.

"Yes, yes, we are," she said. "Though I am still annoyed with you!"

Durkhanai grabbed Gulalai's hands. "Come with me."

She led her to her sunroom, where she promptly called for tea and snacks. Gulalai sat down, getting comfortable, and a short time later, maids brought in trollies of food: a large pot of chai, fried potato samosay with cholay, honey biscuits, and crisp jalebi.

"Oh, I did miss this," Gulalai said. "Perhaps more than I missed you."

Durkhanai laughed, motioning for a maid to pour them both chai before dismissing her.

"We'll have chai every day while you're here," Durkhanai said. "Speaking of, how long have you been here thus far?"

Gulalai stirred sugar into her tea. She released a long breath. For the first time since Durkhanai had been back, things felt right. Her heart squeezed. She had missed her.

"I've been here for about a week, now," Gulalai said. "I arrived for the wedding and, as you should very well remember, as part of Kurra's treaty with the Badshah. You *were* the one who negotiated to have me stay here as your guest, yet when I arrived, you were nowhere to be found. Quite rude. I expected better from a princess, but it seems standards are going down everywhere."

Durkhanai laughed. "Do forgive my terrible manners. Here, have some more jalebi."

"Bribing me with sweets," Gulalai said, putting two more on her plate, "is the perfect method to earn forgiveness."

"Though not nearly enough," Durkhanai said. "Words cannot express how sorry I am for what my grandparents did: informing the Kebzu Kingdom about the unification summit, leading to the attack. I will make it right by your father, by everyone affected, I swear it."

She would make everything right again; she would.

Durkhanai bit the inside of her cheek, watching carefully how Gulalai would react. Say Gulalai never forgave her?

Durkhanai's grandfather was the reason Gulalai's father would never walk again. And Durkhanai had withheld that information from Gulalai, when Gulalai had been nothing but the truest friend: providing her with comfort, advice, company, trust—everything.

Gulalai sipped her tea, then set down the cup. It made a slight clinking noise against the saucer as Gulalai inhaled a deep breath. Durkhanai waited.

"Well, that is nice," Gulalai replied. "But you are not accountable for the mistakes of your grandparents. What you are accountable for is what you do now."

Durkhanai breathed a sigh of relief. "Thank you, Gulalai." But still, Durkhanai worried. Even if she wasn't accountable for her grandparents' sins, was it only a matter of time before she repeated them? Already, Durkhanai had been so selfish, hiding away for so long.

"I believe in you," her friend said firmly.

"It was wrong of me to stay away so long," Durkhanai said. "But I am back now. And I will set things right." She was reinvigorated. "How have you been these months?"

"Well enough," Gulalai said. "I went back to Kurra, spent time with my parents. I helped organize the troops as part of the negotiation. . . " She paused, frowning. "It was a bit of a strange ordeal, however. Lots of meetings behind closed doors. Very hush hush."

"You weren't allowed in those meetings?" Durkhanai asked. Gulalai shook her head.

"Why not, I'm not sure," she said. "I assured my father you and I were friends—though, if I am being honest, at the time, I was furious with you—and I even told him you had invited me back to stay as your guest. I didn't tell him that the Badshah was guilty; I didn't want to cause war any more than you did."

"Thank you for not telling your father," Durkhanai said. "But that is strange. Perhaps they needed to be sure which soldiers to send?"

"It is true that the soldiers would need to be extremely level-headed," Gulalai said. "If any had ulterior motives in coming to Marghazar and decided to do something risky—well, I imagine it would not end well for them."

"Hm."

They continued eating their little snacks. Gulalai regarded Durkhanai closely.

"One last thing," Gulalai said. Durkhanai had a bad feeling that she knew what Gulalai would say before she said it. "Asfandyar."

Durkhanai fell silent. Even hearing his name hurt, like a physical blow to her chest. Steam billowed from their teacups, thick at the base, then thinning out as unfurled upward. Gulalai waited. Durkhanai took a deep breath.

"I suppose I do have some explaining to do," she finally said.

"Yes, I rather think you do."

"Where to begin?" Durkhanai said, releasing a little laugh. "I love him."

"I think that much is obvious." Gulalai reached over and squeezed her hand. "Take your time with the rest."

Durkhanai nibbled on her lower lip. She took a deep breath, and the story unfurled, like steam uncurling, spreading, taking shape.

She told Gulalai how Asfandyar had been a spy for her father—who was alive—because of what had happened with Naina. She told her how he had used her and so, in that final, fatal moment, Durkhanai had motioned to the door with the lion.

But it wasn't even that—not really. The truth was far more insidious.

All this time, she had been in denial, hoping she had made the right choice because she was never wrong. She was arrogant and proud and always got what she wanted.

But now she realized she *had* been wrong.

"I should have fought for him," Durkhanai said, eyes welling with tears.

How she missed him.

It wasn't just desire, but comfort and companionship. He was her match, her equal. In such little time, he had become vital to her.

It wasn't that she couldn't live without him—for she was whole entirely on her own—it was that the world would not burn so bright. He was the extra sweetness, the necessary beauty, in life.

She couldn't stop thinking about him, memories flitting in and out of her mind like horses racing by; there for a vibrant moment, gone in the next, but the aftermath lingered in the soil, in the air. She recalled once the way he had looked at her.

She had seen him from a distance, across the room. Candlelight had illuminated his stark features, and she had noticed the instant he saw her, his eyes filling with their usual amusement and warmth. He had approached, gaze fixated entirely on her, and as he grew closer, she had felt her cheeks flame.

His eyes had never left her, a faint smile tilting his lips. As he came near, she wondered why he did not say hello, or make some quick remark, or say anything at all. And then she had realized—the way he looked at her.

He was captivated speechless. He did not look away.

What she would do to have him see her again. In a way she was afraid that if he could not see her, nobody could—as if she might cease to exist the way she had for him, in what she had seen as one of the best versions of herself.

The thought troubled her immensely.

At the very least, she hoped he was all right. Who knew where he might be by now.

Hadn't he said he would see her in the war?

But perhaps he was sick of her family and had gone far, far away, run away as he had asked her to, what felt like centuries ago now. Perhaps they would never meet again. She was wretched enough to wish for the war, if only it gave her the chance to see him again.

"Shehzadi, a message for you," a voice called from her door.

"Come in," Durkhanai called, setting down her teacup and sitting up straight. The messenger entered, but he avoided her gaze. He simply handed her an envelope of papers.

"Is this from General Rizvi?" Durkhanai asked, taking the file. But as she turned it over, she saw her own seal, broken and returned to her. Her grip on the papers tightened. "Well?"

The messenger looked from Durkhanai to Gulalai, unsure of whether to speak or not. Durkhanai made an impatient sound, urging him on.

"General Rizvi thanks you for the orders but says he cannot carry them out without the permission of the Badshah," the messenger said, voice hardly audible. Durkhanai set her jaw.

"Is that so?"

The messenger shuffled on his feet. She dismissed him, then sunk back into the sofa.

"Goodness," Gulalai said, taking in the cross expression on her friend's face. "What will you do now?"

"What I must," Durkhanai replied.

"Can I aid you in any way?"

"No, but shukria." Durkhanai squeezed her friend's hand. "I will see you in the evening."

"Of course," Gulalai said, taking her leave, and Durkhanai went to her bedroom, though it was not her final destination.

After learning that her grandparents were out for a stroll, Durkhanai gathered the correspondence she had sent to General Rizvi and the key. Making sure no maids were watching, she then slipped into the passageways.

The moment she entered, a chill ran through her body. It was freezing in here. She clutched her shawl close as wind whistled in the air, echoing through the empty passageways. With a match, she struck a torch, and the warm glow illuminated the space around her.

Durkhanai made her way to the Badshah's private office. A chill ran through her again, and it wasn't just the cold, but remembering when she had done this last, and with who. Asfandyar and her, pressed against the frigid walls, listening.

She didn't know where he had gone now, or if she would see him again, but she prayed she would.

Durkhanai released a long sigh, and the flame of the torch flickered in front of her.

When she arrived at her destination, she unlocked the door and entered. It was empty, as expected, but seemed messier than when she had been here last. More correspondence and treaties and papers and maps—she would have lingered to shuffle through them, but she didn't know when her grandparents would be back.

She needed to be quick.

Durkhanai took out the Badshah's seal and lit a wax candle. She poured the wax beside her own broken one and pressed the Badshah's seal into it.

As the wax seal dried, Durkhanai's gaze caught on the portrait behind the Badshah's desk. Agha-Jaan, holding a baby on his forearm, her feet in his palm and her hand curled around Dhadi's finger.

An ember of guilt burned within her, but she snuffed it out quickly. She was doing what she must for her people.

Strangely, in that moment, she felt closer to Asfandyar than she had before—she could understand what he must have gone through when he had done this exact thing.

He, too, had stolen the Badshah's seal. Despite it hurting the people he loved, it could not have been avoided.

As she slipped the seal and wax back to their designated spots, blowing to let the wax dry quicker, a sharp pain settled across her chest, quick and bright, but she ignored it.

He had done what he had thought was right, and she must, too.

Durkhanai considered why she did not just join Wakdar's side, and she realized it was because he was driven by vengeance, and such a man would not make a good ruler.

Surely, he did not truly care for the people, or he would not have left in the first place, or stayed away so long. And if he did not care for her people, Durkhanai did not care for him.

At the end of the day, her people were the most important thing. Not her desire for love or family or anything else. What mattered was that her people were taken care of and had a good ruler who cared for them. However Agha-Jaan was—proud, stubborn, callous—at the very least, he cared about the people.

Though it was becoming less and less evident, judging from his behavior. Durkhanai made haste to leave the palace grounds at once, mounting Heer and traveling down the mountain. She made her way to the gates, her anger growing as she did.

She had planned to visit more villages in the evening, to speak with her people, reassure them that she was here and she would fight for them, but now she could not.

What a waste of time this was. If General Rizvi had merely accepted her orders, she would not have had to spend hours traveling down to speak with him directly.

"Shehzadi!" The guard on duty cried when she arrived, surprised to see her at the gates. "What—"

She glared to silence him, entering without a word into the gate's tower. She made her way up to General Rizvi's office, and no one tried to stop her. When she arrived at the outside of his office, the guards on duty immediately stood straighter.

"Wha—" The guards stammered, but she pushed past.

Durkhanai entered the office. General Rizvi sat at his desk, papers spread before him. Just as he looked up to see who was disturbing him, she threw her own papers in front of him.

"There is your precious permission," she snapped, as his eyes fell on the Badshah's seal. "Though you won't have use of it now. You are dismissed."

He immediately stood, shocked.

"Shehzadi—" he started. She held up a hand.

"Not only do you defy my direct orders," she said, seething, "you waste both my time and the Badshah's, while time is limited and this mountain is on the verge of war." General Rizvi swallowed. "I have no need for such an insolent general, and thus your career as one has come to an end."

"Shehzadi, please, I did not intend—" he stammered. "Forgive me."

"You have insulted me," Durkhanai said. "You will take your retirement, effective immediately."

"I should not have questioned you," General Rizvi said, face twitching. "Please forgive me. I assure you it was my first and last mistake."

She glared. The door of the office was open. Outside, the guards were watching the spectacle with shock and fear.

*Good*, she thought. She could not have them doubting and delaying her, not now.

"That is enough groveling," Durkhanai said.

She paused, as if contemplating her final decision. General Rizvi waited, perspiration gathering on his brow. Durkhanai released a low breath.

"Very well," she snapped. "I will relent."

"Shehzadi, shukria, shukria," General Rizvi said, his face awash with gratitude. "You will not regret it."

"You should make sure of that," she replied. "I won't have you questioning me again."

"No, never," he said. "I will carry out these orders immediately. Is there anything else you need? Anything at all you wish?"

She ignored him, walking out without another word.

The adhan for maghrib was ringing out; the sun was setting. Half the day wasted, and Wakdar would be here any day now. But with the proper urgency, General Rizvi might still be able to carry out her commands by then, and things could still be salvaged.

She did not regret bullying him. There was a crown on her head. She would not buckle beneath its weight.

# CHAPTER SIXTEEN

As Durkhanai made her way back to the palace, the wind was harsh against her cheeks. Night was falling like a cloak across the mountain, covering it in darkness, but she kept alert, watching, taking note. As she traveled up, she noticed that the mountain was filled with wedding guests. They were clearly foreigners, and while there were not many of them, it was enough to make Durkhanai uneasy.

They must have been barricaded in—no one was to leave the mountain until further notice. It was a nuisance, having all the foreigners clogging the mountain, but it was not the most pressing matter, which was the impending siege.

Just then, she spotted familiar faces. Durkhanai stopped in her tracks, unsure of what to do, just as they turned.

"Shehzadi," Naeem-sahib said curtly. He lowered his head in respect, but when he looked at her, his hazel eyes had lost their warmth. He regarded her coldly, and it was easy to see why when she saw who he was with.

Rashid, his son, the most eligible bachelor in Safed-Mahal—the one she had so callously rejected. It seemed like such a small thing now, compared to everything else, but for him and for his father, it had been a hard blow.

Rashid looked miserable. He was thinner, and his usually bright face had lost some of its luster.

"How are you? Well, I hope?" Durkhanai asked, dismounting Heer to speak with them.

"Thank you for your concern," Naeem-sahib replied, voice clipped. He looked at her with angry eyes. He was still upset about her rejecting Rashid's proposal, then.

Rashid said nothing.

He did not look at her. He was still upset, too.

Durkhanai did feel terribly about it, but she knew in the long run, it was best to reject him then. Better a small heartbreak now then a heart-shatter later.

"We must be going," Naeem-sahib said. He placed an arm on his son's shoulder, steering him away.

Durkhanai had always liked Naeem-sahib for his clever dealings and staunch loyalty, but she did not forget for a moment that he was the most powerful noble and well-aware of it.

Which was why he thought he could get away with treating her so flippantly.

"*Wait,*" Durkhanai said, voice hard. They slowly turned. "There is an important matter I wish to discuss with you, if you have a moment."

"I am afraid I do not," Naeem-sahib replied. His face was cold. "Should the Badshah wish to see me, he knows where to reach me."

"But—" Durkhanai began. She wished to inform him about the siege, so that he could prepare, but Naeem-sahib did not wait to hear what she had to say. He merely turned and walked away, back straight. Rage spread through her.

Rashid lingered for a moment, not following immediately, and Durkhanai's temper flared.

"Will you simply follow your father or be a man of your own?" she snapped. Rashid lifted his eyes to look at her.

She started. He looked so *sad*.

She did not know where the words had come from, and perhaps they were not directly toward him as much as they were directed toward herself.

Would she simply follow her grandparents or be her own person?

It was up to them to decide for themselves who they wished to be.

But did it matter, in the end, what they decided? Were some things not inevitable?

He opened his mouth to speak.

"Rashid," his father called. Rashid released a sigh, then turned and left without saying a thing. She watched him go, heart beating fast.

Heer nuzzled against her, sensing her distress, and Durkhanai stroked her mane.

"Chalo," she said. "Time to go."

She continued on, back to her palace, and just as she made her way to the doors after leaving Heer, someone approached.

Moonlight cast harsh shadows across his features. That sweet, kind boy she had known so long ago was gone, replaced by someone else, someone she did not recognize.

Until she did.

Durkhanai regarded Rashid carefully. Neither said a word, but there was some misery in him that she recognized, that same hopeless, helpless misery that came with being in love.

She remembered what Zarmina had said, right after the trial.

And she understood.

"Ao," Durkhanai said. "Let us have chai."

Rashid followed her inside. She called for chai and hot aloo parathay because she was quite hungry. They sat together and ate, and she recalled a time not so long ago when they had sat in this same area, how he had spilled chai.

How different they both were from then.

"He thinks I have not recovered from your rejection," Rashid finally said. "When the truth is, it is not you I am heartbroken over." He paused, considering something. "Though I think you may be the only one to truly understand the depth of my pain."

"Yes, I think I can," she replied. There was no use denying it. The same marriage that kept him away from his love kept her away from hers.

Though that was not the only obstacle she faced.

"She does not love him," Rashid said, eyes focused somewhere far away. Durkhanai knew this, but it was a relief to hear it confirmed. It settled that childish jealousy in her. "I know it is wrong," he continued, voice miserable, "that she is married, but I could not—cannot—stay away."

"How did it begin?"

"How does any of it? With a glance, a kind word, a smile." He finally looked at her, and his eyes were vibrant once more, warmth settling back into the depths of those hazel hues. "She is so gentle and genuine and kind. At first, I detested her, for she was an extension of *you*, but somehow my poor manners only made her more relentless."

"Yes, she is like that," Durkhanai agreed.

"Then, just as something began to bloom within me, the trial—" He shook his head, looking away. "She said it was only a marriage in name, that she would never be his. I know I should have stayed away, but—" His voice cut off. He smiled weakly. "Well. I suppose you know."

"All too well." Durkhanai sighed. She reached across the table and took his hand in hers. When he looked at her, there were tears in his eyes.

"I love her," he whispered.

"You will have her," she promised. She squeezed his hand. "You will."

Rashid smiled at her. "I suppose I should be thanking you," he said. "Had you not broken my heart, she would not have mended it."

"Glad to be of service," she said, smiling in return. "Love works in strange ways." With that, she looked away, something squeezing in her chest.

"You will have him," he promised, this time squeezing her hand. "You will."

She was not so sure of that. "Look how far we've come."

"Yes, it is rather comical, is it not?" Rashid shook his head, laughing gently. "Now, enough of all that. What was it you wished to speak with my father about earlier this evening?"

Durkhanai gave him the abridged version, ending with the siege she expected sometime in the next day, the day after if they were lucky.

"Can I expect your allyship?" Durkhanai asked. "I'm afraid your father is currently not a fan of mine."

"Yes, I am here for you, Shehzadi," Rashid said firmly. "I am glad you are back. I—I have missed you." His cheeks turned pink. "I didn't realize what a presence you had become."

"I missed me, too," she replied softly.

"The people need someone fighting for them, not politicians with their own interests," he added. "I see it in my own father—ruled by his pride and his hurt—and your grandfather, as well. When, really, their petty emotions don't matter, not at all. What matters is the welfare of the people." He paused. "I think, sometimes people in positions of power forget that they are there as caretakers, not as wardens."

He was right.

"I shouldn't have stayed away for so long," she said.

In a way, she had felt if she could not have Asfandyar, there was no point in anything.

But now she saw there was so much more to live for.

Even if she could not have him, or be with him, she would not wither away. She would work to be worthy of him all the same, and worthy of her people.

She'd had enough of sulking and moping about.

"How can I help?" Rashid asked.

"Come with me," Durkhanai said.

As they walked across the palace to their destination, Durkhanai took a detour to find Gulalai. She sat on her bed, reading over a letter, her fingers brushing across the ink. There was a faint smile on her face as she lifted to page to her nose.

"Gul," Durkhanai said.

"What! Nothing!" Gulalai said, pushing the letter beneath a pillow indiscreetly. Rashid and Durkhanai exchanged a glance.

"Would that be from a certain Wali?" she asked, drawing closer to her. Gulalai's mouth fell open, her cheeks flushing.

"How interesting," Rashid said, sitting beside her. "What's the story there?"

"No story!" Gulalai insisted, as Durkhanai said, "Shirin sent her dried apricots."

"Ah," Rashid said, as if that was all he needed to know. Gulalai glared at them both.

"Surely there are more important matters at hand than an insufferable Wali who must exert her dominance upon me at every turn?" Gulalai huffed.

"Actually, there are," Durkhanai agreed, taking Gulalai's hands. "Come, we have work to do."

Durkhanai went to the stores, where she loaded bags of nuts and dried fruit and wheat onto a cart. A sign of good faith and also to prepare the people for the impending siege.

They went to Dhok-Alfu, one of the villages. It was night, many were asleep, but at the sound of hooves approaching, some people roused from their homes.

At the sight of the Shehzadi and a nobleman, many quickened forward. Torches lit the night, illuminating flashes of faces. Durkhanai caught the surprise evident in their expressions, heard the low hum of whispering and words being exchanged.

Did they hate her? Her chest hurt at the thought. This morning in Kajali, the people had been kind to her, but she was closest with those villagers. Dhok-Alfu was a bit more removed, so they might not automatically default to the love they had for her.

Was she really ruined? What good was a princess who was not beloved by her people?

But that was also why she was here: to see how they would react to her.

"Shehzadi!" a young man cried. "You have returned!" She walked forward, smiling and saying salam to the people.

"How is your health?" a villager asked her, and the silence broke as more voices joined in with replies and questions for her.

"We were so worried for you," someone added.

"I spent every tahajjud for the past two months praying for you, Shehzadi," an old woman said. Durkhanai's heart shifted and tugged, a seed nudging forth from the earth.

She dismounted from Heer.

"It is because of your duas that I am here today," Durkhanai said, taking the old woman's hand. "Shukria. I cannot thank you enough."

She was passed around, taking people's hands and meeting their eyes and seeing their warm smiles.

Her people loved her still. They had missed her. Any gossip that had tied her to Asfandyar must have died down, or perhaps the people did not care to begin with.

"I am back now," Durkhanai announced, voice strong. "And I will protect you until my dying breath."

With that, she and Rashid and Gulalai distributed the supplies and were met with gratitude and even more love. And on they went, to a few more villages close by, and at each, she was met with similar concern and love and eventual gratitude, when she handed out more supplies.

She did not have enough time to linger with the people as much as she would have liked, but still she let her presence be known, let them see the love in her eyes. She needed them to know that she was here for them.

It was not a lot, but it was enough to show that she cared for them. For those villagers farther away, she sent runners from the villages she did visit, people whom she spoke to directly and who could relay her concern and love for her people.

She hoped it would give the people faith that they could hold onto when the inevitable army arrived, hoped that they would know she had not forgotten them.

By the time Durkhanai came back to her rooms in the palace after Rashid had retreated home and Gulalai found her own room, she was exhausted. All she wanted was to seep into a steaming hot bath, but there was a report on her desk from General Rizvi she had to go over and respond to, as well as correspondence from merchants. Durkhanai read and replied to the correspondence first before digging into the General's report.

He had succeeded in carrying out most of her orders, which she was glad to hear. Though time had been short, she had been right in assuming he would not disappoint her again.

As Durkhanai scribbled notes for further instructions and follow-up questions, her eyelids grew heavy. She dozed off on her desk, ink staining her fingers. When she awoke, her neck was badly cramped.

She set the papers down and transferred herself to her bed. She would just take a little nap, she told herself. Just to re-energize. . .

Durkhanai fell soundly asleep, and did not stir until she heard the sound of someone approaching. Tangled in the cobwebs of sleep and dreams, Durkhanai's thoughts first went to him.

"*Durre, wake up,*" he said.

"Do not wake me," she whispered. "Let me dream a little longer."

"Wake up, Durkhanai."

Someone shook her. She snapped awake to see it was not him at all. It was Gulalai, eyes alert with fright.

"What is it?" Durkhanai asked, jumping out of bed. In one movement she slipped on her shawl and shoes, then ran outside where she saw.

It was a messenger, his uniform mangled. The whites of his widened eyes stuck out against the dark blood and dirt mixed on his face.

"What is it?" she asked, though she already knew.

"He's here," the messenger replied. "Wakdar is here."

# CHAPTER SEVENTEEN

awn lit her grandparents' room with a soft, subtle glow. Despite the hour, they were wide awake. Durkhanai was with them, and it was only the three of them in the room. They stood staring at the letter in the Badshah's hand.

The letter was short and direct.

Wakdar was at their borders, requesting entrance into the palace as the rightful heir of Marghazar. If he was not let in peacefully, he would fight his way through.

They had until the next dawn to let him in. Or they would have war.

"Agha-Jaan," Durkhanai began, breaking the silence, and it was as if her words broke whatever trance the Badshah was under.

"Foolish," the Badshah said, discarding the letter and walking toward the doors. Durkhanai caught the letter before it fell. "Bring breakfast to our rooms today," the Badshah said to a maid at his door. She hurried away to fulfill his order.

"Dhadi?" Durkhanai asked, dumbfounded as the Wali lowered herself onto a plush chair in the room's sitting area.

"Yes, jaan?" Dhadi replied, gaze unfocused. Durkhanai followed her grandparents to where they sat in front of her, their backs straight, chins lifted.

"What is to be done?" she asked. The Badshah's gaze shifted to her, but he did not speak.

"About what, jaani?" Dhadi asked. Durkhanai did not understand. Were they going to pretend they did not just receive that letter from Wakdar? Their estranged son? Threatening siege and war?

Durkhanai did not reply, letting the silence take on its own weight, and finally the Wali waved a petulant hand.

"Oh, that," she said, scoffing. "He is not a threat."

"But—"

"Durkhanai, please," Dhadi said, pressing a hand against her forehead. "I cannot deal with you and your questions right now. We will discuss this later."

Indignation flared in Durkhanai's chest, but with it came a sort of relief.

"As you wish." She released a short breath and left. Her grandparents' continuous dismissal of her—despite everything she had done to be a good princess, a good *queen*—made it easier for her to do what she believed.

Yes, she still loved them, in the way that family always loved one another, but she did not rather like them anymore, nor did she respect them as much as she once did, and as the fog of that blind loyalty ebbed, she was blessed with a certain clarity.

She had to do what *she* believed was right, not what she believed her grandparents wished her to do. She had to be better than they were, not exactly the same, or her people would continue to suffer. She had to break the cycle.

But would she be able to?

Durkhanai turned down the hall, heading east. Slanted rays of sunshine cast golden light across the white marble halls, and she quickened her steps. There was less than a day to prepare for the worst.

"You there!" Durkhanai called, when she found who she was looking for. The messenger turned, lowering his head with respect when he saw who addressed him. He had cleaned up the blood and dirt, though his eyes remained bloodshot, worried.

Durkhanai pulled him to the side, speaking in hushed tones. "Who have you told about this message? General Rizvi? The palace guard?"

The messenger shook his head. "I received no orders to do so. The Badshah expressly forbade me from telling anyone before I was dismissed. I was told to retire to my quarters and spend the day resting."

She narrowed her eyes. It was not that the Badshah had plans, and was merely not sharing them with her. Instead, he was self-assured enough to pretend that there was not an army at their borders, that his son was not returning to take his vengeance and his throne.

"Go, rest," Durkhanai said, dismissing the guard. She would handle it from here.

She rushed to her rooms, changing into a velvet suit of shalwar kameez, keeping the embellishments to a minimum. She had a long day ahead of her.

When she was ready, she went to the stables, then rode Heer down to the base of the mountain. By the time she arrived at the gates, the mountain was awakening, the bustle and business of the day underway.

"Shehzadi," a guard said, lowering his head as she approached. He opened the door, letting her into the building, and she made her way up to General Rizvi's office.

As she entered, her line of sight was bombarded by the mess: papers strewn across the floor, figurines toppled on the map. At least the general was taking matters more seriously, though he was nowhere to be found.

She looked around, and her gaze happened upon the spiral staircase, leading up to a small latch that she assumed would lead up to the apex of the watch tower, as his office had no windows. She climbed up the stairs, then opened and entered onto the watchtower, where General Rizvi stood in silence with his back to her, her shoulders rigid.

An arctic breeze rushed against her, and she steeled herself against it, standing. There was a long list of things to discuss with the general, but as she went to his side, the words died on her lips as she saw.

The valley was filled to the brim with Wakdar's army. Her heartbeat quickened, a sick feeling settling deep within her. And it was not merely the size of the army, which appeared now as much larger than what she had seen when she had escaped a few days ago, but it was the sight of what lay at the forefront of the army which made her mouth dry.

Canons.

Durkhanai swore beneath her breath. She had seen canons before, but none directed toward her, toward the gates that kept enemies away from her home. Maybe she should have ordered the army to meet Wakdar on his route here, rather than let it get to this.

But it was too late for that.

She resisted the urge to put a hand to her mouth in horror. Instead, she clenched her hands into fists at her sides, taking measured breaths.

"Preparations are being made," General Rizvi said, breaking the silence. He turned to her, heavy dark circles beneath his eyes. "Most of the merchants have returned and were able to buy food, but not all of them returned before we had to close the gates. Many villagers also refused to leave."

Durkhanai huffed in disapproval, stretching her fists into a neutral position. That was not good.

While most of her people lived on the main mountain, there were some villages down in the valley, mostly with citizens who were shepherds who needed more space for their livestock.

She was sure Wakdar would claim all of the villagers' goods for himself to feed his army. He had already swallowed up the land.

"General," Durkhanai said. "I assume you are working through the best strategy for when the siege begins?"

Now, he turned to look at her. "Does the Badshah have any specific requests for how to proceed?"

Durkhanai straightened her back. The Badshah's plan was to do nothing. "He trusts your professional opinion, as do I."

General Rizvi nodded.

They went back to his office and he explained how they would handle the attack the next morning. While Durkhanai did not exactly understand military strategies, she was reassured by the general's instructions. At least he had a plan, though he was still working through the details.

It made her feel better as she left the gates to return to the palace. Rather than taking the back route, she traveled through the villages, hoping to gauge people's reactions.

As she walked, a piece of paper on the ground caught her eye. She bent over to retrieve it, then smoothed the leaflet to read. Her heart pounded with dread.

It was a propaganda piece. She could not make out all of the words, for it was crumpled and covered in dirt, half torn, but she saw Wakdar's name, and as she walked, she heard the rest, whispered between the villagers.

"Did you hear?" someone asked, tone hushed. "They say Wakdar is alive, has been all these years."

A gasp, a hand clutching another.

"Nahi! Can it be?"

"But how?"

"That fateful night our beloved Shehzadi was born, he was thrown from the palace."

"Sachi? Thrown from the palace!"

"Thrown!"

"But why?"

"Who can say? The Badshah is infamous for his temper."

"And what of his wife, the beloved Shehzadi's mother?"

"Yes, what of her?"

"Murdered!"

An exclamation, another chorus of gasps.

"Murdered?!"

"*No*, yeh kaise? How could it be?"

"Sachi!"

"They murdered her and kept the Shehzadi all to themselves."

"Yeh toh zulm hai, this is not right."

"There's more, did you not read the leaflet?"

"But from where did these leaflets come?"

"Haan, how can we trust them?"

"Wakdar is alive, my son's wife's brother saw him!"

"And how is he sure that was him?"

"There is no mistaking him, he looks just like the Badshah, just like our Shehzadi."

The people tsked.

"What more?"

"Yes, tell us what more?"

"The Badshah was behind the summit attack on the other zilla leaders. He has aligned himself with the Kebzu Kingdom. Do not make such faces of disbelief! There is evidence! A letter from a high-ranking Kebzu general himself. . . "

Durkhanai froze, heart pounding.

It was the letter Asfandyar had shown her, the one she had burned. It must have been a replica. *Damn* Asfandyar. Damn him.

As Durkhanai traveled home, taking the long way, passing through as many villages as she could, she heard the rumors, again and again. She could almost see how quickly they were spreading. Wakdar must have kept in touch with people in Safed-Mahal, people who were still loyal to him and who spread these rumors and leaflets, now.

When Durkhanai arrived back at the palace, she went directly to her grandparents room, adamant on confronting them.

Did they really try to have Wakdar murdered the night he fled? Did they really murder her mother?

But when Durkhanai entered, she was surprised to see her uncles already present with her grandparents. For a moment, the sight of them made her pause—they looked so like Wakdar: the same blue-green eyes, the same hefty build, those striking features and the honey-colored hair now streaked with gray.

But there was something different about them still. Their eyes were more green, like Dhadi's. She always thought she looked like her uncles, but now that she had seen her father, she knew she was more Wakdar than them.

"Zmarack Chacha, Suweil Chacha, salam," she said, greeting them. They placed a hand on her head in a sign of affection, though the warmth of the gesture did not reach their eyes. They had come from Trichmir and Dirgara for Zarmina's wedding, an occasion which would of course no longer be happening, and now their childhood city was being laid siege to.

"Abu, you must relent," Suweil Chacha said. "You must stop this siege before it begins."

"You cannot win this," Zmarack Chacha said, running a hand across his beard. "Retire to Mianathob. It is the only way for this to end with peace, for you to escape unscathed."

"You have had a good reign," Suweil Chacha continued.

"It is time to bow out gracefully," Zmarack Chacha finished.

Wakdar had clearly spoken with them, as he had with her. While Durkhanai had refused the idea at first, she now saw reason in it. She was not fond of the idea of Wakdar ruling, but perhaps it was the only way.

After he had the throne, surely he would not run their country to destruction?

Durkhanai shook her head, realizing the irony of such a thought when Wakdar was literally at her gates with an army.

He did not care about destruction. All he cared about was his desire for retribution.

War was inevitable, now. She wished she did not have to pick a side, but not picking still put her on one side, whether she liked it or not.

"*Bas!*" Agha-Jaan snapped, voice harsh. "That is enough! I will not give up my throne, the throne I have worked fifty years for, the country and people I have endlessly toiled for. If Wakdar was an admirable successor, perhaps it could be considered, but he is not. He will end Marghazar's centuries' old traditions and show weakness in front of the Lugham Empire, rather than crush them. He had no sense of duty or honor."

"Please, there must be another way," Durkhanai said.

"There is not," the Badshah said, and that was final. He was too stubborn and too proud. He would not relent.

With nothing else to say, Durkhanai returned to her room, rubbing her temples, dread and horror spreading through her stomach. She had heard of war her entire life, but it was always in the background, always far away.

Tomorrow, it would be here, in her home. There was no running from it. She would have to face it.

That night, she prayed. Again and again.

There was nothing left to be done. The least she could do was rest. She collapsed onto her bed without changing, waving off her maids until she was alone in the darkness, nothing but the low glow of a candle to illuminate the room in a soft light that did not reach the room's corners. The doors were all closed to keep the cold out but she wished to lean on her balcony, to find some sort of peace.

Instead, she stayed in bed, curling into herself, trying to fall asleep.

And it was in the land of half-consciousness that her heart cried out, that she found that she was exhausted and that she missed Asfandyar. She wished he was there with her, just that he was there.

Though it was impossible for him to be. They were on opposite sides of this war.

Yet, still she ached for him, loved him, missed him, and she felt it everywhere, from her teeth to her toes. In the darkness, she imagined him beside her, just like that one perfect night they spent together, exchanging stories, holding on to one another, and the sound of his breathing when he'd fallen asleep, the lazy, possessive way his arms had held her close, and the way that when she had tried to shift away to see what his reaction would be, his arms had tightened.

Though it was winter around her, in the heat of her memories, she was surrounded by summer, surrounded by him, and in that warmth, she slept.

After Fajr the next morning, the mountain shook.

# CHAPTER EIGHTEEN

*G*uards appeared at Durkhanai's door.

"What?" she snapped, barely sparing them a glance as they approached. She was transfixed on the letter General Rizvi had sent the Badshah this morning, which he had barely paid any mind to. *Inevitable*, was all he said, though none of it was.

"We are to escort you to safety," one guard said. She narrowed her eyes, this time looking at him. He had the good graces to bristle. "They are the Wali's orders."

"No," she said simply, looking back to the letter, her mind spinning as she considered what there was to be done. Undeterred, the guards entered her room. "What. Are you doing." She spat out.

"Apologies, but we were told to escort you to safety," one guard said, not looking into her eyes. "Even if we had to use force."

"I sincerely would like to see you try," Durkhanai challenged. The guards exchanged a look. Before either party could see who would win this particular tiff, Dhadi appeared at Durkhanai's doors.

She looked calm and regal as ever, her hair in a tidy knot, her sari crisply ironed. Rubies hung from her ears.

"Jao, Durkhanai," she said calmly. "Go."

"Why?" Durkhanai asked, voice hard. "Why should I, when currently my home is being laid siege upon?"

"For precisely that reason," Dhadi said, trying to coax. "You must be kept safe."

"I do not want to be kept *safe*," Durkhanai said. Her temper flared. "I want to *do* something. Someone must." She paused, then strode forward to take Dhadi's cold hands. "Dhadi, please. Tell Agha-Jaan to make peace with Wakdar. End this battle before it can get worse, for I fear this is only the beginning. He will not stop until he has succeeded."

Dhadi withdrew her hands. When she spoke, it was as if she did not see Durkhanai, not really. "You must go, now."

"I am the Shehzadi!" she cried, but it was like screaming at the wall for all the difference it made.

"Which is why we must keep you safe."

Durkhanai clenched her jaw, suppressing a scream. She did not want to go, she wanted to help. They were trying to decide the fate of her people—yes, *her* people—based on *their* pride and what suited *them*. No one was thinking about the lives that would be lost in the coming hours, the coming days.

The Badshah refused to relent to his son, Wakdar wanted to punish his parents, and Safed-Mahal and the crown were just prizes to be won between them, not thousands of lives, thousands of people who trusted the crown to ensure their livelihood.

"Don't look at me like that," Dhadi said, and Durkhanai realized she had not tried to mask the unadulterated fury she felt toward her grandparents. "We must take a stand. The people are a necessary sacrifice for that. They will die with honor." She paused, then shook her head. "I don't expect you to understand. Guards, take her."

The guards seized her arms and began carrying her forward.

"Stop treating me like a child!" Durkhanai yelled at her grandmother.

"You *are* a child," Dhadi replied.

Durkhanai let them take her in silence, take her down to the private quarters within the mountain, where the jewels and valuables were hidden, where the room of the lady lay.

They led her into the lavish suite, then locked the door.

Durkhanai was alone. She clenched her hands into fists, resisting the urge to destroy the room's contents. For a moment, she felt an intense sense of vertigo. She did not, as she expected to, feel suffocated by the memories of when she was in this room last, when Zarmina was the lady and Asfandyar was to sit trial.

Instead, she felt a weightlessness and heaviness all at once, as if this was a dream, as if *she* was a part of the trial, though not the lady—she was the monster behind the second door.

She squeezed her eyes shut to stop the room from spinning, and in the darkness, she saw that nightmare now familiar to her: the woods, in the dead of night; the moon; her bleeding heart, blood dripping onto snow; the funeral shroud.

Her eyes flew open; she clutched the table, knuckles turning white.

After she steadied her breathing, she spent the next few hours trying to escape.

But there were no windows, no passageways, only one door, locked. It was not like when Zarmina had been here, when only the door at the end of the hall was locked and she could move freely between the dressing room, bathing room, and suite.

Durkhanai was locked with nothing but a small vanity and a bed and a bowl of assorted nuts and dried fruit. She tried to persuade the guard at the door, but he would not relent. Not when she talked sweetly, not when she threatened. He said nothing at all.

Eventually, Durkhanai grew tired from her efforts, and she sat down, trying to think. She surveyed the items of the room once more, running through scenarios. They played out in her head, each of them failing, even as she adjusted and replayed the situation again and again.

Finally, an idea shifted into place.

She went to the vanity, rummaging through the contents, and as she'd assumed, there were some cosmetic products. Durkhanai took a tube of red lipstick and crushed it into face cream, resulting in a thick mixture tinted pink. Adding perfume, she thinned it out, achieving the result she desired, but it was still not dark enough for blood, however, and the smell of perfume was too strong.

Picking up a rose, Durkhanai pricked her finger, and true blood bubbled to the surface, but it was not nearly enough for her purposes. Clicking her long nails against the table, she thought.

Durkhanai surveyed the rest of the objects before her, eyes falling to a hairpin. The silver glistened, but the end was too blunt; it would take too much strength to draw blood. She met her gaze in the mirror, chewing on her bottom lip as she thought.

She noticed the sapphires dripping from her ears. She clenched her jaw. This would be unsavory, but she was nothing if not determined.

She undid one of her earrings, holding it steady between two fingers. Swallowing hard, she lay her left hand flat on the table, then raised her right hand above it. She took a deep breath and drove the earring down.

At the last moment, she shuddered, drawing her hand back.

Making an irritated noise, Durkhanai rolled her shoulders. She had to do this.

Self-preservation itched in her throat, but she brushed it away, laying her hand flat again. This time, as she drove the finding forward, it sank into the soft flesh of her hand.

She winced, biting down on her tongue to stop from crying out, biting down so hard in fact, she drew blood in her mouth. The taste was sharp on her tongue.

Blinking away tears, Durkhanai removed the earring's finding from her palm. A rush of blood spilled across the creases of her hand as she took measured breaths.

She dripped as much as she could into the mixture, then hurried to the door. It was not bleeding too much to be dangerous, but her hand did throb and ache.

Durkhanai set up the scene: She brought a vase in front of the door, then lay down on the ground. There, she spread the blood across her wrist and down her hand, across the floor. It was not a perfect mix, but it would provide an illusion enough for what she needed.

Showtime.

Durkhanai kicked the vase. As it fell to the floor with a crash, she cried out, then spread the rest of the fake-blood mixture to the crack at the base of the door. Last, she put a heavy shard within reach.

"Shehzadi!" the guard cried.

She closed her eyes.

She heard him fumbling for the keys, then unlocking the door.

"Hai Allah, Shehzadi," he cried, falling to the floor where she lay limp. Only when she felt him crouch over her did she reach for the heavy shard of the broken vase and attack his head.

The shard shattered on his skull. He fell back, and she rushed forward, grabbing the keys from his hands. As he made to sit up, she kicked his stomach, and he doubled over in pain.

Before he could recover, she stepped out of the room, closed the door, and locked it.

"Ay!" he cried, pounding on the door. It rattled on its hinges, but did not budge.

The hall was empty. Only one guard had been spared, operating under the assumption that she could never escape.

Well.

Durkhanai rested her brow against the door, breathing heavily, until eventually the pain in her hand subsided. She straightened her shoulders and made her way back to the main palace. Impossibly, when she emerged, the halls were dark and quiet. Night had fallen.

"Durkhanai!" a voice called. She turned.

"Gulalai," replied Durkhanai, running over to meet her.

"Where have you been?" Gulalai asked. "And what's all this blood?"

"Not real," Durkhanai said, though her palm was aching. Her hand was clenched in a fist, which had stopped most of the bleeding.

Durkhanai made an irritated noise. "Dhadi thought to lock me up."

"Her mistake," Gulalai said.

"What's happened?" Durkhanai asked. Dread filled her chest like iced talons scraping against her ribs. There were too many things that could go wrong, and would. "The gates haven't fallen, have they?" She paused, her voice dropping to a whisper. "Did they find Asfandyar?" Gulalai shook her head. "What is it then?"

"Come, let's get you cleaned up," Gulalai said. "I'll tell you on the way."

"What could it possibly be?" Durkhanai asked, and she and Gulalai made their way to her rooms, where her maids would clean her up. The wound wasn't deep enough to need stitches or anything so dramatic.

"It's the wedding guests," Gulalai said, both of their paces brisk. Durkhanai raised a confused brow. "They are actually Jardumi soldiers."

"No," she exhaled. Durkhanai recalled the guests she had seen all across the mountain when she'd returned from Mianathob. That meant enemies within the gates, already.

"That's not all," Gulalai continued, as they turned down the hall to Durkhanai's wing. Her guards looked surprised to see her, but no doubt imagined Dhadi allowed her out, rather than Durkhanai finding her own way.

"What else?" asked Durkhanai. Now Gulalai stopped.

"There's no easy way to say it . . ." Gulalai bit her lip but met Durkhanai's eyes. "The other zillas have declared war."

"*What?*" Durkhanai blinked. "Gulalai, are you certain?"

Her friend winced, nodding. "There was a letter, something incriminating the Badshah of alerting the Kebzu Kingdom of the summit."

Durkhanai swore under her breath. This was Asfandyar's doing. *Fitteh mu tera.*

And this was the man she was madly in love with. Foolish, foolish, foolish.

"Wakdar must have planned this in advance," Durkhanai said. "And that means . . . the troops."

She stopped, recalling the treaties that had been agreed upon between the Badshah and the ambassadors: the armies the Badshah had called for.

The armies the Badshah had been calling to Safed-Mahal in the past few months, those same armies would turn on him now, as the treaties dissolved.

"Wakdar's forces have nearly doubled with the support of the other zillas' armies, which were already here," Gulalai said. The Badshah and Wali would not have expected this.

"Can you stop the Kurra forces?" Durkhanai asked, mind spinning. Gulalai chewed on her lip, shaking her head.

"They have orders from my father directly, I didn't even know," Gulalai replied. "I was angered by it, as well. I don't want my troops in any war, regardless."

Durkhanai pinched the bridge of her nose, and as she did she caught the smell of dried blood on her fingers.

"Let's clean you up," Gulalai said. "Then take matters from there. But truthfully I don't know if there's anything to be done."

"There is always something to be done."

Taking a deep breath, Durkhanai entered her rooms and quickly allowed the maids to help her wash up while she considered her next move. A negotiation would need to be struck between the Badshah and Wakdar, but the Badshah would not listen to anyone.

Perhaps there still was someone who he would listen to.

"That's enough, thank you," Durkhanai said to her maids. She did not change, instead, walked straight out, Gulalai at her side.

They went outside, in the frigid night, and from up here, from the peak of the mountain where the marble palace lay, it was easy to pretend there was nothing amiss. This far up, she could not even hear the cries of the battles waging down below, could not even see them.

As closely as she listened, all she heard was the rattling of frozen branches, the howling wind.

She and Gulalai rode the short while to Rashid's estate.

"Durkhanai, Gulalai," Rashid said, greeting them both the instant they entered. "This way," he said, walking quickly until they were in a private room. Only when the door was closed did he speak again. "My father and the other nobles are . . . upset to learn that Wakdar is alive, as well as the rest of these rumors. Some have even refused to send in their men to fight, saying the Badshah should sort out this family affair himself."

Durkhanai tried and failed to suppress a groan.

"That isn't all," he said, seeing her angered expression. "The rumors have well and properly spread, and by now, everyone knows that the Badshah was complicit in the summit attack and that he has allied himself with the Kebzu Kingdom. They aren't happy."

"As if I am overjoyed!" she interrupted.

"Which is why many refuse to defend the Badshah now against Wakdar," he finished.

Durkhanai rubbed her temples. "I cannot blame them. It was an egregious act, but they must understand that Wakdar won't be much better as a ruler. At the very least, the Badshah has been here, fighting for his people, for the past two decades while Wakdar has been in hiding."

Rashid winced. "The way he has been fighting may well make it worse. Some believe things may be different with a new king."

"They're wrong." She shook her head. "At least, in regards to Wakdar they are. He seeks to punish his parents, nothing else."

"So your allegiance still lies with the Badshah?" Rashid asked.

"Yes," she said. "I can still get to Agha-Jaan, I think. I can get him to understand. One day, maybe ten or twenty years from now, I will be ruler of this land, so I am still his legacy. He may discard me now for being young and petulant, but with more time, I can get him to change his ways."

"Are you sure of it?" Gulalai asked.

Durkhanai shook her head. "No, but I must hope. There is no other way. I know I can be a better ruler than Agha-Jaan or Wakdar." At least, she hoped such a thing was true. She needed it to be true; otherwise, what was the point? "It is just a matter of getting the chance, and I have better chances with Agha-Jaan. He does love me, and respect me, too." She sighed. "With Wakdar, I am nothing more than a showpiece. There may be some sentimentality in me being his daughter, but because he had another, even that emotion is not strong."

Rashid's mouth opened in shock. "Excuse me, did you perchance just say *another*? As in, Wakdar has another daughter?"

Durkhanai and Gulalai exchanged a glance. "Let me handle this," Gulalai said, holding up a hand. "While I did appreciate the detail with which you related the story to me, we need to expedite past the dramatics right now." Insulted, Durkhanai's mouth popped open. "Don't look at me like that! It was very moving, jaan, but we just don't have the time for your tears at the moment."

Gulalai faced Rashid then, cracking her neck. She took a deep breath.

"Brace yourself, Rashid, dear." Her gaze was determined. "After Wakdar fled from Safed-Mahal, he went to Jardum, remarried, and had a child—Durkhanai's half-sister, Naina. She grew up with Asfandyar and they fell in love. Naina wished to reunite her father with his estranged family, so Asfandyar brought her to Safed-Mahal, but she was killed by the Wali for attempted insurrection. As such, Asfandyar pledged his life to Wakdar and the two plotted revenge.

"Then, Asfandyar came to the palace as a spy to distract Durkhanai, make her fall in love with him, and get evidence about the Badshah's collusion with the Kebzu Kingdom, which would lead to the war we are witnessing now." Gulalai said all of this very quickly, without stopping for breath. When she finished, she looked at Durkhanai. "Did I miss anything?"

"I don't think so, no." Durkhanai was actually impressed by how succinctly Gulalai had relayed the tragic tale.

Rashid was truly dumbfounded. He turned to Durkhanai. "And you're still in love with this man?"

Now it was Durkhanai's turn to wince. That was his one question? She smiled weakly. "Yes."

He shook his head, then surprised her by laughing out loud. "You really do rub salt in the wound. If I understand correctly, you rejected me for a spy who was in love with your half-sister, plotted revenge against your beloved grandparents, and is responsible for the war against your homeland?"

Durkhanai glared.

"When you put it that way, it truly does sound insane," Gulalai agreed. "Rashid may be on to something."

"I hate you both," Durkhanai said, pouting. "Besides, we are entirely going off topic when there are more important matters to discuss than my depraved tastes in men."

"Right, right, war and siege and all that," Gulalai said.

"Do continue," Rashid said. "What do we do now?"

"Whatever the Badshah and Wakdar's quarrels, we cannot let the villagers lose faith in the crown," Durkhanai said. "I must go speak to them, assuage their worries."

"Good idea," Rashid said. "I will join you."

"Your father won't like it," Durkhanai warned.

"It is what is right."

Together, they three went to the villages, and it was just as Rashid said. Everyone had heard, and they were confused. Durkhanai did her best to reassure them.

"Whatever occurred in the past is irrelevant now," she told them. "We must stick together now; we cannot falter! Do not lose faith in the crown, I beg you. I promise we will do right by you all; we must stay united!"

"The Shehzadi is right!" Rashid said. "We must stand strong together against these foreign forces!"

"This seems to be a family affair," someone grumbled. "Why should we put our lives at risk?"

"Why does the Badshah not speak with his son?" another added.

"We are tired of war!" voices cried out.

"Please!" Durkhanai said. "I ask that you trust me! Nothing good can come from our disunity! Defending our mountain is of the utmost importance right now. I ask that you please cooperate with the commanding officers' orders!"

While some seemed to understand, others did not. They didn't dare argue further with Durkhanai, but she could see it on their faces. At the end of the day, the villagers would do as they saw fit, and in a way, Durkhanai could not even blame them.

This war was ridiculous. She did not even believe in it herself, how could she ask these villagers to risk their lives defending a crown she herself was losing faith in?

When they returned to the palace, exhausted, the trouble wasn't over for the night.

A set of guards spotted Durkhanai, and they were highly ranked enough to know she was not where she was supposed to be.

They quickly approached her, expressions tense.

"You were meant to be in the lady's suite, kept safe," the guard said, voice hushed. She was sure Dhadi would be angry with her, but she did not care. "Come with us, now."

Durkhanai's heart pounded rapidly. The guards could take her, lock her away again, and she would not be able to escape a second time.

A guard reached for her arm and in the same moment, Rashid unsheathed his sword.

"Do not even try," he said, gaze hard. The guards glanced at one another, then back at Rashid, who did not waver. "Be on your way."

The guard muttered something under his breath, then, huffing and puffing, they retreated. Durkhanai let out a breath.

"Thank you," she said, feeling a bit unsteady on her feet. She hoped the guards did not try to take her again. She prayed, too, that Dhadi would be too busy to make them. She would not be able to ward them off if she were alone, and she did not think she would be able to escape again.

"Anytime," Rashid said, putting his sword away.

"I am impressed," Gulalai said, giving Rashid an appreciative glance. "Durkhanai, Rashid is right—you rejected him for a spy, and look how nice he is! I cannot believe you broke this poor boy's heart."

"How long will that be held over me!" she cried, but still, she felt a little embarrassed, even if Rashid himself was joking about it a little while ago.

But then Rashid laughed, and the tension dissipated. She laughed, too, then squeezed his hand. He would be reunited with Zarmina, he would.

"I really ought to learn to fight," Durkhanai said, muttering to herself.

With her city under siege, she really needed to know how to defend herself—but it was too late, now.

Three days later, the gates fell.

# CHAPTER NINETEEN

*D*urkhanai received the reports.

Once the canons broke down the boulders surrounding the gates, the gates fell easily, quickly. Wakdar's army was merciless, as was the combined army of the other zillas. They advanced up the mountain quickly.

Most villages surrendered to Wakdar once they found out the Badshah was colluding with the Kebzu Kingdom. They now accepted Wakdar as the Badshah.

Durkhanai was hurt by this, but she understood why. How could she blame them? Especially when the consequences were so clear for denying Wakdar what he imagined was his birthright.

The consequences she saw before her now, in Kajali.

Or, what was *once* Kajali.

The entire village was in ruins. The fields were burned down, houses destroyed, and everything was muddy, though upon further inspection, it was clear the dirt was not wet with rain, but blood.

The blood of *her* people. The people she could not protect.

Durkhanai stood there, alone in the quiet night, the sights etching into her memories. Leaves rustled above her, and the moon was a harsh, white curve in the dark sky.

It was a small village, perhaps twenty families, a little over a hundred people, and there were none left. No survivors. The rancid smell of decaying bodies filled the air, and Durkhanai resisted the urge to gag, to cover her nose. Instead, she breathed it in.

The people of Kajali had refused to bow to Wakdar. They had been the first village to do so, to reject him, and this was the result of such loyalty to the Badshah.

Loyalty to the Badshah—or loyalty to her? For hadn't she said once that while her grandfather wore the crown, she was the face the people knew?

What good was it? Their love for her? All it brought them was ruin.

Had she not held these same children in her arms just a few days ago? Had she not conversed with the women as they hung their laundry, and listened to the mens' singing as they tended to their animals? Their love had renewed her, given her the flare of life and motivation she had needed, and now they were all gone.

This is what their love for her had brought them—death and destruction. This was her fault just as much as it was Wakdar's. What did her intentions matter when the end result was this? Didn't her father, and her grandfather for that matter, also believe they had good intentions? What did any of that matter, when all they did was hurt people?

How was she any different? Any better?

Was there even any point in trying?

"Shehzadi, it isn't safe for you here," a guard said, appearing by her side. Durkhanai turned to see a group of guards, all on high alert. She had snuck out after hearing the news, and now they were here to collect her.

Nodding in compliance, Durkhanai strolled forward, and the guards created a formation around her. She went with them, mouth dry. The quickest way out was through, so they walked along the carnage. She did not look away.

Blood and broken bodies and charred skin and destroyed homes. Each sight was a fresh pain, a new cut across her skin, and by the time she made her way through, it felt her entire body was covered in gashes.

When they reached the edge of the village, they veered right to the quicker, back route. As she traveled through the darkness, staring up only at the moon, Durkhanai thought of Wakdar.

He would know these routes, this land, as well as she did, if not better, for the near decade more he had spent here than she had.

He could easily come to the palace.

But deep down, she knew he would not take the quiet, back routes to arrive. He would continue his ostentatious siege, wreaking havoc, and play this game to its end, for that was all it was to him—a game. Durkhanai had secretly hoped Wakdar was better than his desire to exact revenge on his parents, but in that aspect, he was his father's son.

Was she her father's daughter?

The same blood rushed through her as it did in her father, in her grandfather. She felt it singing within her, the greed for destruction, for punishment, for pain.

She could not remove this blood from her body, and for a moment, she was suffocated by the thought. Was she destined to be just like her father? And her grandfather? For the first time, she felt burdened by her lineage, as though . . . cursed.

But she would not use her people to accomplish any of her goals. She knew that with certainty. Not as the Badshah did with the Lugham Empire. Not as Wakdar did now with this war.

She would always put her people first.

She would be different.

But no matter how many times she told herself the statement, she wondered if some things were simply unavoidable. That no matter how she fought it, perhaps some things were simply fated.

Ignoring the lingering discomfort from the thought, she went to see her grandparents. Though it was late at night, they were still awake and allowed her into their chamber, where they both sat in their night clothes, large shawls wrapped over their bodies.

The Badshah sat reading a letter, while the Wali rolled a tasbeeh between her thumb and forefinger, though her lips scarcely moved.

"You know you should not have left the palace," Dhadi said, voice scolding. "I wonder why we bother to tell you anything at all when you no longer listen to us." When she gazed upon Durkhanai, her eyes were weary, as if she was tired of her granddaughter.

"Wakdar is advancing, and it is only a matter of time before he reaches the palace," Durkhanai said. "What is your plan for when he does?"

Dhadi looked at Durkhanai with those same weary eyes, as if looking straight through her.

The Badshah did not look up.

"Well?" Durkhanai asked, raising her voice to draw their attention. "You must have some plan. Something you will say to him." She paused, thinking it over. "Perhaps if you apologized—"

The Badshah looked up. "Now you are talking nonsense," he said. "What do we have to apologize for?"

"Just because you are elder does not mean you have done no wrong," Durkhanai said, voice hard. "You do not realize the anger that has festered inside of Wakdar all these years, inside of Nazo Phuppo. But they are still your children, your blood. I believe they can still be reached. If you just *talked* to them, made things right, perhaps—"

"Enough!" the Badshah yelled. "I will not be lectured at by a child whose only grievance in the world is that she was not allowed an unsuitable match."

Durkhanai's heart rattled by her grandfather's raised voice, but she remained undeterred.

"I am not a child!" she cried. "And you *will* listen. This is not merely about him, not merely about him and I. It began decades ago, with Yaqut, then continued on with Naina, and Asfandyar. You cannot control everyone, and you cannot control everyone's love. You did not learn the lesson then, and you are still paying the consequences, as are our people!"

The Badshah looked away, repulsed by her.

So that was how it was.

She was adored so long as she stayed in line, but dissent earned her disgust. Very well.

"You should have abdicated in the beginning," Durkhanai said, shaking her head. "They were all right, and I couldn't see it, then, but it was the best course of action. It would have saved us all this."

"Get out," the Wali said, voice deadly.

Durkhanai was already on her way.

Regret seeped into her as she left her grandparents' chambers, going over the last words she had spoken. But it was not regret for what she had said, rather for the timing. It was too late for those words, now.

She should have forced them to abdicate earlier. It would not have been so bad. She had so many chances to do so, but thought back to the first one, the vital one, when Asfandyar had told her about the Kebzu alliance.

How different things would be had she not been so blindly loyal to her grandparents.

She would not keep making the same mistake, but she could not let Wakdar win, either. He would take the palace soon; it was only a matter of time.

When he did, she could side with him, just like Nazo had asked her to all those weeks ago. Then, before any further damage could be done, she could make him see reason.

It hurt her to even consider siding with him, but the Badshah wasn't doing nearly enough, and something had to be done.

It prickled within her, contemplating betraying her grandparents, but while family and tradition were important, at some point she had to break free and decide for herself who it was she wished to be.

And she no longer wished to be led by the Badshah or the Wali, the way her instincts coddled her to, the way she had during the trial.

It all came back to the trial, the decision she made, and how wrong it was.

But was siding with Wakdar the wrong choice, too? After what he did to Kajali?

How did she find a third way—her own way?

Possible solutions played through her mind. If she sided with Wakdar, the Badshah could be forced to abdicate, as he would lose all his standing. The last of those loyal to the Badshah would follow Durkhanai, she knew they would.

Once the Badshah and Wali were gone, things could be sorted further. Durkhanai was sure Wakdar did not actually care about Marghazar, and once he had won, and had his vengeance, she could convince him to go. Or at least, retire into the shadows.

She could rule.

But did she deserve to? Would she be any better than those before her? She could not run from her ancestry. Would it only be a matter of time before she became just like them?

She cut the thoughts off at their inception; there was no room for doubt. *Yes*, she deserved to, she convinced herself. At the very least, she loved Marghazar, loved its people. That had to count for something. It had to.

It would take some maneuvering, but Durkhanai could manage it. She would. Though she hated that it had to get to this point.

Durkhanai stood out on her balcony, thinking, thinking. The frigid night air was brutal against her cheeks, and even through her shahtoosh shawl, she shivered, but she was glad for the sensation, the harsh grate of it against her face.

It was not numbness, no, but a throbbing, a constant hurt in tandem with her heart. She closed her eyes against the cold, and all she saw was blood. The blood of the villagers, the blood on the snow, her hands, stained crimson.

She heard a sound.

Her eyes flew open just as she turned, then froze in place as the tip of a dagger kissed her throat.

"Asfi," she choked.

# CHAPTER TWENTY

He was here.

He stood before her, both his beard and hair grown out, and the sight of him struck her like a blow. She staggered back, as if physically hit, and clutched the balcony railing. He did not lower the dagger, eyes blazing with something she could not place.

"What are you doing here?" she whispered, unable to keep the tremor from her voice. Sudden euphoria filled her to see him, to feel him so close, but it was quickly replaced by fright.

There was still a bounty on his head.

"Dimagh toh nahi kharab? You can't be here," she snapped. "They'll kill you if they find you!"

She pushed the dagger aside with her hand and went to cup his face, her fingers sinking into the hair that curled at his nape. He flinched, but did not withdraw.

He was so near, yet still so far away.

Her heart ached, deep, deep into her bones.

"Please, you cannot be here," she said. The pulse on his neck raced beneath her hands. He made no attempt to move.

The wind howled behind her. Their chests rose and fell together, drawing closer and closer.

"I thought you ran . . . I thought you had gone," she whispered.

She was so glad to see him. She thought she would never see him again. And here he was. Flesh and blood and bone.

Something struck her then, about why he was still in Safed-Mahal, why he would not have gone. He had to have been idling nearby. How else would he have spread his evidence of the Badshah's alliance with the Kebzu Kingdom?

Durkhanai's stomach twisted. She withdrew her hands, but did not step back. A chill surged forward, and she shivered, before pulling the doors closed behind her, fingers tight on the handles. The cold pinched into her palms for an instant before she withdrew.

"You've been here," she said, working it out as she spoke. "Hiding right beneath our noses." There really was only one place no one would look for him, one place he might stay undetected. "The passageways?" she asked, though by then she knew. The small nod of his head confirmed it.

"Wakdar will win," Asfandyar said, voice hoarse. "Tell your grandparents to surrender."

"You think I have not tried?" she replied. "They won't listen to me."

"*Make* them listen."

"If I could just do that . . . " She shook her head, then brought her eyes up to look at him. He closed his eyes.

Silence hung between them, heavy and damp like clothes set out to dry in the cold. She watched him, the muscle moving in his jaw, the slow rise and fall of his shoulders as he took measured breaths.

She took a step forward, then another, until she was before him. His throat bobbed, and she tilted her chin up to look at him, the fan of his lashes, the low pout of his lips. She reached out—

He stopped her, dark eyes open. He clutched her hand, and she felt her pulse beating against the press of his thumb, warm and steady against her skin.

"Why are you here?" she asked, voice low. Had he only come to command her to tell her grandparents to surrender?

If she knew him at all, that was not merely why he had come. And she hoped she still knew him, prayed she did.

"Asfandyar," she said. His grip on her wrist tightened, while her pulse quickened against his thumb. Something flickered across his face—conflict? Hesitance? Uncertainty?

When he looked at her, it *hurt*, but she did not look away. The hardness in his eyes gave way. He opened his mouth to speak—

A low noise rattled from the doors of her bedroom. Without thinking, without hesitating, Durkhanai grabbed Asfandyar by his kurta, pulling him behind her.

Her heart beat furiously against her chest as she waited for the doors to open, for guards or Dhadi to enter. She braced herself, protecting him with her body.

But there was nothing. No one. It was just the wind.

Releasing a deep breath, Durkhanai turned, to where she still clutched Asfandyar's kurta, where his hand was wrapped around her forearm, anchoring her to him.

"You must go." She released his kurta, but he did not release her.

"Ask me again," he said, voice gruff. The way he looked at her—it unearthed something ancient within her.

"Why are you here?" she whispered.

"I wanted to see you."

A secret, glimmering between them like a shooting star. She sucked in a breath.

"And now that you have seen me?" she dared to ask, drawing closer as inevitably as the sun stretching across the horizon, lighting all in its path.

"Why did you warn me?" he asked. She blinked.

"You know," she said. "Surely, you must know."

He waited.

"I love you," she said, as though it was the simplest thing, and it was. What else did she know? Perhaps it was the only thing she knew for certain, against the backdrop of war, amongst these shifting loyalties stood out this one, singular truth.

His eyes burned into hers. Then, she was in his arms, his lips upon hers like a key locking into place. She gasped, but did not hesitate as she kissed him back, mouth greedy for him, always greedy for him.

Just as quickly as it began, he pulled away. His lips were red, his breathing heavy, and Durkhanai was sure she was in a similar state. She felt starved and sated at the same time.

"This changes nothing," he said, voice ragged.

Of course it did not. For she had loved him before and loved him still.

Before she could conjecture that the same could be said of him, before she could gaze into his eyes and seek out the truth, before she could hope—he was gone.

Durkhanai sat on her bed, hands tied into her sheets, then fell backward, sinking into the cushions. With him gone, the cold returned to the room. She pressed a frozen finger to her mouth and winced.

It hurt, but she did not withdraw. She couldn't help herself. And that was how she slept, tongue across her swollen lips, as if to trap his kiss within her.

Three days more, and Wakdar took the capital.

# CHAPTER TWENTY-ONE

urkhanai stood by her grandfather's throne, waiting.

It was just like that day all those months ago, as they stood waiting to greet the ambassadors.

But when Durkhanai turned to her grandparents this time, she was not met by any reassuring smiles. No hand reached for her.

Guards were spread out in the throne room, all poised for action. It was only a matter of time, now. Durkhanai's heart raced, and she resisted the urge to fidget. She contemplated what was to be done now, her mind going over her plan to side with Wakdar.

Could she manage it? Would she be able to out-maneuver the king and queen and their banished prince?

Suddenly, the door swung open loudly, cutting off her thoughts. Durkhanai tensed, but the Badshah made no movement. He sat perfectly still, the Wali a mirror beside him, both expressionless as enemy guards piled into the room, fanning and spreading out until finally, Wakdar entered.

His blue-green eyes glittered.

"The prodigal son returns," he said, spreading his arms wide. He grinned. He looked every bit a prince and not like a general who had just fought his way up this mountain.

The Badshah's eyes slitted. His hand made the slightest movement, as if to send a command. In a flash, the palace guards lifted their swords, and Wakdar's did the same. It was a standoff, and the Badshah's guards were outnumbered.

"Aise toh nahi hota," Wakdar said, tsking lightly. "Come, let's be civilized."

"Decades gone and still the little prince cannot bear being overlooked," the Badshah said, face unimpressed, unamused. "I assume that is why you went through all this effort for an audience."

Emotion flashed in Wakdar's eyes—hurt, quickly masked by anger. Silence hung in the air as the Badshah and Wakdar glared at one another. It had been nearly twenty years since they had seen one another, and the pain and rage in both their eyes made even Durkhanai bristle.

"Agha-Jaan," she murmured, voice low. There was no need to exacerbate the situation.

"Speak your piece, boy," the Wali said, jaw set. But Durkhanai could see her grandmother was close to tears, close to breaking. Whatever quarrels they had, Wakdar was still her son.

Durkhanai's heart softened painfully. How had it come to this? But the ordeal was like experiencing a landslide or avalanche; she could do nothing but watch in horror as the destruction fell.

"Oh, he will," a voice said, and the guards parted to let someone forward. On her right, Durkhanai's uncles sucked in their breaths as Nazo stepped forward. On either side of her were Zarmina and Saifullah.

Durkhanai's heart gave a lurch to see them, especially to see them standing across the divide, on the opposite side. They would not meet her eyes. She regarded them closely. Saifullah looked thinner than when she saw him last, and there was a hollowness beneath his eyes. Zarmina did not look physically any different, but there was something sullen about her aura, which forced her shoulders to crumple forward, her hands to lay limp at her sides.

Where had they been? *How* had they been? She was on opposite sides to them now, but still, her heart called out to her beloved cousins.

"Look, the whole family is here," Wakdar said. "The great Mianguls, reunited at last."

"Indeed," the Badshah said thoughtfully. "If this is in fact a family affair, why not do away with the guards? And I will do the same." Wakdar hesitated for a moment, and the Badshah smiled, a challenge in his eyes. "Is your bravado so easily shaken?"

Wakdar set his jaw. "Very well," he said. With some silent gesture to one of the guards—the leader, she assumed—Wakdar's soldiers piled out, and the Badshah's followed.

The throne room was empty save for her family members, her blood.

She did not know how this day would not end in bloodshed.

Durkhanai tried to catch Zarmina's eyes, tried to communicate something, anything, but she would not look at her. Instead, silence hung between them all.

Until someone moved.

It was her Zmarack Chacha. He strode across the throne room, toward Wakdar, and lowered his head with respect.

"Bhai," he said. Wakdar smiled, placing a hand on his younger brother's shoulder. The way the pieces fall one after another in a game of chess, Durkhanai watched her Suweil Chacha do the same, crossing over, being taken.

The Badshah's side had dwindled: All that remained were the king and his queen. But the Wali was not his queen in this game—Durkhanai knew that. The Wali was not a separate entity from the king.

Durkhanai was the deciding factor.

If she switched sides, the king would fall immediately. If she didn't, there could still be a chance . . .

She did not know what to do. It seemed so simple, the plan she had in her mind, but now that it was here, pledging allegiance to Wakdar seemed a deplorable choice to make.

She was frozen in place, unsure. She would not act on instinct and emotion as she had during the trial.

She knew Wakdar needed her on his side. If he really wished to rule over Marghazar successfully, he would need her. But what was he willing to do to get her?

"There must be another way," she said, looking at the Badshah, looking at Wakdar. It was her final attempt. "Please. You are family. We are *all* family."

"There is no other way," Wakdar said. "Durkhanai, my daughter, meri jaan, come."

But Durkhanai did not move.

"Agha-Jaan," she said, looking at him one last time. She searched his blue-green eyes, her own eyes pleading. There had to be another way. "Please."

Something in her grandfather's face gave way. He opened his mouth.

But before he could speak, Wakdar did.

"Fine," he said, stepping forward, closer and closer. "I can see your regard for them, dearest Durkhanai. Would it make you happy if I spared their lives today and instead they were exiled? It is more than they deserve, but for your sake, I can make it so. They can publicly abdicate, hand the throne over to their capable heir, and there would be no risk of badnami, either, no shame incurred."

Durkhanai blinked. "Do you swear?"

"On my life," he replied, reaching out a hand. "Now, come."

But still, something kept Durkhanai rooted in place.

"Durkhanai," Wakdar said, losing his patience. "This offer is a rare display of kindness. Conversely, I could just kill your beloved grandparents and take the throne. Consider that. You would have no choice but to support me."

Durkhanai narrowed her eyes. "If that is true, why don't you try?" she dared. Wakdar's eyes flashed with anger. "You will not because you must know I would never forgive you for such a thing. And I can cause a great deal of hardship for you if I am not on your side."

"Then I can just kill you, too, no?"

Durkhanai raised a brow. "The people might forgive you for killing Agha-Jaan and Dhadi, after the business with the Kebzu alliance, but they would never forgive my death." She knew this for a fact.

Wakdar may have taken the mountain, but to keep it, he would need her support and her help, birthright or not.

"But if you do not believe me, try your hand at it," Durkhanai said, stepping down toward him. She lifted her chin, baring her throat. "Do it."

Wakdar smiled. "Daughter dearest."

At first, she thought it was with her he was pleased with: her tenacity and her courage and her confidence. But it was his next move that satisfied him, not her.

He whispered something in Saifullah's ear, something which made Saifullah stiffen, then exit the throne room.

"And if I had something you would not refuse?" Wakdar asked. Durkhanai raised a brow.

"What could you possibly—"

But the words died on her throat as the door opened and Saifullah returned.

With Asfandyar.

Her stomach twisted. She immediately scanned to ensure he wasn't hurt, but that was ridiculous; he was on Wakdar's side, wasn't he?

"He told me you couldn't hide your emotions, little red," Wakdar said. She bristled, remembering that day so many months ago when Asfandyar had called her that. Her stomach lurched, and she realized she had lost all her bravado the moment Asfandyar entered the room.

"You cannot think of threatening him to get to me," Durkhanai said crossly. "You know I would not forgive it."

Asfandyar stepped closer, across the room until he was standing beside Wakdar, until he was just across from her, close enough for her to reach out.

"Your father is not so narrow-minded, no," said Wakdar, putting a hand on Asfandyar's shoulder. "What I *meant* was that you could marry."

Durkhanai's heart stopped.

"Surely by now, everyone is aware of the love you have for him," Wakdar said. "And though he has tried to hide it, anyone can see the love he has for you. Was it not evident all those months ago?" Wakdar spoke slowly, letting the words sink in, their claws settling deep into her. "But your dearest Agha-Jaan would not allow it, would he?" Wakdar asked.

Durkhanai turned to look at her grandfather and saw that he was standing, genuine fear on his face. "I would allow it, Durkhanai. What else do you want?" Wakdar asked. "You would remain princess of your land, your beloved grandparents would keep their lives, and you would have your love. Again I ask, what else do you want?" He paused, considering her. "Though I sincerely suspect you would do anything for just one of those things, and we all know which one that is."

Durkhanai looked to Asfandyar, willing him to say something. But he would not speak. He stood entirely still, as if holding his breath. Was he waiting to see if she would choose him?

Of course she would.

She took a step forward—

"Durkhanai!" Agha-Jaan cried, suddenly beside her. He grasped her hand, stopping her. "What are you doing?"

"Did you tell her how you slaughtered her mother?" Wakdar asked the Badshah. "Poisoned her as punishment for my fleeing?"

Durkhanai jolted. She recalled how Wakdar had told her this tale when he had captured her from Mianathob. She had not believed it, then, but. . .

"What is it you speak of?" the Badshah replied, and there was genuine confusion in his voice.

"Did you tell her how you tried to have me killed?" Wakdar continued.

The Badshah shook his head. "You are speaking lies to confuse her now," he said. "But even if Durkhanai joins you, the only way you will be the next Badshah is over my dead body."

Wakdar growled. In a swift movement, he unsheathed his sword. "That can be arranged."

The Badshah unsheathed his sword, as well, rolling his shoulders back to prepare for the fight.

"No, stop!" Durkhanai cried, standing in the middle. Neither of them would hurt her. But it was as if they did not see her.

"Apologize!" Wakdar cried, and tears shone in his eyes. Durkhanai was startled by the emotion on her father's face. "Admit your fault! For Yaqut, for sending assassins after me when I ran because I could not bear the thought of killing *you*."

"What are you saying?" the Wali cried, coming forward as well. "We did not kill your wife, nor did we send assassins after you." She held her hands to her heart. "Even though I swore to Allah we would kill her, we did not wish to rob Durkhanai of her mother. But when we found her, she was already dead . . . she took her own life, Wakdar."

There was no mistaking the honesty in Dhadi's voice, and for a moment, Wakdar faltered. Dhadi reached for him.

"You're lying," Wakdar said, shaking his head, tearing his gaze away from her. "Nazo told me! She told me about the poisoned naan!"

Durkhanai couldn't make sense of this. She caught Nazo shifting nervously.

"Enough of this nonsense!" Nazo cried, her voice an octave too high. "Wakdar, stop dawdling. Finish this!" She took two steps forward, coming beside her brother. "For *Naina*."

Upon hearing his beloved daughter's name, Wakdar did not hesitate.

Time slowed around Durkhanai as Wakdar lifted his sword. Sunlight glinted off the steel. Behind him, Nazo's eyes widened in anticipation, and behind her, Saifullah's and Zarmina's confused faces slowly turned to one another.

Wakdar set his jaw, blue-green eyes wild with grief and reckless fury. Durkhanai did not see the Badshah but she heard the rustle of his clothes as he took a step forward.

A sound rose in Durkhanai's throat, her hand twitching with movement.

But she was too late.

Wakdar plunged the sword into Dhadi's heart.

# CHAPTER TWENTY-TWO

*A* scream tore through the air, and Durkhanai fumbled back.

She watched in horror as Wakdar pulled the sword from Dhadi's chest. Dhadi crumpled to the ground, crimson spilling across the silver gray of her shalwar kameez, soaking it completely.

She clutched at her heart, as if to contain the spillage. Her head fell back, eyes wide with shock.

Wide and emptying. *Dying.*

"Dhadi, *no*," Durkhanai cried, falling to the floor beside her. She pulled off her dupatta, bunching the fabric together against the wound. Dhadi sputtered for breath, and Durkhanai held her grandmother's head in her lap, just as Dhadi used to do to her when she was a child.

"Dhadi, please," Durkhanai said, voice breaking. "Please don't leave me."

She looked around, but everyone was frozen, in shock, in horror, whatever it was. No one came to her aid. Durkhanai did not know who to call, for it was Dhadi she always turned to in times like these.

"Dhadi, please," Durkhanai whispered, stroking her grandmother's hair. Dhadi's bloodied hand came around Durkhanai's wrist, imprinting her skin with fingerprints. "Please don't go," Durkhanai pleaded. "You cannot go. You will not die. You—You will do better, you must."

"I'm sorry, janaan," Dhadi choked out. "But you must do better for me."

And with a final breath, the light left her eyes.

A scream tore through the air.

Durkhanai raised a hand to her mouth, and it was then she realized the scream had not come from her, but Agha-Jaan. He was on his knees before Wakdar, grief distorting his features into someone unrecognizable to her. The sword clattered from his right hand; the dagger fell from his left. As the blood emptied from Dhadi's body, Agha-Jaan grew more and more pale.

"What have you done?" Durkhanai cried to Wakdar, her voice hoarse. He seemed to be in shock, as well. He swallowed hard, then took a heavy step forward, toward his father.

"*No.*" Durkhanai stood, standing between her father and grandfather. "Don't. You said you would let them go."

"I did not mean it," Wakdar said quietly.

"Stop!" she cried, pushing him away, but it made no difference. He cast her aside, and she fell to the floor beside Agha-Jaan.

Asfandyar ran to her side, helping her up, a fierce expression in his eyes, something that said he was with her, though he did not know why.

Wakdar lifted his sword. "No!" Durkhanai cried, throwing herself in front of Agha-Jaan.

"Enough!" Wakdar said. With an irritated noise, he raised his hands to push her aside again, but Asfandyar deflected the blow, standing in front of her. He held one hand behind his back, holding onto her wrist. "Boy, get out of my way," Wakdar warned.

"Make me," Asfandyar said, feet locked in place.

Wakdar shook his head. "You'll never learn, will you?"

With alarming speed, Wakdar elbowed Asfandyar in the face. Asfandyar stumbled back, and Wakdar punched him in quick succession: two to the gut, one to the face. With the hilt of his sword, he struck Asfandyar's temple. Asfandyar crumpled to the floor.

"Asfi!" Durkhanai cried. She went to where he was lying unconscious and pressed a finger to his bloodied cheek. As she did, Wakdar had a clear shot at Agha-Jaan. Before Durkhanai could return her attention to her grandfather, someone grabbed her from behind and held her back, their grip tight as steel.

"Be still now," Nazo snarled. Durkhanai struggled, but Nazo held her in place with surprising strength. "Do it," she said to Wakdar. "Finish this."

"For Yaqut," Wakdar said, voice low, but still he hesitated as he brought his sword up.

Agha-Jaan met Wakdar's gaze.

"Go on," he pleaded. Durkhanai understood. He did not want to live a life without his wife. The king and queen were irrevocably tied.

"For Yaqut," Wakdar repeated, but his hand was shaking.

*"For Yaqut,"* Nazo said. The pressure on Durkhanai's arms was gone as Nazo took her brother's hand, and together they plunged the sword into their father's chest.

The crunch of bones filled the air.

This time, it was Zarmina who screamed. Durkhanai turned just as Saifullah pulled Zarmina against his chest, muffling her cries. Stunned, Durkhanai fell back as Agha-Jaan hit the floor, blood spilling across the white marble.

It was done.

Wakdar and Nazo both withdrew.

"Agha-Jaan," Durkhanai cried, going to his side. She couldn't help it, seeing him killed right before her. She did not agree with all that he had done, but he was her grandfather: He had held her in one arm when she was a baby, her feet cradled in his palm.

She went to place a hand on his cheek, then saw blood smearing his beard. Her hands were bloodied. She did not know whose it was.

"Agha-Jaan," she said, and he lifted his eyes to hers one last time.

"Khush rao," he said. "*Be happy.*"

Just like Dhadi, he died.

Wakdar stood with his back straight, vindicated at last, but his eyes were downcast.

Pulse roaring in her ears, Durkhanai sat between the bodies, blood seeping into her clothes, hot and sticky. Although life had left them both, their blood still flowed. She would drown in it, she thought distantly.

Everything felt distant. As if this was just another one of her nightmares. And perhaps it was, for there was the usual sign: Asfandyar out cold on the floor, laying so still and silent, blood on his white shalwar kameez.

In a daze, Durkhanai watched Nazo approach, thinking she was coming to stand over the bodies of her dead parents. But then she lifted a dagger.

"*For Zarmina,*" she said, voice low, and brought the dagger down to Asfandyar's heart.

"No!" Durkhanai did not think. She grabbed Agha-Jaan's sword and sliced it through the air.

Nazo's scream filled the room as the hand that held the dagger severed from her body. Blood spurted out, spilled onto Asfandyar's chest, just as he sputtered awake, eyes wide.

"Ammi!" Zarmina cried, her and Saifullah ran to their mother's side as she fell back, clutching her wrist.

"What have you done?" Wakdar spat to Durkhanai, approaching her. He looked to Asfandyar. "You dare attack *us*, your blood, for him!" He shook his head. "Just like with Naina, he has ruined you."

Durkhanai let out a bitter laugh at the irony. She was standing now, the sword still in her hands. "Us?" she asked. "What *us* is there?"

"I am all you have left," Wakdar said, gaze hard. "I will make sure of that."

He attacked, his movements swift. She held the sword up to defend herself, then realized all he aimed to do was disarm her, which he did quickly. He struck her hard in the face, and she fell back, head swimming. Her vision darkened, splotches bubbling and bursting across her eyes.

In a blur, she watched as Wakdar attacked Asfandyar.

He was on his feet now and much more skilled with a sword than she was, but even so, Wakdar had two decades of fighting on him, and Asfandyar swayed on his feet, still recovering from his previous blows.

"Asfandyar," Durkhanai called, her voice quiet and hoarse. She reached for him from her position on the floor, feeling too weak to stand. "Asfi."

She staggered to her feet as Wakdar disarmed him, kicking the sword backward. Undeterred, Asfandyar lifted his fists, quickly blocking the curve of Wakdar's sword.

Asfandyar fell back, ducking just in time to save his throat. Instead, the sword cut across his chest, and Asfandyar grunted in pain. He scrambled back on the floor, inching away as Wakdar approached, and Durkhanai knew what she must do.

She lifted the sword. It was heavy. She did not realize just how heavy it would be.

With all her strength, she brought the sword up, every muscle in her body straining as she sliced it through the air.

Steel met Wakdar's throat, met skin and tendon as the sword severed her father's head.

Blood spurted into the air, landing across her face, in her mouth. As the sword finished its arc, the tip clattering against the marble floor, Wakdar's body crumpled one way, his head rolling the other.

The taste of blood was nauseating on Durkhanai's tongue. Bile rose in her throat. Breathing heavily, she leaned on the sword for support. Her hands shook.

Wakdar was dead.

There it was, the simple solution, so obvious. The option she had been seeking.

But she hadn't wanted it to come to this. Now, it seemed there was no other way.

And so, Wakdar fell, too, fell just beside his parents, and his blood joined theirs across the marble floors.

"Durre," Asfandyar choked, shock and a thousand other emotions on his face. She could not look at him.

"My debt is repaid," she said quietly. "I have given you back the life I tried to end last summer."

But even still, could that debt ever truly be repaid? Did she deserve to be exonerated?

"Forgive me," she whispered, though she did not know who it was she spoke to as she closed her eyes. "Forgive me."

She took a deep breath. Remembered who she was. Who she had become.

There was nothing she could not do.

She was Durkhanai Miangul, the Badshah of Marghazar.

She straightened, lifted her chin. When she opened her eyes, the others were waiting, as she knew they would be. Durkhanai turned first to her uncles.

"Let it be known this war is over," she said to Zmarack Chacha. To Suweil Chacha, she said, "Call someone to clean this mess and prepare the bodies for burial. The janazah will take place as soon as possible."

Her uncles nodded. They did not challenge her, tell her she was still a child. It was always known Durkhanai was to be the next Badshah of Marghazar. There was no questioning it.

When they left, guards and soldiers piled into the room. As they took in the scene of carnage, they all stilled, shocked. Some of Wakdar's soldiers went to flee, but Durkhanai's guards stopped them.

"No more fighting," Durkhanai said. "Wakdar is dead. Return home. I will be speaking to your Walis soon."

Slowly, the soldiers made their way out, followed by the guards to spread the message. A few guards remained, lingering around Durkhanai. They were sworn to protect her.

It was as if their presence in the room had broken a trance, and suddenly, Zarmina cried out. She left Nazo's side and instead went to the bodies of her dead grandparents.

Saifullah did the same, his face stricken with horror and grief at the massacre. Tears rolled down his cheeks, and he did not wipe them away, while Zarmina openly cried, her sobs filling the silent chamber.

The sound grated through Durkhanai. She wished to strike them both, to blame them.

But she knew there was no way forward if she behaved in such a manner. She was no longer a spoiled, petulant princess, but a queen.

She turned to the remaining guards. "Lock her in the dungeon," she commanded, gesturing to Nazo. She turned to her cousins. "Join her if you wish, or help me clean up this mess. The decision is yours."

The guards went to Nazo as Saifullah and Zarmina exchanged a glance.

"No!" cried Nazo. "Don't let them take me!"

She screamed as they lifted her, eyes rolling back in her head. She writhed in their arms, resisting, sobbing, shaking. She had gone mad.

"We'll stay," Saifullah said, swallowing hard. "Durkhanai—"

She held up a hand to silence him. She did not wish to hear anything, not now.

"Saifullah, tell the nobles I am the Badshah now," she ordered. "Zarmina, find Rashid and Gulalai and tell them the same."

Saifullah looked as if he wanted to say more, but he merely lowered his head, accepting the order. He left, and Zarmina followed behind him, casting a worried glance over her shoulder, which Durkhanai ignored.

She had sent them all away, left alone with the dead, but Asfandyar remained. She could not bear to look at him right now. She knew that if she did, she would see kindness in his eyes, and she would break.

Slowly, Durkhanai made her way toward the windows, toward the light. If she could just breathe, she could move forward, and she had to move forward.

Her ears were roaring with the sound of blood rushing by, and it sounded so similar to the current of the river. She felt she was drowning.

When she arrived at the windows, she realized it was snowing, and had been for some time now.

She stared out at the image for a long while, the blanket of white: so like a funeral shroud, but so like a new beginning, as well.

*Would she drown, or would she swim?*

It was up to her to decide.

# CHAPTER TWENTY-THREE

*A* few hours and two baths later, the scent of blood still clung to her skin. She did not feel cleansed of it, did not feel cleansed of anything that had occurred this morning.

She still heard the shrieks ringing in her ears; the hot, wet blood seeping into her clothes; the moon-white snow, the crimson blood; the heavy sword in her hands. Each memory stitched into her, hanging around her like tethered ghosts.

The servants had already moved her things to the badshah's chambers, and she half-expected Agha-Jaan to walk in any moment, to chide her for taking up all the space on his bed. He would tell her to move over, and Dhadi would come on her other side, and she would be cocooned in the center.

It had happened so many times—Durkhanai expected it to happen now. Instead, she was alone on the massive bed.

She got up and went through the connecting chamber to Dhadi's room. She would need to go through her grandparents' things—she cut the thought off. If she began thinking of all she needed to do, she would surely collapse.

One step at a time.

For now, she was adjusting to her new rooms. The badshah's chambers were larger than the shehzadi's, of course, but they never felt so large, for her grandparents were always there to fill them. While Dhadi had her own room, she stayed in Agha-Jaan's rooms.

Thus, Dhadi's rooms did not have so many memories. Durkhanai would stay here, she decided. It was still haunted, but less so. She could think a bit clearer.

Of course, there were already preparations set for such situations, for it was always known Agha-Jaan would one day die and that the throne would pass to Durkhanai. She was glad for that, for it meant she did not have to be the one to handle sorting out what would come next: the janazah and funeral, the coronation.

A guard appeared at her door. People had been coming in and out for the past few hours, getting final decisions approved by her. In a daze, she had been approving them all.

"Gulalai of Kurra, Your Excellency," the guard said. Durkhanai waved a hand, and he let her through. Gulalai had heard, of course she had heard. By now, everyone knew.

She wondered how this story was being told; was she a hero, or the villain?

She wondered further how this story would end.

"Oh, Durkhanai," Gulalai said, coming to sit beside her. Durkhanai held her hands together in her lap, folded tightly. "You will get through this, you will."

Durkhanai made a noncommittal sound in response.

"Your grandfather, too, took the throne in terrible circumstances, did he not?" Gulalai said. "Take strength in that—that all those who came before you also held grief in their hearts."

It was true. Agha-Jaan had lost his father and brothers all at once.

"But that was different," Durkhanai said, looking out the window. The world was covered in white. It burned too bright. It hurt to look at. "That was unavoidable."

"This, too, was unavoidable," Gulalai told her.

"Was it?" Durkhanai asked, voice distant. She kept going back to it, those images still so fresh in her mind, and perhaps it was inevitable.

Wakdar would have killed her grandparents, no matter what he promised her. He would have been a tyrant had he taken the throne. Perhaps his fate and her hand in it were irrevocable, and it had merely been a matter of time. But she did not know.

"He did terrible things," Gulalai said. "You need not feel guilt over what you did for the protection of your people and your land."

And Durkhanai had killed before, it was true. Even inadvertently, she had done it, all those months ago when she poisoned Rukhsana-sahiba. Then, too, she had done it to protect her people. She had felt regret at the taking of a life, even though it had not been intentional.

But what Durkhanai felt now was not remorse, exactly, for she did not really know Wakdar, nor had he been a good father, or a good man, even, after what he had done in the village of Kajali.

What she felt was fear for herself.

"It feels wrong," Durkhanai said, voice quiet. "To have killed my own blood, though he never behaved as my father. It feels worse still that he killed his father."

She broke off, not wanting to say too much. It was too horrifying to say aloud to her friend. What would Gulalai think of her?

What was wrong with all of them, the famed Miangul leaders? Once, she had thought their blood sacred; it had been a source of pride for her, this thing that linked her to her proud and brave grandfather. But more and more, she was beginning to find that very link cursed.

The fact that her family and her blood were inescapable had always seemed to her a blessing: It meant she would always belong, always know who she was. But now, she felt trapped: as if she was destined to always be haunted by the sins of her forefathers, destined to be just as wretched as they once were.

Perhaps it was embedded in the very essence of who she was, and there was nowhere she could run or hide.

Perhaps it was only a matter of time before she became just like her father . . .

"You know who you are," Gulalai said. "Do not let such things muddle you now."

"But how can I not?" Durkhanai asked, looking at her friend's kind eyes. She knew Gulalai wished to comfort her, to say the right thing, but what was it that Durkhanai wanted to hear? What was it she would listen to?

"I do not even know if I should mourn for them," Durkhanai said honestly. "My grandparents, not Wakdar, for I never loved him, but my grandparents—I loved them with the whole of my heart." Her voice broke. "But do they deserve to be grieved?"

Yes, they had been her beloved grandparents; they had raised her, adored her, spoiled her with love. But they had also done terrible things, cruel things. Things they could not atone for now that they were gone.

Gulalai sighed. "Honestly, I do not know," she said, thinking on the matter carefully. "You cannot forgive them for their affronts against others, for that is not your place. But you can still remember the love they had for you, and you for them, and try to do better than they did. Be better than they were. Do not make the same mistakes."

"I hope I can be better," she said. But if her blood truly was cursed, was it futile to even attempt such a feat? Did Wakdar not think the same thing? That he would be better than his father? And look what he had become.

Where did she begin?

There was too much to be done.

Durkhanai was struck by how alone she felt. For Agha-Jaan, it had always been easier, for he had had a life partner in Dhadi; they had worked together, seamlessly.

"It's all too much," said Durkhanai, feeling overwhelmed.

"I am here for you," Gulalai said. "I know I cannot do much, but I am here."

She reached out her hand, and this time, Durkhanai took it.

"Shukria," she said. "Truly." She thought for a moment. "And, actually, there is something you can do."

"What is it? Tell me and it is done."

"Will you stay?" asked Durkhanai. "I am in desperate need of allies." She paused, reconsidering. "No, I am in desperate need of my friends. And I cannot think of a friend more dear to me than you."

Gulalai smiled. "Of course I will stay. I will help however I can." Durkhanai squeezed her hand. "But first, I must go write to my father."

Durkhanai nodded, and Gulalai went away. It would be good to have her around.

After Gulalai had gone, Durkhanai pondered what to do next. There was a long list of things awaiting her attention: she would have to meet with the nobles, answer their questions and concerns; she had to deal with the aftermath of this war; decide whether to reconstruct the gates; communicate with the other walis; formally apologize for the Kebzu alliance her grandfather participated in . . . the list went on.

And she would tend to them, but first, there was something else she needed to do.

She left her rooms, and a small company of guards fell into place, shadowing her at varying distances. She would have to grow accustomed to that. The security protocols were much more intense for the badshah than for the shehzadi.

As she made her way to her destination, Durkhanai kept her gaze straight ahead. Even as she passed people by, her gaze did not stray.

No one approached her. No one would, until she addressed them first. Another part she would need to grow accustomed to.

Finally, they reached their destination. At the threshold, Durkhanai hesitated, but then she steeled herself and entered.

Nazo sat defeated.

In the dungeon cell, behind the iron bars, Nazo sat still in her bloodied clothes, the stub of her wrist bandaged where her hand had once been.

When she saw Durkhanai approach, Nazo hardly stirred.

"It was you, wasn't it?" Durkhanai asked, sitting down. All the little signs had been there. "You were the one to kill my mother, the one to send assassins after Wakdar."

"Yes," Nazo said. There was no emotion in her voice, just simple truth. "As for the assassins, I knew Wakdar would defeat them, and hoped it would solidify the hatred in his heart. When still he did not turn on our parents, I killed your mother, in hopes that would turn him over. Still, it did not."

"Why did you not take your revenge yourself?" Durkhanai asked.

"I never got the chance," she said. "After the trial, I was married off and sent away, and whenever I visited, your grandparents made sure I had no opportunity to lay harm to them. Once daughters are married away, they are no longer part of the family; I had no standing in this palace. The only one who would listen to me was Wakdar, but even he could not take that final step." She clenched her jaw. "He loved Yaqut, but not like I did. No one loved him as I did."

"All of this, for revenge?"

"He was the great love of my life," Nazo said. Her eyes filled with tears, even twenty years later. "You understand. I know you do. You're just like me. I know you understand."

Perhaps she did. In a way, Durkhanai did not even blame Nazo. For if the blood that coursed through them was the same, were they not equally cursed? Were they not the same?

And Durkhanai did not know what she would have done had Asfandyar been unjustly taken from her as Yaqut had been from Nazo. She did not know.

*But don't you?* A little voice in her head sang. *Don't you?*

Didn't she see just what she had done when his life was threatened?

Durkhanai's stomach twisted in revulsion, but there was no escaping her link to her aunt, just as there was no escaping her link to her father, her grandfather. She could not run from her bloodline.

"Then, when Dhadi killed Naina, you had your chance," Durkhanai said.

"Finally," she said. "Had I known, I would have brought Naina to her death sooner." Durkhanai shook her head. "Do not look at me like that," Nazo said. "We are all pieces in a game. It is only a matter of who is playing. Surely you know that and know it well."

Durkhanai could deny it, but of course it was true. She was not thinking of her people when she killed Wakdar; it was all for Asfandyar.

It was a game, and surely she had won.

But then why didn't she feel like she had?

"I understand," Durkhanai said. She did. "But where does that leave you now, Phuppo? Where does it leave you?"

Emotion broke across Nazo's face. Tears spilled over her cheeks.

"Empty," she whispered. "It leaves me empty." She shook her head, horrified. "There is nothing left."

Suddenly, she cried out, shrieking with pain. She had had her revenge—her parents were dead—but it did not bring Yaqut back, nor did it bring her any peace. Her life had been built for seeking retribution, and now that she found it, her life lost its meaning.

"It's over," she sobbed. "It's all over."

"It isn't," Durkhanai said. "Think of your children. You still have much to live for, Phuppo. It isn't over."

Durkhanai needed to see it—she needed to see Nazo recover, not succumb to madness. It meant there was hope for her, yet.

But Nazo rolled to her side, curling into herself, and sobbed. And there she would remain. Fear thrummed through Durkhanai at the sight. Would this be her future?

So Durkhanai left.

She began walking back to her rooms, and it was only halfway there that she realized she was heading in the wrong direction.

She rerouted, going to the badshah's chambers, not the shehzadi's. With a start, she realized her old rooms would probably remain closed for a long while now, and a certain sadness ran through her at the thought.

When she returned to her rooms, she found Rashid waiting to speak with her, and she told the guards to let him through.

"Durkhanai, I am so sorry for your losses," he said, holding a hand to his heart in condolence. She moved her head, accepting, but could tell that was not why he was here. He was fidgeting, nervous and stressed.

"What is it?" she asked, gesturing for him to sit.

"I hate to bring this up now, but it is pertinent for you to know," Rashid said, running a hand across his beard. He worked his jaw. "The nobles are immediately requesting an audience with you. My father, especially, is particularly . . . awaiting speaking with you."

It sounded like he was more so "demanding" it than "awaiting," but Naeem-sahib and the other nobles were not high on her list of priorities right now. She knew they would never do something so drastic as oppose her claim to the throne, so whatever else it was they wished to discuss would have to wait.

"Thank you for informing me, Rashid," she said, nodding. "I will try to find time to hold a meeting soon, but I cannot guarantee it before the janazah. There is much to be done. Do you know what it is they wish to speak about?"

"Of course," he said. "And no, I do not know. I heard my father talking about it and thought to tell you directly. They won't cause trouble, but it is something to be mindful of. These nobles—my father especially—are going to be a headache for you if allowed to grow fussy."

"Yes, I understand," she said. "Please manage it for now, Rashid. I will attend to it, soon, but until then, do console them, however you see fit."

She knew she could not ignore the nobles thus—that they would be a headache for her later, even a problem—but just now, she could not manage them. She trusted Rashid to do so.

"Of course," he said. Rashid stood to leave but hesitated before he did so.

"Was there something else?" she asked.

"I don't know if it is my place to say."

"Rashid, we are allies and friends, both," she told him. "I trust you as I trust few others. You must feel you can speak to me freely if we are going to work together."

He nodded gratefully, but still his voice was soft when he spoke, "It's only that . . . please speak with Zarmina. She—just speak with her, please."

With a quick bow of his head, he left, and a guard came to tell her that Zarmina was in fact here already, standing outside Durkhanai's doors, waiting. Durkhanai gave the signal to allow her entrance.

When Zarmina entered, her face blotchy and red, Durkhanai was overcome with a sudden surge of anger and hatred, blistering and burning—but then she saw the tears in Zarmina's eyes, and the rage faded quickly.

"Durkhanai," Zarmina said, trying and failing to keep her voice steady. "I am sorry. For all of it."

Durkhanai stood and met Zarmina halfway. "I am, too."

They did not know exactly what it was they were apologizing for, not precisely, but it was the language of sisters and they were versed in it well. Zarmina put her arms around Durkhanai in a hug, and Durkhanai squeezed back quickly.

Zarmina lingered, but Durkhanai let go. She had to. If she held on any longer, she would well and truly break, and she could not lose face. A guard entered to inform her Saifullah was here, and Durkhanai said to let him in.

"Whatever you need, I am here," Saifullah said, voice strong. She smiled gratefully, and they three went to sit.

"Not just like that," Durkhanai said to him. "I know you have ideas and plans, so you must be honest with me. You must communicate and tell me if there is something I am doing wrong—the both of you. It isn't just me who has to do better, but all of us."

"You can count on it," Saifullah said. He rested a hand on her head, and the brotherly gesture of affection made tears spring into her eyes. She blinked them away, feeling less alone.

"What can we do now to help you?" Zarmina asked.

"Before that, there is something else I need to say to you both," said Durkhanai. "I will say it once and then we do not have to speak of it again, but it is something that must be made clear if you are going to stay here and help me."

Saifullah and Zarmina exchanged a wary glance, then agreed.

"I love Asfandyar," she said. "I suspect I will always love him, even if he does not feel the same. And if you cannot accept that, if you cannot accept him, I would prefer if you left."

She knew they might find it deplorable that she had killed Wakdar for Asfandyar's sake, and she could not live with that hatred festering between them.

They had to understand. She had not chosen Asfandyar that first time, but she would spend the rest of her life choosing him.

"We are in this entire mess because Agha-Jaan and Dhadi tried to keep Nazo and Yaqut apart," she said. "I will not keep making the same mistakes. If you cannot love me with my love for him, you may

leave, and I will not harbor any ill feelings. We will be family, always."
She paused now, allowing herself to hope. "But if you wish it, I could
use your help in rebuilding our nation—in forging a new path for the
future."

"We will stay," Zarmina said, without hesitating. "We love you,
all of you. We will stay."

Durkhanai looked at Saifullah, and he nodded in agreement with
his sister.

"Good," she said. "I am glad." She took a deep breath. "Now,
the janazah and burial is tomorrow. The coronation is in four days. I
could use your help in overseeing these matters before we move forward with anything else.

"Zarmina, speak with the villagers on my behalf. Inform them
that I did what was necessary and while it was an egregious act, it was
unavoidable. Tell them I will do my best as caretaker of this land.

"Saifullah, please write to the other walis to inform them of the
events that transpired today and send back all foreign troops, even
those that were sent as part of the ambassador negotiations. We are
not taking any prisoners. Our goal now is to move forward beyond this
entire mess."

They both nodded, understanding, and for a few minutes discussed what the best tactics would be to manage such tasks. After they
had decided what was to be done, Saifullah was the first to go. Zarmina lingered, as if she had something else to say.

"What is it?" Durkhanai asked, arching a brow.

"Asfandyar divorced me," she said. "I thought you should know.
I am free. And so is he."

Durkhanai blinked, caught off guard by the knowledge. Zarmina
took her leave.

It was good of him. But she could not feel glad, she realized, for
it meant that he was now free to leave. There was nothing tethering
him to Safed-Mahal, no reason he should stay. If anything, he should

have been hurrying away, after all the horrors he had to witness in this palace.

Would he leave?

If he did, she had to say goodbye. She had to see him, if just one more time. She left her rooms, wandering the palace, searching for him, but she could not find him.

She quickened her pace, a slight panic seeping into her. What if he had already gone?

Then it struck her, where he might be. She turned and immediately went forth.

How did she know? She just did. Love without intuition was not love at all.

She went to her private library. And there he was, standing by the window.

"Asfandyar," she said. He turned, and something broke on his face. A beat passed between them, and in the next, she was in his arms.

And there it was, the peace she had been seeking, the peace that comes only after the war.

He whispered her name into her hair, holding her, and after a moment, she meant to pull away, too close to shattering, but he held on tighter and did not let go.

She broke.

Her tears soaked into his chest, but he did not let go. Stroking her hair, he whispered her name, again and again, as if anchoring her.

Eventually the tears subsided, and his arms eased around her. Still, she clung to him, their chests rising and falling together as they breathed. Slowly, she detached from him, wiping at her cheeks.

Durkhanai was suddenly self-conscious. She had cried in his arms, she had killed for him, but what did he feel for her?

She found she could no longer read him, or perhaps, she was too afraid to. He did not hate her, that much was clear, she supposed, but did he forgive her?

What did forgiveness look like?

"You have divorced Zarmina," she said, playing with the ends of her hair. She did not know what else to say. "You are free to leave."

But, by Allah, she wished he would stay.

"Yes," he said, and he ran a hand through his curls. The gesture softened something inside of her. It had been so long since she had seen him behave so normally.

Perhaps it was this which caused her to blurt out, "Stay."

She held her breath, watching as he blinked, surprised.

"I know you do not have to, but please," she said, "just stay."

*Stay with me*, she wanted to say. *Never leave me.*

"I will stay," he said, and for now that was enough.

No—that was everything.

# CHAPTER TWENTY-FOUR

*L*ate in the night, after everything was done and Durkhanai was collapsing from exhaustion, she slept.

She dreamt she was in the woods, surrounded by towering, dark trees. The snow was piled on the ground around her and still falling heavily, drifting against her bare cheeks and hands. She went to pull her shawl around her but found she wore none.

Shivering, she walked along the path, her feet sinking into the snow. Ahead, she saw a child, playing, and as she neared, she realized the child was her. The world around her shifted, and suddenly, she *was* the child, her old, young self.

"Ah, I've been hit!" Agha-Jaan cried, as a snowball collided with his chest. Durkhanai squealed with joy as she chased Agha-Jaan, her steps clumsy and wobbly.

Dhadi laughed at their antics, throwing a snowball Durkhanai's way. It hit her face, and she fell back, giggling. She sat up, sticking her tongue out to taste the snow, but when it melted on her tongue, the taste was metallic. Durkhanai pressed a finger to her mouth, and it came away red.

She was no longer laughing. Blinking, she looked around and found that she was surrounded by bodies, lying in the snow. She stood to approach, but as she did, she saw the snow was drenched crimson with blood. There was so much blood.

She screamed, crying out, deathly afraid. She did not know who she was crying out for, but still she cried and cried, and no one came.

A lion roared.

Durkhanai awoke with a start. But she could not move. Her body was frozen, her clothes matted down with sweat. She was suffocating beneath the heat of the blankets, her skin aflame.

She was paralyzed still from the nightmare and felt trapped in her body. Her heart beat anxiously against her chest, and she willed her limbs to move.

She could not even breathe deeply; her chest would not lift and expand. She lay there, taking quick, short breaths, feeling more and more confined.

Finally, her body began tingling, until she could command her muscles once more. She took a deep breath, shaking, and reached for a glass of water at her side table.

But once her fingers wrapped around the glass to lift, it slipped from her fingers and fell, shattering. She jolted from the noise.

Within a moment, her doors were opened and guards piled in, assessing the danger.

"It's fine," she tried to say, but her voice was scratched. She cleared her throat. "It's all right."

Still, she was inspected, the room checked for any breach in her security. Her maids attended to her, ensuring she was not hurt, ensuring she was comfortable, and Durkhanai said, over and over, "It's fine, it's all right."

She was lying. Shame burned within her. She hated to let her guards and her maids see her so weak. They left her, and she was alone. She lay back down in bed, but she was afraid to close her eyes, afraid to sleep and dream once more. But she was so tired . . .

Her eyes drooped closed, and as she neared sleep, she jolted awake, before another nightmare could approach. After an hour more of such back and forth, Durkhanai got out of bed.

She slipped on a shawl and her shoes and left her room. Immediately, guards appeared behind her, following her in silence as she walked to her destination. She knocked on the door, hoping she wasn't disturbing the sleep of the one inside.

Zarmina opened the door.

Durkhanai's face broke, and Zarmina pulled her close.

"It's okay," Zarmina said. Durkhanai couldn't catch her breath. She tried desperately not to hold on to Zarmina, trying to hold herself together, but she was so tired. "It's okay," Zarmina said again, but it wasn't. "Will you sleep with me?"

"Yes," Durkhanai said, voice weak. "I would like that."

But before she could enter, the guards came forward to check the rooms. They had to ensure Zarmina wasn't a threat, which Durkhanai found ridiculous, though she supposed it wasn't so farfetched, after today's ordeal.

Had it just been today? It felt like a lifetime had passed already.

"All clear," the guards said. Durkhanai had the ironic thought that perhaps they ought to be checking that *she* wasn't a threat to Zarmina.

Durkhanai followed Zarmina into the room, and they both laid down together, facing one another.

"Bad dreams?" Zarmina asked. Durkhanai nodded. She listened to the sound of their breathing in the darkness. "I never wanted this," Zarmina whispered.

"Me either," Durkhanai agreed. "I wish—" she broke off. She wished for too many things. It was a silly thing to say.

"What?"

"I wish Agha-Jaan and Dhadi could be here, to make things better," she said. "To atone."

Perhaps then she could have grieved them properly.

"Me too," Zarmina agreed, and she began to cry. Quietly, but Durkhanai heard. She silently brushed away her own tears. "Everything will be different, now," said Zarmina. "We are no longer children."

It was true. Durkhanai had lost the only parents she had ever known and even the father she hadn't. Zarmina, too, had lost her grandparents and a parent; Nazo was practically gone to them.

And along with those losses, they had lost themselves. Zarmina was right. They were no longer children and never would be again.

"I'm scared," Durkhanai admitted in the dark.

"As am I," Zarmina said, voice distant. "But we will face it together."

She reached over and clasped Durkhanai's hands, both their fingers wet with tears, but they held on tight. Zarmina squeezed, and Durkhanai squeezed back.

After a little while, Zarmina spoke again.

"Will he stay?" she asked.

"Yes."

"Shukr hai. Good."

They slept, clutching each other.

The next day was the janazah.

Outside, the world was covered in white. The snow did not stop until the morning, and now everything was buried. It took them quite some time to dig the graves. All the women sat separately from the men, crowding around the three coffins. Everything was covered in white sheets, and the women, too, wore white as they sat doing dhikr with their tasbeehs or reading saparahs. When the men returned from the janazah prayer, which was led by the maulvi, it was time for the coffins to be taken and buried.

All the women stood as the men entered, their faces severe. Zmarack Chacha and Suweil Chacha led the group and knelt to lift the coffin of Agha-Jaan up. There were four corners to be lifted for each coffin, and to do so was a sign of love and respect for the deceased.

Saifullah and Rashid also lifted Agha-Jaan's coffin, though it was not so much out of love for Agha-Jaan as it was for her, and she held both their gazes, hoping they saw how grateful she was. For Dhadi, some of her distant male cousins took the four corners and followed after Agha-Jaan's coffin.

There was only one coffin left: Wakdar's.

As she had no more family members left to take the coffin, Durkhanai expected the nobles to fight over who would have the honors of lifting and taking the body to the graveyard. But the men stood stoic, silent.

Durkhanai narrowed her eyes. Whatever Wakdar had done, he was still a Miangul, being buried here. It was unlike the nobles to let such a ripe opportunity go.

Yet, none of them came forward.

There couldn't be a more humiliating fate. Before further fuss could be created, Durkhanai motioned for guards to lift Wakdar's coffin, and they did so without complaint. The bodies were removed. As the women didn't go to the graveyard, they sat back down, resuming their prayers and reading of the Quran.

The men went to the graveyard, and Durkhanai and Zarmina followed. Close female family members were allowed such things, and it wasn't as if anyone would stop her, anyway.

Durkhanai grabbed Gulalai, as well. She needed them both by her side, though she did not cry. Strangely, Durkhanai felt nothing, just a vast emptiness in her.

They walked in silence, and Durkhanai caught a glimpse of Asfandyar ahead of her. He had not spoken to her, but she felt his presence the entire time. As they walked to the graveyard, as they lowered the bodies into the ground. As the coffins were covered and buried, as rose petals were spread across the surface of the graves.

Through it all, she felt him, as though he were just beside her. It helped her breathe. Whenever she felt sadness threaten to take over, she took a deep breath of the frigid air, and the grief subsided enough not to overwhelm her. But still she felt it, like a rock lodged into her stomach, lodged right where it could never be removed.

Would she carry it with her always?

The funeral was over. Durkhanai almost felt relieved that it was done. The people dispersed, and Asfandyar passed by her. As he did, she felt the brush of his fingers against hers, just for a moment. His skin was warm where hers was cold, and she wished to hold on, but he did not linger. There were too many people watching.

Slowly, everyone left, and it was just Durkhanai, standing before the three graves. Further along the plot, she saw the empty land where one day she would be buried. Suddenly, it all seemed so futile: life, existing at all.

What was the point of any of it, when in the end she would be buried beside her father and grandfather? Even in death, there was no escaping.

She went back to the silence, back to the warmth inside the castle, but still she felt cold, as if the winter chill had settled deep into her bones and would not shake.

Back inside, she changed once more, and began sorting through reports on the casualties and damages incurred by the war. At the very least, most of Wakdar's armies had pulled back.

Durkhanai was interrupted from her reading by a guard. She looked up, awaiting who it was here to see her. She had already informed the guards that certain people did not need to be announced: Saifullah, Zarmina, Rashid, Gulalai, and Asfandyar. They could enter as they pleased. But it was not one of them now.

"It is Naeem-sahib," the guard informed her. She let out a long breath.

"Let him in," she said. She could only ignore him for so long.

He entered, his gaze cold. Durkhanai did not stand. He bowed, and she gestured for him to sit.

"My sincerest condolences, Your Excellency," he began. "Your grandfather was not only my respected king, but a dear friend as well. He and his wife will be missed."

Durkhanai had no need for such talk, though she assumed much of her adult life would be wasted by people not getting straight to the point. She waved her hand.

"Please be brief," she said curtly. He clenched his jaw, and she saw him bite back a rude remark.

"I understand that this is a big adjustment for you," Naeem-sahib said. "From princess to queen, and I would just like to make myself available to you. I did advise your grandfather on a number of matters, and I assume you will follow in his footsteps just as he followed in his father's."

For some reason, these words made Durkhanai pause. She did not wish for her rule to merely be a continuation of her grandfather's, not a repetition.

She wished to do better.

But were some things merely inevitable?

"I am well-attuned to how things run and how they run smoothly," he continued. "You must be overwhelmed, and you are still quite young. However, it is pertinent for you to make the right decisions, especially early on, or the repercussions could be insurmountable."

"Thank you for your concern, Naeem-sahib, but seeing as it has only been a day, I do not think I have made any bad decisions thus far," she said, narrowing her eyes. She did not need for him to condescend. "And I am not so young or inexperienced. Though I am sure you meant no offense."

"No, no, of course not," he said. "You were a radiant princess and will be an even better queen." She resisted the urge to roll her eyes; flattery would not get him far. "There is nothing wrong with getting a little bit of help, that is all I wished to say."

"Thank you, Naeem-sahib," someone said from the door, and they both turned to see Saifullah entering. He came to stand beside Durkhanai. "We appreciate your offer and will of course bear it in mind."

Perhaps Naeem-sahib would take the hint that his advice, for now, was not wanted.

"Good, good, I am glad," he said, but made no move to leave. "You have many matters to attend to, and I would hate to see you make the wrong move. For example, it seems you have acted quickly regarding Wakdar's armies. You have allowed them to go, when it could be said that they could have been used as a ransom and kept as prisoners while you figured out some other use for them."

"I do not recall asking for your opinion on the matter," Durkhanai said, voice hard. "If I require your guidance, I will ask for it."

She did not think there was much else to say after that. She expected Naeem-sahib to fall in line, but he worked his jaw, prepared to speak further before Saifullah cut in.

"That is a good suggestion," he said.

"I am filled with good suggestions," Naeem-sahib said. "Please, let me help you."

While the words were innocuous enough, Durkhanai could see in his eyes he wished to seize power from her. He thought he could enter here while she was grieving and overwhelmed and that she would willingly hand over her power to him. But she would not.

"Again, if I need it, I will be sure to ask," she said, tone dismissive. "I hate to repeat myself. Is there anything more? As you said, I do have a great deal of matters to attend to."

Saifullah took a step toward the door, gesturing to show Naeem-sahib the way out.

"Yes, but—" Naeem-sahib started, standing, but they all turned as another entered.

"Abu," Rashid said, voice pleading. "Come, let us go."

Anger flashed in Naeem-sahib's eyes, but Rashid was not chastised, and Durkhanai was glad to see it.

"Naeem-sahib, I do appreciate how eager you are to help," she said, this time softening her voice. "Rest assured, I am already working closely with your son to find solutions to our problems."

She had hoped such a statement might appease Naeem-sahib, but it only made him further irritated. Rashid said something too low for her to hear, but Naeem-sahib furrowed his brows.

"Shukria," Rashid said, taking his father's arm. They both bowed their heads quickly, and Rashid all but pulled his father away.

When they were gone, Durkhanai slumped back in her seat. She rubbed her temples. She was sure Naeem-sahib would cause problems, but at the very least she had Rashid to manage him.

Saifullah came to her side and put a hand on her shoulder. She covered it with her own hand and sighed.

"I'm already tired," she said. "I think I will be tired for the rest of my life."

"At the very least, even fatigue becomes you," he said, a half-smile turning his lips.

"Yes, at least there is that," she said, nearly smiling herself.

"Now that you are appeased, do tell me what needs to be done," Saifullah said. "Or will you dismiss me, too?"

She rolled her eyes. "You know you and Naeem-sahib are not comparable."

They sat, and Durkhanai reiterated her previous stance: that all of Wakdar's armies were free to leave. She was not going to take any prisoners, for it might result in prolonging a fight she wanted to end quickly. There would be no ill feelings, and no more bloodshed.

She would give them a few days, watching carefully how they would act. She would need Saifullah to keep an eye out for unrest or discontent on either side, her people or Wakdar's. If there was, she would deal with it then. But she did not think she would receive quarrels. It was simple, and she had not hidden the truth: Wakdar had killed the Badshah and she had killed Wakdar. Thus, the leaders of both sides had fallen, and there was not much else to be done.

If Wakdar had been the only one killed, she could see those loyal to him being driven by vengeance; but since there had been casualties on both sides, it seemed best for all parties involved to lay this battle to rest and move on.

While the troops cleared from the mountain, the palace was thrown into preparations for the coronation, which would take place a few days after the burial.

The palace floors were scrubbed, then scrubbed again, every inch of the marble sparkling and pure and untainted.

Hundreds of candles were lit; massive floral arrangements strewn everywhere. The finest feast was cooked for those at court, and food packages were distributed in the villages. It was a time of celebration, and the perfect distraction.

After Wakdar's troops had gone, and clean up parties were sent in, and the dead buried, all the people lay waiting for the coronation ceremony. It marked a new beginning, and who better to lead the cause than their beloved princess?

Yes, it was a time of sadness, for they had lost their king and queen, and yes, it was a time of confusion, after the war and the revelation of the Kebzu alliance, but the people were confident that if anyone could handle it, it was Durkhanai Miangul.

Had she not killed her warrior father? Survived where no one else had? She was beautiful, yes, but not merely a pretty little fool.

She was a queen.

And when the day of her coronation arrived, she was dressed as one.

In her rooms, Durkhanai's maids applied the final touches. She wore a heavy velvet lengha and choli, both the deepest black and shadowless. They were embroidered with the finest dabka kaam, the deep gold embellishments subtle and opulent.

It was the first time she had dressed up in a long, long while. She felt more like her old self, indulged and spoiled and beautiful, but she also felt like a new person, too. The clothes were not ostentatious, but regal. Even her jewelry was more delicate, though there was no mistaking the richness of it.

She wore onyx jewelry encased in gold, three stones along her neck, two dripping from each ear, and one in a teeka on her forehead. Her eyes were heavily lined with kajal, making the blue-green irises stand out in stark contrast. Her lips were painted ruby red, the same deep color as the mehndi that swirled across her hands and feet. Her hair was pulled back in a simple knot, the heavy dupatta covering most of it as one half trailed behind her and the other fell in front.

The last touches: Agha-Jaan's sword, strapped across her waist; Dhadi's tasbeeh, wrapped around her wrist, the beads bumping against her palm. The advisors told her such things would be a good look for her coronation. It showed she carried her grandfather's strength, her grandmother's wisdom.

But Durkhanai had not chosen them for that. She just wished they were here. And more than that, she hoped to do better than them. To wield her strength in the right direction.

To use her wisdom correctly.

She loved them, but she would not forget their mistakes. She would not repeat history.

Ready now, she exited her rooms, her guards trailing around her. The palace was quiet. Everyone would be in the throne room already, waiting for her.

It was the middle of the day, and the sky outside was a clear, perfect white, the same as the snow on the ground, the same as the marble of her palace. As she walked, the black of her clothes struck a stark contrast to the white, and then she saw her hands, the maroon mehndi.

For a moment, her vision blurred, and she was reminded of blood.

She slowed, trying to catch her breath. She held her hands to her sides, holding them in tight fists. After a few measured breaths, her heart rate steadied. She continued on.

They opened the doors for her, and she entered.

The throne room was full, as she expected. But she had not been there since that day, and suddenly, all the figures began spinning. Vertigo overcame her and she saw blood spilling across the marble floors, though of course they were completely clean.

She clenched her jaw, willing the world to calm, but it would not heed her pleas.

She searched the crowds, searching for who or what, she did not know, until she saw Asfandyar.

His gaze was entirely fixed upon her, and when their eyes met, the spinning slowed. He nodded once, forcefully, as if to say she would be okay.

Something within her calmed. She took a deep breath. And the world stopped spinning.

Durkhanai made it across the room and arrived at her throne. She sat, holding her back straight.

"Bismillah hir rahman nir raheem," the maulvi began. He recited some verses of the Quran to begin, then took her oaths. "Do you, Durkhanai Miangul, promise to uphold peace and justice in this land?"

"I do solemnly swear."

"Do you, Durkhanai Miangul, promise to care for the people of this land as your own?"

"I do solemnly swear."

"Do you, Durkhanai Miangul, promise to commit to this work and never forsake this crown?

"I do solemnly swear."

"Let us pray for you and your rule. Ya Allah, you are the Guider of People, so guide our queen in her endeavors. Ya Allah, you are the Protector of People, so protect our queen in her rule. Ya Allah, you are the Savior of People, so save our queen. Make her a kind and just ruler. Have her lead with wisdom and grace. Give her a long, healthy life, and help her in her rule. Ameen!"

The room filled with the chorus of *Ameen* as everyone said it together.

"Ameen," she said. "Ameen."

She promised it. She promised.

The maulvi placed the gold crown upon her head. It was heavy. She flinched from the weight but lifted her chin all the same.

"Takbir!"

"Allah hu Akbar!"

Thus, she was crowned.

Despite everything, she missed her grandparents. As if by habit, she wished they would be proud of her.

Everyone was watching her, and for a moment, she had the thought that she had never felt more alone. But then she looked and saw Zarmina and Rashid, she saw Gulalai and Saifullah, she saw Asfandyar. She steeled herself. She knew who she was.

She was Durkhanai Miangul. She was the daughter of the mountains and river S'vat. She was a leader to this valley and the purest tribe. Durkhanai straightened her back and raised her chin.

She was Durkhanai Miangul, the Badshah of Marghazar.

There was nothing she could not do.

And she would need to do it all. Being crowned was the easy part.

# CHAPTER TWENTY-FIVE

*T*he real work began.

Throughout the chaos of the ceasefire, the funeral, and the coronation, everyone was too preoccupied to be fussy, but after the coronation, Durkhanai knew she needed to act efficiently and precisely. Things needed to return to normal.

No, things needed to move *forward*.

There was much to be done. After the coronation, her uncles had returned back to Dirgara and Trichmir, of which they themselves were the walis. They had their own zillas to tend to.

"We will of course be in touch, janaan," they assured her, and it was a comfort, to know she still had some family upon whom she could depend. Though she had never been close to her uncles, it was still a reassurance.

They did offer to send along some of her older cousins for help, as advisors, but she promptly refused that offer. Support was one thing; spies were another. She didn't need her elder cousins breathing down her neck. She knew what they were all thinking: that she was too young and inexperienced. She knew they thought it, even though Agha-Jaan had been younger when he'd taken the throne.

But he had not been the "famously spoiled princess," coddled and adored.

She was more than that now. She would prove it.

First, she would choose her own advisors. Naeem-sahib wasn't the only one eager to grow close to the new Badshah, but she needed people she could trust. She would create an inner circle. It was decided.

Agha-Jaan had not had one. He had thought he knew best, and when he did occasionally need another opinion, it was Dhadi's he would seek.

But Durkhanai would not follow along that path. She did not wish to have a myopic view of things. Truly, she wished to do her best, which meant she needed people who *knew* her and were not afraid to be honest with her. She needed her advisors to uphold the important task of keeping her in check, to ensure she would not be corrupted by the power bestowed upon her.

And she knew that if they all worked together, they could forge a better future for all of their people.

The first she asked to join her was Saifullah.

"That you even have to ask," he replied. "Of course."

"Excellent. First meeting after Maghrib today in the war room," she informed him. "I want to hear all your ideas for our international affairs, and I am sure the other advisors will be eager to hear them, as well."

"I look forward to it," he said. She blew him a kiss, though her heart was not entirely in such frivolous behavior, but for things to return to normal, she would need to *act* normal, too. Then she was off to find Zarmina.

Durkhanai found her in the gardens with Rashid, both sharing a shawl as they sat before a bonfire. They spoke in hushed tones, eating roasted nuts from a bowl. Durkhanai watched as Rashid cracked open pine nuts and deposited them into Zarmina's open palm, the tips of his fingers growing black from the charred shells. Zarmina's cheeks were flushed red, though Durkhanai suspected it was not merely from the fire. Her heart squeezed, painful and quick. She was happy for them, but it was hard not to feel a little jealous, though she did not allow herself to dwell on the slippery emotion.

Rashid looked happier and healthier. Durkhanai had promised him that he would have his love, so she was glad to see them together. She reminded herself to ask Zarmina how their relationship came about the next time they were alone.

Quietly, Durkhanai walked around until she came behind them, careful to be hidden from view.

"Kya chalra hai?" she asked, throwing her arms around them both, sticking her head between theirs. "What's going on?"

"Oh, nothing, nothing," Rashid said, cheeks turning pink, and he tried to discreetly move away from Zarmina. But since the shawl was wrapped around them both, he did not get far. Zarmina tsked.

"It's cold!" she said. "Don't pull."

"I'm not, I'm—ah!"

Zarmina and Durkhanai watched as, in his fervor, Rashid fell off the edge of the bench.

The twist of jealousy inside her disappeared, replaced by warmth and genuine joy as Durkhanai laughed. Properly laughed. It felt like years since she had last laughed. Her chest hurt from the force of it, but it was a pain she would gladly welcome.

"It is good you are here together," Durkhanai said, when their laughter subsided. "Saves me a trip. I'd like you both to be my official advisors."

"Oh, how fancy," replied Zarmina. "But while Rashid may be eminent, I do not know if I am distinguished enough to warrant such a role."

"Hush, you." Durkhanai tsked. "You are both equally important, and I need your support."

"If you are insisting," Zarmina said, voice good-natured, "though do not say we are *equally* important. I am at least one degree more important than Rashid."

"Chanda, you undersell yourself," Rashid said. "You are at least a dozen degrees more important than I, not to mention immeasurably more beautiful."

Zarmina grinned, eyes filled with light. She giggled.

"Well handled," said Durkhanai, impressed. Rashid lifted a shoulder. "I expect to see you both tonight."

She told them the details of the meeting and a bit about what would be expected of them moving forward.

Zarmina would handle the domestic affairs that had once been Durkhanai's territory: meeting with the villagers, hearing their complaints, being a lending hand. While Durkhanai would still attend to such duties, she would not have enough time to be as thorough or attentive.

As for Rashid, he was tasked with keeping the nobles in check. Of course, she, too, would interact with them, as was her role, but she did not have the mental fortitude to keep tally of who was cross about what at any given time. That was where Rashid would come in.

She trusted him, and more than that, she liked his ideas. She knew that he, too, was striving to be his own person, independent of his father or his family's views, though that did not mean he would forsake tradition entirely.

It was all about balance.

"I expect a feast for chai," Zarmina said, as Durkhanai was leaving. "A feast!"

Durkhanai waved, then was off to find Gulalai, who would undoubtedly make the same request. She found Gulalai in her room, reading over a letter while she chewed on dried apricots.

When she saw Durkhanai approach, Gulalai hid the apricots. Durkhanai gave her a strange look.

"My father," Gulalai said, holding up the letter before Durkhanai could ask. She gave a sigh and put the letter aside. "But how can I help you, jaan?"

Durkhanai sat beside Gulalai on the chaise.

"I have something to ask," she said. Gulalai straightened.

"Goodness. Should I be worried?"

Durkhanai smiled. "That'll be up to you to decide. I'd like for you to stay here in Marghazar and act as my advisor."

"You know I am here for you," Gulalai said, her gaze warm. "But I don't know how my father will respond to this." She chewed her bottom lip. "He is already cross that I have not yet left."

"I understand," Durkhanai said, heart sinking. Of course she understood.

Gulalai was to be the Wali of Kurra one day, and it was a lot to ask for Gulalai to be away from her home, perhaps indefinitely.

"How would it work?" Gulalai asked. "I do wish to stay and help you however I can."

"However you would like for it to work. I'll take as much of you as I can, in as much time you will give. Just come to the first meeting. Please. Don't decide until you've come."

"All right. I will see you then."

Thus, Durkhanai had her allies, save for one.

Once, she could talk to Asfandyar about anything. But now, she was hesitant. She avoided finding him, until a few hours had gone, and the meeting was fast approaching.

He said he would stay—but what did that mean? Surely he was waiting for her to elaborate.

They hadn't talked.

He had held her while she fell apart, she had killed her father for him, but they hadn't talked.

She went to find him. He was not in the library or his rooms or the gardens. He was not in the halls or the stables.

Suddenly, she had an idea of where he might be.

As she ambled through the halls, she saw light coming from a rose-scented room. Her heartbeat quickened.

As she neared, she heard the soft creak of the chains.

She entered the doorway, and there he was. Asfandyar sat on the jhula hanging from the ceiling in the center of the room, his back to her.

He did not notice her, or he pretended not to, until she went to sit beside him, and he quietly made room for her. Still, they both fit perfectly. Silently, their hands found one another. His skin was warm where hers was cold, but he did not flinch; he held on.

She let go first.

Unsure and nervous, she nibbled on her lower lip. She did not know how to speak to him anymore, which frightened her.

Once, he was her favorite person to talk to; the easiest.

Now, she didn't know where they stood.

She never would know until she asked. She was being a coward, now, she knew, and she hated to be a coward.

"We should talk," she said, breaking the silence.

"I don't know what there is to say," he replied quietly. Insecurity twisted within her. She knew it would be difficult—no, impossible—to forgive her.

But she wished for them to be friends, or allies at the very least. She wanted him in her life, and if that was all she was allotted henceforth, she would be grateful.

"Will you be one of my advisors?" Durkhanai asked, looking at him. He considered it for a moment, then nodded, accepting the offer without speaking. "Are we . . . can we be . . . allies?"

He looked at her. She wondered if she had said the wrong thing. Her hand tightened on the jhula's chains.

Already she felt she was asking for too much of him, but she could not show restraint, not when it was him.

"Actually," she said, swallowing the lump in her throat, "I wish for us to be more than that." He looked up, alarmed. Her heart knocked against her chest. "I wish for us to be . . . friends."

He blinked, and regret pooled through her. She bit the inside of her mouth, unsure once more.

Before she could retract her words, he said, "Of course." He cleared his throat, speaking louder. "Of course."

She let out a sigh, relieved. *Shukr hai.* Her head dipped, landing on his shoulder, and he adjusted, fitting against her once more. Where words were failing them, at least there was this.

They swung on the jhula a bit, and slowly, she felt she could breathe again. Things were on track. Things would be okay.

If she told herself that enough, she would believe it. She would make it true. Despite the haunting creeping through her. Despite her cursed blood. She just needed to convince herself. She just needed to keep going. She would never stop running.

But deep down, she knew some things could not be outrun.

Durkhanai left a little while later, to finish preparations for the meeting. Zarmina had requested a feast, so Durkhanai had the cooks make a special chai spread; hot potato samosay with cholay; cold egg sandwiches; dahi bhalle; almond cake; crisp jalebi.

"I am not disappointed," said Gulalai, the first to enter the war room. She immediately flocked to the table of food and began making herself a plate while a maid poured her tea. Sometime later, Saifullah entered, and shortly after, Zarmina and Rashid did, as well.

"Someone should take notes," Saifullah said, looking around.

"Do it then," Zarmina said, while Rashid crushed pappar over her dahi bhalle.

"Main pehle se hi kaidoon, I'm not going to do it," Gulalai said, holding her hands up.

Saifullah looked to Durkhanai, and she gestured her approval. He had come prepared with parchment and pen. They all settled in, taking chai and snacks, and Durkhanai wondered where Asfandyar was.

As if conjured from her thoughts, he entered. Everyone turned to look at him, simultaneously falling silent.

Durkhanai winced. She did not realize how awkward it might be. They were all well acquainted with Asfandyar, though not in particularly positive ways.

Saifullah had been the one colluding with Asfandyar, the spy within the palace feeding him information. Zarmina was technically his ex-wife, which would already be uncomfortable for Rashid. Though especially so, since Asfandyar was the reason Durkhanai had rejected Rashid's proposal for *her* . . .

At least Gulalai and Asfandyar did not have any drama, that she knew of at least. Worse still, she was almost certain everyone in this room was aware that she was painfully in love with him, except for Asfandyar, of course.

She would not let him know, either, for she needed this council of advisors to work, and for that they needed to be friends, not lovers. Asfandyar was a strong ally to have.

Marghazar needed her to be a queen, not a girl in love.

"Asfandyar, come," Rashid said, breaking the silence. "Do eat something."

He lifted the plate of sandwiches in Asfandyar's direction.

"Shukria," said Asfandyar. He took a sandwich, then went to pour himself some chai.

"I should kidnap your cooks," Gulalai said, tone light to alleviate some of the tension in the air. "This cake is too good."

Durkhanai smiled, but her gaze strayed to where Asfandyar was making himself chai. He poured the liquid into his teacup until it was half-full, then added milk until his chai had changed from a warm toffee color to a pale, wheatish brown.

They all watched him in silence, until someone broke.

"Ya mere khudaya, what are you doing?" asked Zarmina, clearly appalled.

"Drinking chai," he replied easily. Zarmina and Saifullah exchanged a quick glance.

"That is not chai," Saifullah said. "That's milk with a dash of patti."

"I don't like it too strong," Asfandyar replied. They all watched in horror as he added in four teaspoons of sugar.

*In such a tiny teacup!* She wanted to say it aloud but was hesitant to tease him.

"You are taking this too far!" Gulalai cried. "Even I am not so depraved."

"I am offended on behalf of all chai," Rashid said solemnly. "This is an affront."

Durkhanai bit back a laugh, the tension easing from her shoulders. The mood had lightened considerably.

"Come now," Asfandyar said. "Let us ask our noble and esteemed Badshah her opinion."

He turned to her, his eyes alight with that old mischief, and hope lit within her. Perhaps they truly could heal.

The others looked at her as well. She laughed, feeling a surge of sudden love and happiness to have them all here with her.

"Sorry, Asfandyar, but that is downright deplorable," she said, not afraid to poke fun at him now. "Why not just take a spoonful of sugar and wash it down with a sip of warm milk?"

While the others were vindicated, Asfandyar shook his head.

"You lot truly have no taste," he said, sipping his chai (*if* it could be called that).

Durkhanai smiled to herself. The others sat and looked at her, waiting.

"First, I'd like to say thank you all for coming," she said. "This transition hasn't been easy, but having you all by my side has made all the difference. I know I can trust you, and I am not interested in ruling Marghazar in the totalitarian fashion of my forefathers. That being said, I do hope you will advise me and, more importantly, inform me when I am behaving out of turn."

It could be seen as a humiliating thing, to rely on others to monitor her behavior, to rely on them to correct her, but she knew her pride would not be injured by any of the members here.

If she did make a mistake, she was safe to do so in their company. That was what was important.

"I also recognize that some fundamental changes are due," she continued. "For Marghazar not only to survive, but thrive, we will need to end our policy of isolationism. That means we will not be reconstructing the gates of Safed-Mahal and we will slowly open trade routes to the other zillas."

It was a massive step, one she had spent much time considering, but she was confident it was the right decision to make.

"Good idea," Gulalai said, confirming Durkhanai's thoughts. "I dare say my father is still upset about the Kebzu alliance, and this will do wonders to appease him."

"While I was not responsible for that alliance, I do bear the burden of it," said Durkhanai. "I am prepared to make amends, however necessary." She paused. "Nonetheless, it is also important to note that the walis of the other zillas did support Wakdar in his siege on Safed-Mahal." Gulalai bristled. "I do not mean it as a threat. I mean it to say that I hope both sides can leave behind previous grievances and move forward. Together."

Gulalai released a breath.

"How do you feel about unification?" Asfandyar asked.

"The other walis are still considering it," Gulalai added. "It would be a good way to move forward, as you said."

Durkhanai hesitated to answer.

She wasn't sure.

She had considered it a great allowance to open Safed-Mahal and to open more trade routes. Unification however. . . it was a much bigger step.

"It would be a good idea," Saifullah said, pulling out some papers. "I've done the research and ran the numbers. While it would take some time for Marghazar to reap the rewards, since in the beginning, they would be doing much of the investment, eventually, unification would help all zillas involved."

They all looked at her expectantly. Durkhanai released a long breath.

"It is something I will consider further," she finally said. "I cannot commit to such a monumental decision so quickly, but I will be wanting to see those numbers, Saifullah. Rashid, I will also need your help gauging what the noblemen's reaction to such an idea would be. I will not risk putting Marghazar through more inner turmoil."

So the work began. The weeks blurred together, mixed with the fatigue and satisfaction of hard work. The council met every other day, working together, and quickly, they learned the habits of one another.

Asfandyar and Gulalai wrote to their walis. Zarmina spoke to the villagers. Rashid dealt with the nobles, including his antsy father. Saifullah drafted plans for trade and resource distribution. Durkhanai oversaw the recovery from the siege.

They were all happy to work and happier still to work with one another, which came as a relief to her. She did not know what she would have done if the people she loved most did not love one another.

Saifullah, especially, had lots of new ideas. She, Zarmina, and Rashid hesitated, at first, but Asfandyar and Gulalai were wholly behind Saifullah's modern ideas. They had seen such techniques flourish in their own zillas, and Durkhanai was eventually convinced.

It went against their traditions, but perhaps that was a good thing. Not to give up their history altogether, but to be open-minded and do what was best for the future. To adjust and to grow.

"You must formally end the alliance with the Kebzu Kingdom," Zarmina said at one meeting. "Push for peace some other way." Durkhanai had stopped sending any troops north to be used by the Kebzu Kingdom, but she had not formally ended the alliance.

Zarmina continued. "The people do not blame you—" Durkhanai had gathered as much when she herself went to meet with them "—and they are happy to have you as Badshah, but they also worry. They do not wish for you to repeat the mistakes of your grandfather."

With that, Durkhanai wholeheartedly agreed.

"I will get this done," she vowed. She wrote to the Kebzu general Agha-Jaan had previously been in contact with and awaited his response.

It was no wonder the people were tired of war, and had been for some time. Durkhanai also reached out to the Lugham Empire, seeing if some sort of peace could be reached. Their reply came quickly: they would cease fighting if Marghazar became a colony in their empire.

Something Durkhanai would never let happen.

She refused.

Because she had nothing else to offer them instead, the fighting continued. She tried to figure something out but couldn't. Gulalai remarked that perhaps this was something the other zillas may help her with, should they all unify.

It forced Durkhanai to consider the matter even further. She dithered with unifying the zillas, despite the numbers Saifullah showed her, the data proving that such a political move would only strengthen Marghazar in the coming years.

Her hesitation was perhaps unfounded but still deep-rooted. She knew her grandparents would have balked at the idea and be outraged that she was even considering it. Isolation and self-sufficiency were core values of her grandfather's reign.

But she did not wish to lead as her grandparents had: She wished to be better.

After much deliberation, further reports from Saifullah, remarks from Gulalai and Asfandyar regarding the other zillas' perspectives, consultation with the noblemen and her uncles, Durkhanai finally decided that unification was for the best.

Despite how it made her squirm to do so, she knew it was the best choice. Especially when it meant the other walis were open to forgiving the past and moving forward together.

However, it was not all without quarrel.

"Shirin does not wish to unify," Asfandyar told her, finding her in the stables as she brushed Heer's coat. Durkhanai's hands stopped brushing. She opened her mouth to speak, but before she could, Asfandyar said, "Do not worry. I will convince her."

Durkhanai trusted that he would. Shirin was his wali, after all, and he would have better luck with her than Durkhanai would.

"Thank you," she said, and she resumed brushing Heer's coat. Asfandyar came to stand beside her. He stroked Heer's mane, and Heer nuzzled against him.

Durkhanai shook her head.

It was obscene how much her horses loved him, though not entirely surprising, if she was honest.

With a smile, Asfandyar began patting Heer's coat, and she risked glances at him from the corner of her eye, brushing absentmindedly until his fingers met hers.

His hand settled against hers, bringing the brush higher on Heer's coat, then sweeping down, both of their hands joined. A shiver ran down her spine.

"I missed her," he said. He turned and looked at Durkhanai, his eyes warm. Her heartbeat quickened, blood rushing in her ears. When she spoke, her voice was quiet.

"She missed you, too," she managed to reply, staring up at him. A curl fell across his brow, and she wished to brush it aside, to trace the lines of his face.

He removed his hand from hers and went to retrieve sugar cubes for Heer. Durkhanai shook her head, trying to snap herself out of it. He was just being friendly, she reminded herself.

Sometimes they had moments like these, which made her wonder if they could ever be more than allies, more than friends, but she doubted that.

He and Shirin seemed quite close. Once she saw him reading a letter, just smiling to himself. When she had bitten back her pride and asked who it was from, he replied that it was from Shirin, and he relayed the news that she had agreed to unify.

While Durkhanai was glad from a political stance, from an emotional one, she pouted to see him smiling at words written by another woman, but she vowed not to be dramatic about it.

He was her friend, and she was grateful even for that. She loved him, but she would not push.

Which left her with the question: What did she do with this love she had for him?

She prayed for him. She prayed for his happiness. It was all she wanted for him, even if it was not with her.

After all the pain she had caused him, perhaps it was for the best that she stayed away, especially if she was cursed, as she suspected.

Most days she was fine, but some nights she had such wretched dreams, as if to remind her not to forget. Her sins. Her forefathers. She was not at peace.

Sometimes she felt she would never be at peace.

It was best she was busy then, at least. Most nights she fell asleep so exhausted, she did not dream.

With advice from her council, she also decided to hold a summit where they would all discuss unification. She would host, but the walis had no reason to trust her, especially after her grandfather had been the reason behind the last summit's attack.

And thus she offered Mianathob as the meeting location. It had gone through the siege unscathed; Bari Ammi was right when she'd said the villagers would be fine. Wakdar had only cared about retrieving Durkhanai from the village, and once he had her, he did not pay any further attention to Mianathob, which Durkhanai was glad for.

Now she herself put the village at risk, but it was the only solution she could think of, and Bari Ammi supported her decision. She hoped that offering up her secret, trusted refuge would appease them.

Luckily, it did. The walis agreed to come. They would all travel there in small companies due to the cold and the snow.

Even so, it was a big risk. They could all turn on her, or anything could happen along the way.

"Saifullah, Gulalai, and Asfandyar will come with me. Rashid and Zarmina will stay behind," Durkhanai said as they were finalizing the details. "Should anything happen to me, I leave you two as my successors."

Rashid had been quietly courting Zarmina, and Durkhanai knew soon they would be engaged and married.

"Nothing will happen to you," Zarmina said, frowning. "Don't say such things."

"Insha Allah, nothing will, but just in case," Durkhanai said.

While she was not ready to die, there was a small, dark corner of her soul that courted death. It would be so much easier, so much simpler. At the very least, Naeem-sahib was happy with her decision to name his son and Zarmina successors, which was good, for he had only grown more and more fussy.

"Some advice," Naeem-sahib said, when she had an individual meeting with him. "Do not change so much so quickly. It may appear as though you are trying to outrun your lineage . . . as though you find them unsuitable."

Durkhanai's breath caught. While his words were ambivalent, she felt he understood the deep mechanisms of her mind; that she was running from her father and her grandfather's blood, that she was afraid it would not be enough.

"And do tread lightly with these new ideas of modernism," he continued. "People do not like to have their traditions uprooted, though that is not something I would expect the youth to understand."

Durkhanai narrowed her eyes. "The youth understand perfectly," she said, voice clipped. "People may think that because I am young and aggrieved from the loss of my family members that I may be easy to control. But *people* would be wrong. I am the Badshah, and what I say, goes. People will adjust to modernity well enough."

Naeem-sahib bowed his head when she dismissed him, but he was clearly irritated.

And he was not the only one. Some of the nobles were unhappy with the idea of unification. They were outnumbered, of course, but still she held personal meetings with each of them, accompanied by Saifullah, who went over the numbers and projected advantages to Marghazar.

For the elder ones who were still not convinced, Durkhanai spoke to their children and successors, those who were younger and more open to the new ideas.

It was a new age. They all had to adapt.

# CHAPTER TWENTY-SIX

*D*urkhanai and her party arrived at Mianathob first, to prepare. The snow and unforgiving cold made the trip difficult. The winter in the mountains was always long and brutal, especially this time of the year.

A constant layer of snow covered the landscape, giving no sign of melting soon. Icicles dripped from bare tree branches, sharp as daggers, glittering in the sun. The lake in the village was frozen over, a pale, still gray. Bari Ammi came out to greet them, along with the other women.

"How are you, janaan?" Bari Ammi asked, holding Durkhanai close.

Durkhanai sighed in the older woman's arms, warmth spreading through her. They had not seen each other since before the siege, and how different things were now.

Though they had been in touch via letter, it was not the same as this: looking into Bari Ammi's eyes, feeling her hands in hers.

"Determined," replied Durkhanai. Bari Ammi smiled, brushing a lock of hair behind Durkhanai's ears. She then turned to see Durkhanai's travel companions, hugging Saifullah.

"And who is this?" Bari Ammi said, looking to Gulalai, who smiled in return.

"The life of the party," replied Gulalai, coming to hug Bari Ammi as well. Durkhanai smiled.

That left Asfandyar.

He made to introduce himself, but Bari Ammi waved a hand.

"You, I know," she said, narrowing her eyes. Asfandyar bowed his head, holding a hand to his heart in respect.

"Just as I know you," he replied. Bari Ammi raised a brow. Her gaze was sharp as she scrutinized him. Asfandyar did not waver, standing tall.

Finally, Bari Ammi lifted a hand. Asfandyar lowered his head, where she placed her hand in the gesture of greeting and fondness. He smiled at her.

"Girls, come show our guests their rooms!" Bari Ammi called. A few aunties of the village appeared, whisking Durkhanai's companions away to settle in. Durkhanai would stay with Bari Ammi, as she always did.

"It's no wonder you are pagal over him," Bari Ammi said, looking at Asfandyar's retreating form. "He is quite handsome. And those dimples? Na pucho." Durkhanai's cheeks heated.

"Tch, Bari Ammi," she tsked, trying not to laugh. She did love his dimples.

"Acha, chalo, there is much work to be done," Bari Ammi said. "I did all you asked, but even so."

Durkhanai busied herself with preparing the village for their guests, who would arrive in two days. From the palace, she had brought with her livestock and food for feast, as well as servants to help. She had also brought a small company of guards, for protection, but if anything truly did happen, the guards would not be enough to save her. She did not bring too many, for she did not wish for the other walis to feel threatened, or feel like she did not trust them.

For this to work, they needed mutual trust.

Still, as preparations went underway, as food was cooked and huts were prepared for their guests, Durkhanai grew more and more afraid. She alternated between fearing that they would not come and fearing that if they did, they would turn on her.

What if that was what she deserved? To pay for the sins of her grandfather and father?

Agha-Jaan was responsible for the last summit attack, Wakdar involved these walis' troops into fighting his war.

Well. If it was what she deserved, then she would accept her punishment.

The day of the others' arrival came upon them, and Durkhanai waited. She sat at the edge of the village, staring out into the silence.

Everything was beautiful and white, the trees heavy with snow, the sky a cloudless gray. Despite the freezing temperatures, she was warm beneath her shahtoosh shawl.

She willed herself to feel something, looking out to the beauty of her lands. But she felt nothing. There was an echo of that old wonder, but she could not grasp it.

"They should be arriving soon," a voice said, coming to join her. She turned to find Asfandyar, and there was that echo once more, this time louder.

She turned as he sat beside her. His body immediately warmed her side. She resisted the urge to lean into him, instead smiling up at him. In the past two months, he had been a constant ally and friend. The initial awkwardness and strangeness had faded, which was a relief to her. They were relearning one another. And though she was over-whelmed still, things were heading in the right direction, on all fronts.

"How are you feeling?" he asked. "Nervous?"

She tapped her fingers against her lips. "Hmm. Yes, and no," she replied. "If this summit goes well, things will only grow better and better."

It was enough to placate her, help her feel nearly content. Though she still had doubts.

"You've been a good badshah," he said. His voice lowered. "Your people are lucky to have you."

"Are they?" she wondered aloud, looking away.

"Hey." He tapped his finger to her jaw, turning her to face him again. His dark eyes were warm, the scorching sun amidst the empty sky. "They are," he said, voice fierce enough that she nearly believed him.

He sensed her hesitation, and his brows furrowed together. He still held his forefinger to her cheek, thumb resting against her chin. If she opened her mouth, his thumb would be on her lip. Her stomach twisted.

"What is it?" he asked, voice gentle. His fingers skimmed against her neck, and she shivered.

Should she tell him she suspected she was cursed? Fated to relive the mistakes of her forefathers? Destined to be just as damaged as they were? She had not spoken of it with anyone, but with him, the words bubbled up.

She opened her mouth to speak—

But was cut off by the sound of an arrival.

A horse-drawn carriage entered their line of sight, followed by guards on horseback. They stopped in the clearing before the village. Guards opened the door to the carriage, and out stepped a beautiful young woman. She was a year or two older than Durkhanai and of average height with a thin and delicate frame. Her thick black hair shone like silk, pin-straight and elegantly twisted. She had dark brown skin and arresting black eyes which scanned her surroundings.

Durkhanai prepared to say salam when the girl's face broke into a grin.

"Asfandyar!" she cried. Durkhanai turned and saw that he was grinning. He went to greet her, gathering her in his arms, and they immediately began talking, laughing, and speaking over one another.

Durkhanai's heart sank. She knew right away who it must be; Shirin, the Wali of Jardum.

Taking a deep breath, Durkhanai went forward to greet her.

"Assalam u alaikum," she said, smiling as cordially as she could muster. The warmth instantly vanished from Shirin's face. Her eyes narrowed as she regarded Durkhanai.

"Walaikum assalam," she replied curtly.

Durkhanai blinked. She was the Badshah, not a jealous girl.

"What is wrong?" Durkhanai kept her voice level. Anxiety rose within her, though she kept a straight face. Unification would be difficult to achieve without Jardum. And if she did not wish to unify, why come at all? To stir trouble?

"You sent him to the lion," Shirin replied, straight to the point. Durkhanai's heart ricocheted. "Do not expect kindness from me."

"Tch, Shirin," Asfandyar said, tone a little abashed, and it was clear he had been the one to tell her. She cut him off with a glare.

"Don't take that tone with me," Shirin said, voice fierce and protective. Durkhanai bristled. She opened her mouth to speak, but Shirin turned her glare to Durkhanai next. "Don't worry. Personal censure aside, as the Wali of Jardum, I am looking forward to discussing the ways our zillas can benefit one another. Now, Asfandyar, do show me where I'll be staying."

Before Durkhanai could say anything more, Shirin strode off without so much as another glance. Asfandyar threw Durkhanai an apologetic look, then followed after Shirin.

"Okay?" Durkhanai muttered to herself, watching them go. Gulalai came and stood beside her, looking to where Durkhanai's gaze was.

"Ugh, *her*," she said under her breath. Before Durkhanai could ask for elaboration, another carriage arrived, followed quickly by one more. Durkhanai went to receive the first, while Gulalai went to the second.

From the first carriage came an older woman, Humnah-sahiba, from B'rung, the khala of Palwasha-sahiba. Durkhanai welcomed her, then went to welcome Tanveer-sahib, a middle-aged man from Teer-za, a cousin of Rukhsana-sahiba and the previous wali.

They, at least, seemed happier to be here than Shirin.

"Thank you all for coming," she said. "I hope we can all forge a path forward, together."

The walis nodded, smiling. They seemed open-minded, not hostile, which was a good sign.

Durkhanai had people help them settle in. Her hands shook from nerves, but she clasped them together tightly, refusing to show weakness.

After the walis had been sent to their huts, Durkhanai found Gulalai again.

"What is it?" she asked.

Gulalai huffed. "My father," she replied, rolling her eyes.

"What happened?" Durkhanai asked, alarmed. They could not be splintering so soon. Gulalai made an irritated sound.

"I am not speaking to the Badshah right now, but my friend!"

Durkhanai's heart calmed. "I see," she said. "What is he saying to have you in such a fit?"

"Nothing I haven't heard my entire life!" Gulalai said. "Oh, Shirin is so clever! Look how she arrived here, first. So punctual! So responsible! Why can't you be more like Shirin, she is so accomplished and capable and demure and bak, bak, bak, aisi bakwas."

"Ah."

Gulalai groaned. "I am tired of it! Since we were children, I've always been compared to her, and she has always been so infuriatingly perfect."

Durkhanai nearly giggled, seeing Gulalai so flustered, but then she saw Asfandyar and Shirin stepping out of her hut together, and Durkhanai did not feel so amused.

Doubt crept inside of her, just like the first time she had met Asfandyar and called him Shirin's whore. She wondered if it was true.

"If she wasn't our ally, I would surely fill her bed with cockroaches," Durkhanai said.

Gulalai laughed. "You are a dear friend." She squeezed Durkhanai's hand. "Now I must go check on how Baba is settling in or I will have to hear about what a neglectful daughter I am."

Gulalai rolled her eyes, then was off. Durkhanai's gaze strayed to where Shirin and Asfandyar stood talking outside of Shirin's hut.

Durkhanai couldn't tear her gaze away from them. She watched how he laughed and his face lit up.

Perhaps all this time, he was merely being cordial with her. She did have the sense that they were treading gently around one another, as if both were afraid to pick open a fresh wound.

Or so she had hoped, but she saw now how he was with Shirin and jealousy itched within her. He hadn't laughed like that with her in so long she wondered if he ever had at all.

More than the jealousy, she felt a deep ache.

She missed him. He was right in front of her and still she missed him.

"Durkhanai," Saifullah said, grabbing her attention. "Shall we proceed with lunch after the guests have freshened up?"

Durkhanai took a deep breath to clear her head. She went to check on the preparations for lunch, looking at the big feast that was set out in the largest hut, which had been cleared out to be used as their meeting and eating place. A great wooden table was set with dishes of grilled fish, mutton pulao, chicken karahi, and mixed sabzi, accompanied with fresh rotis.

Soon after, the others entered, all chatting amongst themselves and their advisors. They were not strangers to one another, as they were to her. Immediately, Durkhanai's gaze strayed to Shirin, and she was not the only one.

Everyone seemed to be revolving around her, laughing at her commentary, trying to earn a smile. And it was no wonder: She was clearly a capable leader, not to mention beautiful and clever and well respected.

For the first time in her life, Durkhanai had a rival, and she did not like it one bit.

Understanding that she needed bolstering, Saifullah squeezed Durkhanai's shoulder. She covered his hand with her own, swallowing the lump in her throat.

Durkhanai would not be silly about it. She was a queen now.

As if sensing Durkhanai's gaze, Shirin turned and met her eyes. Durkhanai did not look away; rather, she mustered her most winning smile.

It had no effect. While Shirin did not glare, it was not exactly an amiable glance that she spared Durkhanai.

It looked like Shirin would not forgive her for sending Asfandyar to the lion, and rightfully so. Durkhanai did not know if she would ever forgive herself for that, either, or her many other sins.

But there was no time to think of that now. These meetings would determine the fate of her people. She would not be distracted.

As everyone finished eating, they turned to look at her. She was the host, after all.

Clearing her throat, Durkhanai tapped a spoon against her glass, and the room quieted.

Durkhanai stood, and the negotiations began.

# CHAPTER TWENTY-SEVEN

The meetings lasted a week.

All the walis agreed to unify—that was the easy part. The difficult part was figuring out what that meant exactly. And the first part of that was something Durkhanai had not considered prior to arriving.

"If we are to join together as one nation," Shirin said, "we must all be equals: a Committee of Walis."

The attendees of the meeting all turned to her. While Durkhanai was currently the Wali of S'vat, she was also the Badshah of Marghazar. The only one.

"I understand," Durkhanai told them. "If this is to work, we must stand on common ground." She had to believe that and show it, too. She took a deep breath, feeling frayed at what she was about to do, but sure nonetheless. "Thus, I will abolish the role of badshah. Henceforth, I will merely be the Wali of Marghazar, rather than the Wali of S'vat and Badshah of Marghazar."

The other walis accepted this.

"There should not be so much concentrated power," Durkhanai said, almost as an afterthought, and she was glad for the burden of some of the power to be lifted. It would give her less space to fall into her grandfather's and her father's greed.

While a part of her cried out at such a massive change, she knew it was better this way. She was not a totalitarian leader, but the *wali*, the protector, the friend.

"We should also decide on a capital in a central location," the Wali of Kurra suggested. "We can meet there every third month for a meeting to discuss stately affairs."

Those were some of the big, simpler decisions to be made. The rest were headed by Saifullah, who went through the details of trade, resource distribution, defense, agriculture, transportation, and justice. He was not the only advisor present.

Durkhanai had brought along two other advisors from the palace, and each wali had also brought along two to three advisors. They discussed various strategies and specifics, then turned to the walis for confirmation and agreement. While Marghazar had many advantages, particularly in resources, Saifullah assured Durkhanai that unification would be an investment. The week passed in endless meetings and discussions, and every night, Durkhanai even dreamt of figures and road plans and defense formations.

Through the week, Durkhanai also learned about the other walis, and while they were a bit hesitant around her in the beginning, eventually they warmed up to her. At the very least, they all understood that they needed mutual respect and open minds for this Committee of Walis to work. Mutual respect was easy enough with all except one.

No matter what Durkhanai did, Shirin did not warm up to her. To make matters worse, Asfandyar was constantly with her, and Durkhanai wanted to be above the petty emotion of jealousy, but she simply was not.

"Relax," Saifullah told her at one point, when he saw her pouting over it. When she did not relent, he gave her a stern look, and she sighed, nodding. He was right, of course.

At least, she was not the only one who was not getting along with Shirin. Whenever Gulalai and Shirin were in close quarters, Shirin said something to get a rise out of Gulalai, which was fascinating to behold, since Gulalai was normally so good-natured.

But then one night, late when everyone was asleep, Durkhanai saw the two girls sitting by the fire, under the stars, laughing together. How strange.

The next day, Shirin was back to being her haughty, insufferable self, however, so perhaps Durkhanai had imagined it.

It was Asfandyar's idea to let the Lugham Empire use the Jardum Pass, which would give the Lugham Empire access to fight their enemies in the west. In return, they would cease warring with Marghazar and the other zillas.

Shirin had narrowed her eyes at this idea, refusing outright at first, though it would benefit them all. Durkhanai suspected Asfandyar said something to convince her, for the next day, she agreed.

If the Lugham Empire agreed to the terms, it would ease all their borders in the east, but it would help Marghazar most of all. While the other zillas had managed to keep the Lugham Empire at bay on their eastern and southern borders, Marghazar had been facing the brunt of their attacks as they pushed to take the richer, northern land.

Durkhanai drafted the alliance with the Lugham Empire. She was sure they were just as tired of war as they all were. If this treaty worked, Marghazar would be able to cut their military budget and spend those resources elsewhere, which would only help the other zillas.

It would also mean less people dying in the war, which would certainly make the villagers happy and raise public opinion of her.

While her grandfather would hate to see her "admitting defeat" to the Lugham Empire in such a way, she knew it was the best course of action. She would not keep fighting them purely out of pride. Thus, by the end of the week, a great deal of matters had been attended to. It did grow quite boring and tedious at times, and every night she fell asleep exhausted, but still, it was a productive set of meetings, and the week went by without any major hiccups.

Her previous anxiety faded, and before she knew it, they were wrapping things up and sending people off.

Durkhanai was the last to leave, of course, with Saifullah, Gulalai, Asfandyar, and Shirin, who lingered behind for some reason. Gulalai was returning to Kurra soon, but wished to stay with Durkhanai for as long as she could and promised to visit soon.

"I take my job very seriously," Gulalai reassured her.

"I'm glad," Durkhanai said. "I'd hate to lose my dearest friend."

"Well, I was promised a position as advisor to the Badshah, but I suppose advisor to the Wali will suffice just as well," Gulalai joked.

They all left Mianathob and traveled east together. Durkhanai was with Gulalai in the carriage, while Saifullah rode on horseback, giving the girls some alone time together before Gulalai returned home.

Durkhanai did not know what Asfandyar's plans were. She was too afraid to ask. He had been spending every free moment he had with Shirin. Even now, he traveled with her. The two were in a separate carriage.

They would travel together until the road forked north and south—north to Marghazar, south to Jardum—at which point, Gulalai would go with Shirin and get dropped off in Kurra on the way.

"Time for goodbyes," Gulalai said, when they arrived. Her eyes shone with tears. They stepped off the carriage into the cold day, and in the adjoining carriage, Asfandyar offered Shirin his hand after he dismounted.

"Don't cry," said Durkhanai, tears welling up in her eyes, as well. "We'll see each other soon, I promise."

"I'm not crying because I'll miss you," Gulalai said, wiping her eyes. "I'm crying because I'll have to travel with that insufferable woman." They both laughed. "And we will see each other soon, though this time, it is your turn to visit me."

"I will."

It was time to go. Durkhanai watched Gulalai walk away, and her gaze strayed to where Shirin and Asfandyar were talking in hushed tones. She could not hear what they were saying, but Shirin looked upset.

As if sensing she was being watched, she glared at Durkhanai, her face red. Asfandyar placed his hands on her shoulders, placating, then pulled Shirin into his arms.

The sight speared her, and she felt a childish anger rise within her.

She wished to push Shirin away, to claim Asfandyar as hers—but she would not be so petulant. Not after all she had done to him.

So she stood in silence, waiting.

It struck Durkhanai suddenly that she might be traveling home alone. Just as Gulalai was returning to her home, Asfandyar might, too. He had no more cause to go to Marghazar.

Of course he would return to Jardum with Shirin.

Panic edged all of her senses. She felt that once he left, he would never return. The thought cleaved her.

"Aaj jaane ki zid na karo," she whispered. "Don't go."

He turned, though there was no way he would have heard her. Their eyes met. She took a step toward him, opening her mouth to speak, to be heard.

The words were drowned out by the sound of an explosion.

# CHAPTER TWENTY-EIGHT

The world shook.

Durkhanai reached for Asfandyar just as he reached for her. A slew of arrows rained down, flying free from higher ground. The horses cried out, rearing, and Durkhanai desperately searched for where the attack was coming from.

"Get down!" she yelled.

Everyone was thrown off-kilter, stumbling. Durkhanai fell to the ground, crawling toward the carriage for shelter.

Everything spun with chaos. There was another explosion, this time closer. Gulalai fell on her bad leg, shrieking with pain.

"Gul!" Shirin cried out.

Asfandyar ran toward them, going to cover them or bring them to safety, Durkhanai wasn't sure, but it didn't matter. She watched in horror as arrows hurtled straight toward his back.

"Asfi!" she cried, heart in her throat. She leapt up and pushed him out of the way. He fell over, rolling in the snow. Eyes wild, he stared up at her. Then just as quickly as the attack began, it stopped. There were pieces of paper tied to each arrow. In the distance, she saw Saifullah pick one up and read the message aloud.

"It is a declaration of war from the Kebzu Kingdom," he said, jaw tight. "This was just a sampling."

Durkhanai reached for one to read it herself, then felt sudden pain burst through her body. She gasped. She thought she heard someone call her name, but she couldn't hear properly.

There was a roaring in her ears. She felt dizzy and hot all over, despite the freezing temperature. Something hot and sticky warmed her stomach.

She touched her skin and saw blood drip from her shaking hands onto the snow below. The world tilted.

Asfandyar got up just as she looked down to see an arrow protruding from her waist.

"Asfi?" she said, looking up. "Asfi, I—"

He was the last thing she saw before the darkness took her.

# CHAPTER TWENTY-NINE
## Asfandyar's Tale

Durkhanai made a soft sound. Her eyes closed, and she crumpled. He was already going to her by the time she fell, and he caught her in his arms. They dropped to the floor together, and he eased her onto his lap.

Her blood spilled across his skin, hot and wet.

There was so much blood.

"Durkhanai," he choked. An arrow protruded from her skin, and he felt as though he had been impaled. "Durre," he whispered, feeling like a fool as he held her. He forgave her the day she killed Wakdar for him, and he never told her.

Why didn't he tell her? Now she lay bleeding in his arms.

He pressed his hand into the wound, blood wetting his palm, and his stomach twisted.

For the past week, he had been watching her grow jealous over Shirin, and he had been provoking her on purpose, amused by her adorable pout and scrunched expressions.

He had thought they had all the time in the world; he never considered that they might not.

"Durkhanai, hold on," he said, voice breaking. He couldn't lose her. He loved her. "Promise me," he cried, tears falling. "Just hold on."

Her eyes fluttered, and she groaned. He had to act quick. Asfandyar had spent enough time on the battlefields to know what to do.

He checked the arrow's position. It had entered from her back and protruded out her stomach now, but from an angle that told him it hadn't likely hit any organs.

Asfandyar cringed thinking of what he had to do. He looked around. From where she was at Gulalai's side, Shirin's gaze met his.

"Go," Gulalai said, pushing Shirin away. "I'm fine, go!"

Shirin arrived next to Asfandyar.

"What do you need?" she asked, voice steel.

"Clean cloth and clean snow," he said. "And honey."

Shirin brought him what he needed, and he took a deep breath, steadying himself.

"Stay with me," he said, looking at Durkhanai's face as he broke the arrow from the back. She was so pale. "Stay with me, please."

Her eyes fluttered. "Am I dying?" she asked.

The words twisted within him, painful as a knife.

"Aisi baatein kiya na karo," he pleaded. "Don't say such things."

He pulled the arrow out. Durkhanai's eyes shot open. She screamed, and the sound scraped against his soul, claws raking into his heart.

Then she went limp. Shirin cleaned the wound from the back while he cleaned the front, applying honey to disinfect it. A guard brought him a stitching kit, and he quickly made the stitches.

"Stay with me," he whispered, again and again. "Never leave me," he implored, as he held her against his chest. "Khuda ke liye, open your eyes," he begged, stitching the back of the wound. "Open your eyes, or I will never forgive myself."

He cleaned and wrapped the wound. There was nothing else to do. He had done all he could, but still, he doubted.

What if the arrow had hit an organ and she was bleeding out on the inside?

What if the wound got infected?

What if everything was fine and she still did not make it?

She was light as a feather in his arms, and he prayed she did not fly away. He prayed, saying her name over and over, saying, "Wake up, Durkhanai, please wake up."

# CHAPTER THIRTY

*T*he pain was a constant beat.

It did not increase, nor did it decrease.

It crashed and pulled over her like the current of the river, threatening to take her under.

From a distance, she heard her grandparents.

"Durkhanai, where are you?" Dhadi called.

"Durkhanai, come home!" Agha-Jaan said.

She saw them along the riverbed; she was fast approaching them.

"Dhadi!" she cried. "Agha-Jaan!"

She reached for them, but another voice filled her ears.

"Wake up," he said, voice hoarse, as though he had been crying. "Wake up, Durkhanai, please wake up."

Durkhanai looked to her grandparents. They grabbed her hands and squeezed, smiling. She wondered what it was they were smiling about but did not get a chance to ask.

They pushed her back into the river, and the current took her.

Her eyes fluttered open, just for a moment, and she saw him. Fragmented, covered by candlelight, but alive and before her.

She knew then that it was his voice, calling to her; his hands, reaching for her.

"Asfi," she whispered, her voice raspy.

"Beloved, I'm here," he replied, holding her. "Tell me where it hurts."

"Everywhere," she whispered. Her eyes closed once more.

She took a shuddering breath, trying to stay awake, desperately trying. She did not know if she could manage it. She wished to. She wished it with all her heart.

"I—" she began.

"No, do not speak," he said, hushing her. "You must save your energy."

But she had to say it. Sleep called to her, and she did not know when she would wake again, if she would. If she did not say it now, she may never get the chance.

"I want a different ending," she whispered. "I want you."

He murmured something in response, but she could not understand what the words were, though she was comforted just by his speaking.

In the darkness, there was nothing but the pain and his voice, like a golden cord, anchoring her.

She clung to it, clung to him.

"Keep talking," she whispered, so he did. She focused on it as he dribbled water into her dry mouth, then some small pieces of roti, then some soft nuts. She slept, but even in that dreamless land, she heard his voice, felt his hand in hers.

Slowly, her energy was restored. Though she wished to continue sleeping, she opened her eyes.

Night had fallen. They had set up camp, and her companions huddled around her, while the guards stood watch outside. She seemed to be in the worst condition, which came as a relief to her.

While Shirin, Asfandyar, and Saifullah were scratched and muddy, they were not severely damaged. The only other injured was Gulalai, whose leg was wrapped and elevated.

"You look terrible," Gulalai said, catching Durkhanai's gaze.

"Attempting to compete with you, dearest," Durkhanai replied. They both managed weak smiles.

Shirin was watching Durkhanai closely, and when Durkhanai caught her gaze, Shirin lowered her head in respect, in the first kind gesture she had offered to Durkhanai. At least there was that.

"The people who attacked are either dead or have retreated," Saifullah told her. "It was a small company, meant to serve as a warning."

While the fight was over for now, it would only get worse. The Kebzu Kingdom was declaring war once more. Clearly, they weren't happy with Durkhanai formally calling off the alliance they had made with Agha-Jaan. Now they would attack with full force in the north.

"We need to get back," said Durkhanai, trying to sit up. But as she did, pain splintered through her side. She winced, hands clutching her blanket. Saifullah and Asfandyar both came forward immediately.

"Sambhal jao, easy," Saifullah told her, easing her down. Asfandyar stayed back, his jaw tensed. "You're in no state to travel."

"But the war," she said. "We need to prepare."

"Fikr na karo." Saifullah put a hand on her shoulder. "I'll leave on horseback tonight and handle things. It'll be quicker. You travel with the carriage and come slowly. I already sent one of the guards ahead to warn Zarmina and Rashid. I only stayed back to speak with you before leaving."

"Shukria, Saifullah," Durkhanai said, placing her hand atop his. "Thank you."

While she did not like to be left behind, she also knew there was no way she could travel by horseback in this state. He would have to go in her stead.

She trusted him, and she trusted Zarmina and Rashid.

"I will travel with you," Asfandyar said, looking at Durkhanai. She blinked, not responding, but Saifullah nodded in acknowledgment.

"Good," he said. "Thank you. I will be off."

"Allah de havale," Durkhanai told Saifullah. "Travel safe."

Saifullah left the tent, leaving Durkhanai's side, and Asfandyar came to sit with her. She was puzzled over his last words.

She had thought he would be leaving with Shirin. Durkhanai turned to look at Shirin's reaction to this, but saw that she was at Gulalai's side, on the other side of the spacious tent, the pair too entranced in one another to notice Durkhanai or Asfandyar.

Gulalai was being fussy about consuming her dhoodh haldi, turning her cheek this way and that. Tsking, Shirin clutched Gulalai's chin and forced the turmeric milk into her mouth.

Durkhanai felt the strange urge to laugh at the sight, but she was too tired. Her eyes fluttered as she tried to keep awake. She turned back to Asfandyar and found him watching her, his gaze tense.

"You should rest," said Asfandyar. A muscle ticked in his jaw. He went to stand, and without thinking, Durkhanai took his hand in hers. He stopped, standing entirely still.

Slowly, he turned to look at her fingers in his.

"Your cheek," she said, swallowing hard. There was dried blood across his cheekbone.

Durkhanai sat up. She had enough strength to reach for the cloth on the floor beside her, the small bowl of clean water there.

He sat beside her legs, watching as she dipped the cloth into the water, wringing it. But already she was growing tired, and as she lifted her hand to his cheek, her arm quivered. Before her arm could drop, Asfandyar took hold of her hand, his thumb pressed into her palm.

Her skin was pliant beneath his as he lifted it to his cheek. Where her hand was cold, his was warm, and heat seeped into her skin.

She shivered, but he did not let go.

He lifted their joined hands to his cheek, using her hand to wipe with the cloth. The dried blood rubbed away, but she could not tear her focus from the feel of his fingers curled around her wrist, the scalded imprint they must have been leaving on her skin.

She felt feverish and hot all over.

"All clean," she squeaked. She loosened her grip on the cloth, and it dropped, but he did not release her hand. Instead, he held it, hovering in the air above his cheek. She spread her fingers, touching his cheekbone.

He tilted his head and rested against her hand.

His eyes were molten. She thought she would burn just from the way he looked at her.

"How do I look?' he asked, voice soft.

Without thinking, she said, "Beautiful."

Pain flashed across his face. Immediately, his eyes welled with tears. Durkhanai dropped her hand, a tight feeling spreading through her chest.

"What is it?" she asked. "What have I done?"

"I am still angry with you," he said, and he could not look at her when he said it.

Now, tears welled in Durkhanai's eyes. She should have known . . .

"No," he said, seeing the despair writ across her countenance. "Not— " He shook his head, sighing. "I am angry you threw yourself in harm's way. That arrow was meant to be mine."

The tension eased from her body. If that was all he was angry about, she would not repent.

"I won't be sorry for that," she said. "But I am sorry for . . ."

She trailed off.

"What?" he asked. "You are sorry for what?"

"That you must stay," she said. "You must have been looking forward to going back to Jardum." She paused. "With Shirin."

Asfandyar shook his head, looking away a moment, and when he turned back, she thought she saw a glimmer of mischief in his eyes, but it was gone so quick she might have imagined it.

"Yes, I rather was looking forward to it," he sighed. "But now I must stay. With you."

She frowned.

"You don't have to," she said sullenly, trying not to go so far as to pout. "The guards can tend to me and take me back."

"No, I would not trust them."

"What do you mean? It is their job, after all. Surely they can take care of me."

"Therein lies the problem," he said. "I do not trust anyone to take care of you. Save for myself."

She blinked, confused. Durkhanai risked a glance at Shirin, then back at him, thinking of the way they had hugged just before the attack.

"Won't that be . . . tiresome?" she asked. "Taking care of both me and . . . Shirin?"

He shook his head. "She can take care of herself."

Durkhanai furrowed her brows, still confused. She did not understand.

Her brain already refused to work when she was around him, and it was worse still from the injury and the pain. Before she could interrogate him further, his face grew serious, all mischief gone.

"Tum hi hakdar ho meri," he said. "You are the only one who has rights over me."

Durkhanai's mouth opened. She blinked, taking the words in.

Was she hallucinating? She dug her nails into her palm and startled from the pinch. No, she was not hallucinating.

"What do you mean?" she asked. "What does that mean?"

"I love you, that is what it means," he said. "Main tera—I am yours. Do you understand now?"

Durkhanai was stunned.

"But I thought—" she broke off, flustered. "I didn't know!" She was wide awake now. "I thought I was asking too much even when I said I wanted to be friends." She caught her breath. "Have you truly forgiven me?"

"Yes, I have, I'd forgive you anything, *anything*, Durre," he said, voice velvet. She gasped, hearing him say that name. "I never could stay away, even when I hated you. I've loved you all this time; I never stopped."

Now it was his turn to be flustered.

"I forgave you, but I didn't want to push because I knew how much you were dealing with and how stressed and overwhelmed you were.

"When you said you wished to be friends, I was glad because I was afraid you would never wish to see me again after what happened with Wakdar. I thought you would blame me for his death and the war and everything else, and ya khuda, you've just been through a traumatic injury, and here I am, making a mess of things again, I'm such an idiot—"

"No," she said, shaking her head. "I'd forgive you anything, *anything*, Asfi. Because I love you, too. I am yours. I have always been yours. And I always will be." She realized there were tears in her eyes. "I would have been content to love you from afar for the whole of my life if you didn't feel the same."

He drew near, and the heat of his gaze warmed her to her toes.

"Even now, we are too far apart," he said, and the low timbre of his voice sent a shiver running down her spine.

Durkhanai blushed, suddenly feeling shy. She pulled the blanket up to cover her nose, and his eyes glittered with amusement. A half smile curved his lips.

"I never knew you to be shy," he said.

She bit back a smile, having found a new layer of herself. She rather liked it.

"I really thought you and Shirin . . ." she said, changing the subject.

"Pagli," he said, shaking his head. "Shirin used to be Naina's best friend, which is why she and I have always been close. She is protective over me as a sister would be, which is why before the attack, she was angry when I told her I would be going back to Marghazar with you rather than returning home with her."

Now Durkhanai felt silly. She pulled the blanket higher, covering the rest of her face, and then he did laugh. And no wonder Shirin had hated her from the onset; Durkhanai's grandmother had killed Naina.

"Besides, I suspect Shirin has feelings for someone else," he said. She uncovered her face immediately.

"Who?" Durkhanai asked, surprised by this new information.

"I'm surprised you haven't noticed. You are usually so perceptive."

Durkhanai thought hard, and without the fog of jealousy, it really was so clear. She recalled Shirin's face when Gulalai was struck, her rasped voice crying, "Gul!"

She would have to ask Gulalai about that, but she and Shirin were busy themselves right now.

"Oooh," Durkhanai said, giggling again. "Dried apricots indeed."

Seeing her laugh, Asfandyar laughed as well. He was so very close. She wished to bridge the space between them and kiss him, long and sweet.

He must have had a similar thought, for his gaze strayed to her lips, eyes half-lidded. She closed her eyes with a sigh.

He ran his thumb across her lower lip. "Get some rest," he said, then leaned forward to kiss her forehead instead. This time she did pout, which earned her a wondrous smile.

"Not so shy anymore," he said, then turned to look where Gulalai and Shirin were. *Oh, right.*

When Asfandyar made to leave, Shirin stood as well, her hand lingering in Gulalai's. Before Shirin left, she lowered her head in respect at Durkhanai.

"I hope you recover quickly," she said, the first pleasant exchange they had. At least being shot at had lifted Shirin's opinion of Durkhanai.

"Thank you," Durkhanai replied, then the two were gone.

The tent was quiet. Gulalai and Durkhanai looked over to one another at the same time. They both giggled.

"You two looked *quite* snug," Durkhanai teased. Gulalai smoothed her hair.

"I am sure I do not know what you mean," she said casually. Then her gaze sharpened on Durkhanai. "Though I will say *you* and darling Asfandyar looked quite *cozy.*"

Durkhanai grinned, inhaling deeply. "I won't even pretend," she said. "I was quite cozy."

Gulalai laughed, and so did Durkhanai, her heart so full she could not catch her breath.

There was no need to pretend, and that was the most liberating thing. She could scream it from the rooftops.

She loved him! What a wonderful, terrible thing. It was a thorny rose, delicate and deadly.

She held a hand to her heart, felt it beating against her palm, so quick and desperate. To be in love felt just like the edge of death and the return to life.

She could say that now, for she had been there.

# CHAPTER THIRTY-ONE

When Durkhanai awoke the next morning, her entire body hurt. Groaning, she shifted in the blankets, then lifted up her kameez to inspect the wound. It had been cleaned and redressed, but she had no recollection of it.

The past day came back to her in a haze: the attack, the darkness, then Asfandyar's arms.

With a gasp she remembered what he had told her, that he forgave her, that he loved her.

Had that been real?

It felt too good to be true, and it would not have been the first time she had imagined a perfect reality.

Durkhanai looked around the tent, hoping to ask Gulalai what had transpired, but she was alone.

"Gulalai!" Durkhanai called, but her voice was rasped. She cleared her throat. "Gulalai!"

The mouth of the tent opened. Asfandyar entered.

"You're awake," he said, face soft. He sat down beside her, holding a plate of bread, dried fruit, and achar. When she reached to take it from him, her side stretched, and she winced, falling back.

"Let me," he said, and the timbre of his voice sent a chill down her spine. She nodded, and he came closer. He broke the bread into little pieces and fed her, then he tipped the canister of water into her mouth and she drank, feeling energized.

Then, he lifted the canister to his mouth and turned it to where the imprint of her lips lay, still warm on the steel, and drank, his eyes never leaving hers.

She watched the curve of his throat as he swallowed, and as he set the canister down, a bead of water dribbled down onto his collar.

On her uninjured side, she lifted her arm across and reached to wipe it away. His skin was warm under the collar of his kameez, and her hand lingered there, long enough to feel a little ridge under her finger. It was an old scar.

"Where did you get this?" she asked, frowning. "In the war?"

There was still so much to discover about one another. He smiled.

"Scaling a fence back home," he said, his voice soft. "I'll take you, one day."

"I would like that," she said. "Does that mean you . . . did you mean what you said yesterday?" It felt like a dream. "About me being your hakdar?"

He kissed her palm. "Every word."

Smiling, she held her hand against his face, her heart swollen with love.

She had always thought they were star-crossed, seeped in bad luck, but she realized she was the luckiest of all, for fate had brought them together, and it has brought them together again.

What a rare thing, to love and be loved in return!

She caught the pulse of fate quickening beneath her fingertips, and she would not let it go this time.

She had thought Marghazar needed her to be a queen, not a girl in love, but she could be both.

Was it selfish of her? Perhaps *she* was still ill-fated, and she would only bring him down. How could she rid herself of this cursed blood? Exorcize it from her body?

Her thoughts spiraled, but before they could take her into the abyss with them, Durkhanai pulled Asfandyar's mouth to hers.

He kissed her hard, stealing her breath, devouring her until her lips were throbbing and her mouth was aching, but still, she couldn't get enough. All thoughts left her mind, and she gasped as he pulled her closer, his mouth warm and honey-sweet.

He pulled away. His mouth trailed over her throat, fitting just beneath her jaw. Her pulse quickened against his lips. She caught her breath, but it was not merely the breathlessness of desire. Her torso ached, and her heart was beating so fast it hurt.

Asfandyar's brows crinkled in concern.

"I apologize," he said, holding her face in his palm. "You need to rest. It will take a month or so for you to truly recover."

"A month!" she cried. "How will I ever survive?"

He shook his head, laughing. "Foolish."

"But I am always foolish when it comes to you," she replied. His cheeks turned pink, and though the sight was unbearably sweet, the words she had said played again in her mind. And there it was again.

She *was* foolish when it came to him. And selfish.

Despite being inexorably overjoyed, she felt dread freezing within her. It was a sinking feeling, and she was taking him down with her.

Before, she had been determined to come to peace with being cursed—but now? If he loved her, and she loved him, if they were together, as they both wished, they would be fused.

Would she curse him, too?

But the answer was already clear. Had the Kebzu attack yesterday not nearly killed him?

Perhaps he was better off away from her. She could not run from her blood, but she could keep from fusing it with his.

But she was too selfish to push him away. She wished to hold him close, always. She did not have the strength to be estranged from him again. The front of the tent opened, and Shirin entered, interrupting Durkhanai's thoughts.

"How are you holding up?" she asked, coming to sit beside Durkhanai. She gave Asfandyar a look, seeing how close he was. "Tum toh piche ho," she told him, narrowing her eyes in a way that said she knew exactly what they were getting up to. "Stop trying to exert her."

"I wasn't—"

Shirin cut him a glance, and he bowed his head. She waved a hand, shooing him away, and he complied. Durkhanai smiled to herself. Shirin really was like a sister to him, and Durkhanai was glad he had that.

After he exited the tent, Shirin turned back to Durkhanai. "I've known him my whole life, you know," Shirin said. "I adore him. There's no one with a better heart. Yesterday . . ." she trailed off, at difficulty for words. "You saved his life. I will forever be indebted to you. Please forgive me for not being a friend earlier, but from here on, you can always count on me to be on your side—on both your sides."

Durkhanai reached over and took Shirin's hand, squeezing tightly. "Thank you," she replied. "It means the world to me."

"Goodbye, for now," Shirin said, standing. "Take care of him."

"I will," Durkhanai promised. Gulalai entered to say goodbye as well, hugging Durkhanai tight on her good side. Her injury was not as drastic, and already Gulalai seemed to be feeling better.

"I'll miss you dreadfully," said Gulalai.

"Yes, I can see just how cut up you are to be traveling back with Shirin," replied Durkhanai. Gulalai grinned, wiggling her brows.

Then Durkhanai was left with Asfandyar. They traveled together in the carriage, with the remaining guards. Because of her injury,

Durkhanai spent much of the journey sleeping, and they stopped often to rest.

Whenever they did stop, Asfandyar made a small fire to warm them, and when she returned to the carriage, she saw that he had placed warm stones wrapped in cloth beneath her feet and behind her back to keep her comfortable.

She slept, in and out, and every time she woke, she saw Asfandyar sitting in front of her, sometimes asleep himself, other times, just gazing out the carriage window, and each time she saw him, she felt at peace.

But it was quickly followed by a more sinister feeling she could not place—a feeling she ignored as she slept again.

They finally made it back to the palace.

They dismounted from the carriage at the entrance, and though she had been sitting for all this time, Durkhanai found she could not walk very far without tiring. She called for a guard to bring her a chair and sat down just as Zarmina and Rashid arrived at the entrance to greet her.

"Alhamdulillah, you are home safe," Zarmina said, hugging her tight. "And don't worry about a thing," she added, when she sensed Durkhanai would begin discussing stately affairs. "We have it entirely under control. I dare say Saifullah is in his element, and you cannot think of robbing him of his usefulness at this time."

"I am glad you're all right," said Rashid. "The both of you."

He clapped Asfandyar on the shoulder. Before anything else could be said, Durkhanai saw someone fast approaching. As the figure neared, she realized it was Naeem-sahib. She braced herself.

"Abu, please," Rashid said to his father, trying to keep him away from Durkhanai.

"No, let him speak his piece," Durkhanai said. Naeem-sahib re-leased a short breath.

"I thank you for your magnanimity," he said, voice tinged with sarcasm. "I have come to say you must marry." Durkhanai blinked, taken aback. "Again, I will push forth the match between you and my son. He handled things excellently while you were gone, but without an official relation to the crown, he can only do so much. Marriage to him will even combat your cursed blood, for our family's lineage is unmarred."

Durkhanai's heart stuttered. Cursed. He had said her blood was cursed. She could not even fault him for it, not when she agreed. But to hear it aloud, from another—it filled her with a suffocating dread.

Would she never know peace? Would she never be rid of this haunting?

"Abu—" Rashid warned, but Naeem-sahib held up a hand to si-lence him.

"If you do not wish to marry a suitable match, I suggest you ab-dicate to Zarmina, who can then marry Rashid," he continued. "The people must be united right now. They need strong leaders, and after your ideas of decentralizing powers from the crown, this concept of unifying, and god knows what else it is you have gotten up to with this Committee of Walis of yours, I think it best for you to step down."

"Is that all?" Durkhanai asked patiently, ironing the emotion from her voice. She would not let him see her rattled. Naeem-sahib blinked, but said nothing further. "Good." She took a breath. "Quite frankly, I do not *have* to do anything. I am the Wali of Marghazar, the throne is mine. I wear the crown, and you cannot tell me what to do, so I sug-gest you stop trying. Out of respect for Rashid, I will not punish you for such insolence, but effective immediately, you are retired. Stay at home and relax. Rashid will handle all further affairs."

Naeem-sahib's face turned red. He opened his mouth to speak once more, but this time, Durkhanai let Rashid cut him off.

"*Enough*, Abu," he said.

With a final glare, Naeem-sahib left.

He was silenced, but Durkhanai feared this was not the last she would hear of him.

Exhausted, Durkhanai let out a sigh.

"I am sorry," Rashid whispered. She looked up at him to see his head bowed, his mien tense. "What he said, about your blood—"

"We are not our forefathers," she said, cutting him off before she could hear him repeat his father's words. He squeezed her hand in gratitude, and she wished she could find similar comfort from her own words.

But while Rashid's father was simply irritating, Durkhanai's father had murdered both his parents in cold blood. She reckoned that was a deeply rooted problem, deep in one's marrow. And that could not be so easily overridden.

"I couldn't marry you, anyway," Rashid said, a small smile turning his lips. Zarmina came to his side and laced her fingers through his, grinning. Durkhanai narrowed her eyes on both of them.

"If you've gone and eloped, I'll kill you both," Durkhanai said, voice deadly.

"No, silly! I would never. I need all the pretty clothes." Zarmina laughed. "But he did formally propose, which he hasn't told his father about just yet."

"*Wow.* Without me?" Durkhanai pretended to be cross.

"Yes, with you gone from the palace, it was so quiet and peaceful . . ." Zarmina took Durkhanai's hand in hers. "I jest. I missed you so desperately and suspect Rashid proposed to lift my spirits."

"Either way, I am glad for you. I must hear all the details!" she replied, but her head was lolling to one side.

Oh, she was so tired.

"Another time," said Zarmina. "You should go see Doctor Aliyah, then rest."

"Yes," Durkhanai said. She intended to stand, but her body did not move. "I can't seem to get up," she said, after another failed attempt at standing.

"Should I carry you?" Asfandyar offered. Zarmina and Rashid exchanged an amused glance.

"Let's not scandalize everyone just yet," Durkhanai said.

"I'll call for a palanquin," Rashid said. When it was brought, they helped her onto the cushion. The four guards lifted her and carried her to her rooms. There, Doctor Aliyah was already waiting.

"Come, let us see," she said. Durkhanai lay down on her bed, Zarmina sitting beside her. The boys crowded at the foot of her bed, waiting anxiously until the doctor turned to them. "Do wait in the other room, gentlemen," she said, hands waiting at the edge of Durkhanai's kurta.

Suddenly realizing she would be in a state of undress, the boys quickly dispersed, though Asfandyar lingered in the doorway, concerned. She waved a hand at him, and he went.

Doctor Aliyah lifted Durkhanai's kurta, then peeled back the cloth wrapping the wound.

"It looks good," she said, as she cleaned the wound. "It isn't infected and looks to be healing already, which is ideal, but it will scar."

Durkhanai did not mind. She would wear it as a badge of honor.

The bravado wore off quickly as Doctor Aliyah and the maids helped Durkhanai bathe. Her whole body ached from the injury and from traveling.

By the time she was cleaned and changed into fresh clothes, she was ready to sleep once more. She lay still as Doctor Aliyah applied a salve to the wound, massaging the surrounding skin, then wrapped the wound.

Durkhanai bit back tears, and Zarmina held her hand.

The pain was excruciating, so Durkhanai shifted her attention to the conversation happening in the next room, between the boys.

"I'm handling him," Rashid said, but he sounded tired.

"He is getting out of hand," Saifullah replied. "We don't want him to do anything rash."

"Let Durkhanai rest, now," Asfandyar said. "We'll deal with Naeem-sahib. Besides, now that he is retired, what can he possibly do?"

"All set," Doctor Aliyah said, bringing Durkhanai's attention back. The doctor pulled Durkhanai's blanket up around her torso, then stood.

"I've applied a salve which should help with accelerating your body's healing, but you must rest often," Doctor Aliyah said. "I will check in with you every day to reapply the salve, and insha' Allah, you will be all right."

"Shukria," said Durkhanai, and the doctor was off.

As the boys reentered the room, Durkhanai settled more comfortably into her bed despite herself. Anxiety spread within her to be resting when there was so much to do, but before she could call for a meeting or find papers to peruse, Zarmina tucked her in more tightly.

"Don't even think of doing anything but resting," she said, voice stern. For a painful moment, it reminded Durkhanai of Dhadi.

"But—" Durkhanai started.

"Tch, Durkhanai, please," Saifullah said.

"We will handle it," Rashid reassured her.

"You must focus on getting better," Asfandyar told her.

"Yes," she mumbled, eyes drooping closed. She was exhausted.

That evening and night, Durkhanai rested, waking only to eat and pray. It did work wonders.

The next day, she felt much restored, and after another visit from Doctor Aliyah, she had enough strength to get out of bed and move about.

She had a pile of papers on her desk to go through, and today, she would be productive. But first, she needed to get dressed in proper clothes.

In her changing room, Durkhanai pulled out a lengha, choli, and shawl to wear. It would be easy to slip into and would keep her warm. She was half dressed when she heard someone enter her room.

"Durkhanai?" called Asfandyar. "Where are you?"

"In here," she called. With a wave of her hand, she dismissed her maids, who did not even look particularly scandalized as they quickly made their exit.

One moment, she was alone, standing in front of her mirror, and the next, he was there.

Asfandyar stopped in the doorway, hands frozen on the curtain he had brushed aside as his gaze snagged on the bare skin of her back. The top was backless except for three tiers of strings which tied the blouse together in the back.

"Will you help me?" she asked innocently. "My injury . . ."

He strode forward in two steps and was behind her, the warmth of his body cocooning her. She watched in the mirror as he brushed her hair aside with a soft touch, his fingers skimming the bare skin of her shoulders.

She shivered. He moved to the first set of strings, pulling them to tie, pulling her closer to him as he did.

Her breath caught in her throat. He moved to the next set of strings, pulling them tight, and she leaned back into him.

As he moved to the last set of strings, their gazes met in the mirror and held for a tense moment.

Durkhanai did not dare breathe.

His ears were tinged pink, and her cheeks were flushed a bright red against her winter-pale skin. She had asked him for help thinking it would tease *him*; now she was just as flustered, if not more so.

*Goodness,* she had to get her head straight.

As if thinking the same thing, he pulled away, exposing her back to the cold air of the room. He gathered her shawl from the chair and set it across her shoulders, hands lingering on her skin.

"There is work to be done," he said, voice hoarse. She pouted, earning her a smile. But he was right.

He kissed her cheek as she sat down to work.

# CHAPTER THIRTY-TWO

*T*hings settled over the next month.

Durkhanai's injury had healed nicely, and she adjusted to her role as Wali, not Badshah. The Lugham Empire accepted the Committee of Walis' treaty, and thus the fighting on their western borders ceased. However, the war in the north intensified, and it was only Marghazar who fought it. The worst of winter was upon them; it was February, where everything was frozen solid. The winter was always long and brutal in the mountains, and while the weather helped to slow down the progression of the war against the Kebzu Kingdom, domestically, it was not so helpful.

Some villages had lost entire stores of food to Wakdar during the siege, but thankfully, through quick thinking and redistribution, Durkhanai was able to manage it, with Saifullah as her chief advisor. The Committee of Walis was also a success, and while there were a few hiccups in the beginning, they slowly eased into working together, and unification proved to be fruitful.

Because they were no longer fighting the Lugham Empire in the east, the war against the Kebzu Kingdom in the north did not hit Marghazar as roughly, and it seemed to be going in quite a manageable fashion.

Rashid and Zarmina were officially engaged, planning their wedding for the summer, which was good in that it kept Naeem-sahib busy. He did not approach Durkhanai again, and she hoped this time, he was silenced for good.

As for she and Asfandyar, they loved one another.

Through the oceans, she searched for a mountain. Beneath the mountain, she entered a marble house, and in that house lay a stone crate. The stone crate cracked open to reveal a wooden box, and in the box, she found a velvet pouch. With shaking hands, she opened the pouch and held her beating heart in her palm.

Yes, it could still be broken, still bleed, but the risk was worth it.

So they loved each other, and loved each other well.

Durkhanai knew she could marry Asfandyar if she wished, but she was afraid. Her people were still in recovery, and she did not wish to further cause disarray by marrying a foreigner.

In another way, too, it felt wrong to choose him now. As if she were benefiting from her grandparents' deaths.

But she wouldn't be a coward. Not again.

That night, as she slept soundly in her bed, a noise stirred her from her sleep. For a moment, she was afraid, but then she saw it was him. She could not discern his features in the darkness, but the outline alone was instantly recognizable to her.

"What is it?" she asked, worried.

"I just wanted to see you."

He lay beside her and instinctively, she wrapped her arms around him.

"You shouldn't be here," she murmured.

"Okay, I'll leave." He got up, and she whimpered.

"Come back."

"These nakhre of yours," he said, shaking his head. "They're—"

"Killing you?" she said, teasing herself.

"No, they are the reason I live."

He slipped into the space beside her. Peace spread through her, having him there. Sleep called to her again, and she closed her eyes, until he tsked, waking her.

"First, you tell me to go, now you sleep and ignore me," he said, voice cross. "Very sad."

She smiled to herself. "Are you angry with me?"

"Yes."

She lifted up on one arm and kissed his cheek, and when he made no response, she kissed his other cheek, again and again until his mouth spread into a smile and she felt him laugh beneath her lips.

"Who can stay angry with you?" he said, more to himself than her. She settled back, and she was really very sleepy, but she latched onto his arm so he would not leave. He winced.

"Your hands are freezing," he said, squirming, but she held on tighter, pressing her toes against his calf. He swore.

"Too late to escape, now," she told him. He held her hand to his chest, and she fell asleep to the steady beat of his heart against her palm.

In the morning, she woke up entwined with him. The sun was far along the sky, a drop of gold amidst the white. They slept in, but there was no rush.

She stretched, breathing deeply. Asfandyar did not rouse when she got out of bed and called for breakfast.

She was being scandalous, but such allowances were afforded to the queen, and anyway, who could scold her? This was her palace, and she was his entirely.

It was a quiet, peaceful morning. Durkhanai hummed to herself as she dressed.

She was pulling her hair back into a simple braid when he roused. Still sleepy, he came up behind her, wrapping his arms around her waist. She smiled at their reflection in the mirror, tying her hair with a ribbon.

"Shabba khair," she said. "Good morning."

"Good morning," he replied, twirling her to face him. She threw her head back and laughed. He kissed her throat with smiling lips as she wrapped her arms around his neck.

They swayed together, dancing, and she was so happy she felt untethered to this world, as if she was floating through air.

"Marry me," he said, breathless. She laughed, and he continued on. "Marry me. I cannot bear another morning without you now that I have tasted this bliss, nor can I imagine another night alone. Be my beginning, my end, the sweetness in between, marry me, marry me," he said, kissing her cheek, her throat, her collar. "Marry me," he said, again and again.

She laughed, and kept on laughing, until finally, he laughed, too.

"Won't you give me a response?" he asked.

She pretended to consider it. "I may need some more convincing."

He grinned, lifting her up in a hug, spinning her around and around, and she cried out in glee. She held his face in her hands and said, "Yes, I will marry you, yes, a thousand times, yes."

She kissed him, long and sweet, for they had all the time in the world. His mouth trailed over her throat, fitting just beneath her jaw. Her pulse quickened against his lips.

Someone knocked on the door, bringing them back to the real world, which was all right, as long as he was by her side, and as long as they had mornings like this, nights like last night, and everything in between.

Servants brought breakfast into the room, then retreated, leaving them alone. Durkhanai sat across from him, watching as he poured her chai, watching as he broke his puri and dipped it into the cholay.

She couldn't stop looking at him. His every movement was beautiful to her; his very existence was.

She held a hand to her heart because it hurt to feel so fully. But she was glad for it all the same and wouldn't give it up for anything. And she remembered Agha-Jaan's last words to her; *be happy*.

She intended to.

The rest of the day progressed, meetings and the business of being a leader. In the evening, she met with her advisors, but they were more her friends, and they must have noticed something.

"You won't stop smiling," Saifullah told her. "It's unnerving."

Durkhanai grinned, looking at Asfandyar. He nodded.

"We are engaged," she said. Rashid, Zarmina, and Saifullah exchanged a three-way glance, not reacting. Her lips turned down into a pout. "Oh, hello," she said, snapping her fingers. "Did you hear me? Asfandyar proposed, and I accepted. Where is the excitement?"

"Are we meant to be surprised?" asked Saifullah, smiling.

Zarmina laughed. "You two aren't exactly subtle."

"It's true," Rashid agreed. "About damn time!"

But even so, they all laughed, standing to congratulate and hug both her and Asfandyar.

Durkhanai was missing Gulalai desperately, but she would write to her and tell her to come immediately.

"Wait a second," Saifullah said, as if realizing something. "Out of the five of us, there are now two couples. This is insufferable!" He shook his head dramatically. "You must find new advisors to even us out."

In response, Durkhanai laughed. She would tease him about finding someone himself, but she knew he wasn't interested in romantic relationships, that he was perfectly content in the other relationships he had.

"Bako mat," Zarmina said to Saifullah. "You're ruining the mood. This is so exciting!"

Zarmina hugged Durkhanai again, and they jumped up and down, while Rashid clapped his hand on Asfandyar's shoulder. Everyone was grinning ear to ear. They spent the rest of the meeting making jokes and teasing one another.

There was so much happiness—but something else, too.

There was this cloying feeling she couldn't shake. It had been with her all day and all last night, and she did not understand what it was exactly.

She tried to ignore it, but it was getting harder to overlook. That evening, Asfandyar took dinner with her in her room, and the strange feeling only intensified, making her distracted.

"What is it?" he asked. She realized he had been talking and she wasn't paying attention. She tried to offer him a lighthearted smile.

"We must stay apart now until we are wed," she told him.

"Because you enjoy tormenting me?"

"Yes."

With a dramatic sigh, he stood and came to kiss her cheek, then left as instructed.

That night, when she went to sleep alone, it was more torment for herself. She tossed and turned through the dark hours, drifting in and out of consciousness.

It was guilt she felt. After everything she had done, did she deserve such happiness? Did she deserve Asfandyar, or to be the Wali, or any of these blessings?

She felt haunted by ghosts. While she did not have nightmares so often anymore, they still came every once in a while, drenched in blood. Her stomach twisted at the imagery. She suddenly felt disgusted with herself.

Asfandyar was so *good*, and she was rotten to the bone. Would she corrupt him? She was trying, yes, but was it enough?

Would it ever be?

During the day, she was able to keep such insecurities at bay, but at night, more and more, she felt damned. Haunted.

And if she was truly cursed, was it something she wanted to perpetuate by marrying and having children? She would only curse them as her father cursed her, as her grandfather cursed him. When would it end? It never would, not unless she ended it now.

And, oh, she should not have thought of children because there was nothing she wanted more. She loved Asfandyar so much, and to have children born of that love would be a dream—but would she not inadvertently corrupt those children, too?

It wasn't her fault, she knew. She wasn't being emotional about it, but practical. It couldn't be helped.

She wasn't sure.

Perhaps she should talk to Asfandyar about it. In a way, she knew he would say the right thing, that he would not let her go—but was that not selfish of her? To let him do such a thing?

Perhaps the logic was flawed, anyway. For Zarmina was to marry Rashid, and she did not feel the same guilt. But Zarmina and Saifullah were often likened to their father, while Durkhanai was always likened to her grandfather and to Nazo.

Durkhanai even looked just like them. Sometimes she looked in the mirror, and in her blue-green eyes, she did not see herself, but Nazo, Wakdar, Agha-Jaan. Two of which were dead and the one left was rotting away in a cell, driven to madness with vengeance and grief.

Durkhanai was afraid for the future. Right now, everything was good and perfect, but what would she become, should things change for the worse?

What had she become, already?

She had the blood of her father on her hands, and he the blood of his, a vicious cycle. She did not wish to be a part of it, but she was, all the same.

It was as if she had wickedness lying dormant within her, and no matter what she did, she could not expunge it from her veins.

Where did that leave her?

She tossed and turned all night, sleep and peace evading her.

# CHAPTER THIRTY-THREE

Durkhanai slept long into the next day, stirring only when she was jolted awake.

"Durkhanai, wake up," Zarmina said, shaking her. "Wake up!"

The tightness of her voice made Durkhanai instantly rouse, and when she opened her eyes, she saw worry etched across Zarmina's features. Fear crashed over her. She knew it was all too good to be true.

"What is it?" Durkhanai asked, heart seizing. "What is it?"

Tears welled in her eyes and spilled across her cheeks.

"If anything has happened to him . . ." she said. Zarmina blinked, confused, then shook her head.

"No, no, Asfandyar is all right." She hugged Durkhanai close. "It isn't him. It's Naeem-sahib."

The grief was quickly replaced with dread. "What has he done?"

"When Saifullah announced your engagement . . ." Zarmina paused. "He took it as an opportunity. Durkhanai, he's launched a coup."

"*Kya?* He did what? There's no way."

"I did not believe it, either, but he has managed it," Zarmina continued. "He claims that your engagement to a foreigner makes you unsuitable as our leader, and he is using the haziness caused by the unification transition period to support his claim."

"But *you* were married to Asfandyar!" Durkhanai exclaimed.

"Yes, but I am not the Wali, and that was because of the trial." Zarmina paused. "He claims you have no respect for traditions and is calling for you to abdicate to Rashid and I. We have made it clear we do not support Naeem-sahib's coup, but he has garnered some support from other older nobles."

Durkhanai set her jaw. So this was why he had been quiet these past few weeks.

He must have been carefully working toward this, and her engagement to Asfandyar had proved the perfect catalyst for him.

Well, she would not give him what he wanted.

Getting out of bed, Durkhanai quickly dressed and called for a private meeting with Naeem-sahib. There had to be a way to resolve this. She could not merely dismiss him, as she had tried previously. He had proven that by gaining the support of fellow noblemen. Rashid would not be able to deter his father, either.

It was up to Durkhanai to manage.

"Well?" she asked, when he met with her. It was just them two. "What, precisely, is your problem?"

Naeem-sahib sat. "Quite simply, you are not fit to rule."

He did not say the words with malice, but casual certainty. That was what struck her. How sure he was in his statement. It was not driven by petty emotions but *facts*. It pressed deep into the insecurities within her.

"How so?" she asked, trying to keep her voice steady. Her bravado dwindled. She had thought Naeem-sahib had led this coup out of anger, and she would have met his rage with her own. But this—this was different.

"You are guilty of being cursed," he said. "You should have never killed Wakdar. You are cursed, and you will curse the people, as well. Perhaps not right away, but eventually, you will; you cannot run from your blood. And it will lead all of us to ruin. The people have come to believe this, too."

Durkhanai's heartbeat quickened as he gave voice to her innermost fears. She had come to this meeting expecting to clash with Naeem-sahib based on trivial sentiments—she assumed he did not like her because she was young and spoiled; or because she had rejected his son; or because she loved Asfandyar, a foreigner.

She did not expect to understand his perspective. Heart hammering, she tried to collect her thoughts, not speaking for a moment.

"You, too, understand this," he said. "It is why you are not immediately denying the claim." His voice softened. When she looked at him, she saw truth written on his face. "I do not say this with malignant intent, but genuine concern for our people." He paused. "Which is why I, and those who support me, believe there is still a solution."

She blinked, considering it, and then she understood. There was only one way to prove such superstition away, and it was with something wrought of the same substance.

Her heart dropped, but she steeled herself.

"Very well," she said. "You have accused me, and there is only one way to discern my judgment." She swallowed. "A trial."

"So you are not so far removed from our customs, after all." Naeem-sahib leaned back in his seat. "Yes, a trial will determine your fate. There are enough people who are suspicious of you being cursed that a trial must confirm or deny it, or your standing as a ruler will never be sure. There will always be that doubt."

"I understand."

He was right, and she knew it.

She did not think she could effectively rule with this doubt living within her, either. Already, peace evaded her in such a manner she felt she would never truly be able to grasp it.

She was haunted, even in her happiest moments. Perhaps the trial would give her the respite she sought.

"But the trial will occur under my terms," she said.

"As you wish," Naeem-sahib replied. He was not doing this with ill-intent, out of greed or spite, she could see that. He and his supporters genuinely believed she might be cursed, genuinely saw she was unfit to rule if that was the case.

Well, the trial would answer the question.

"If I am innocent, I will marry Asfandyar and rule, and you will not attempt to hinder me," she said. "If I am guilty, I freely leave Zarmina and Rashid as my successors."

"Those terms are acceptable."

"I will take it from you in writing," she said. "In front of all other nobles to bear witness." She turned to a guard and ordered him to gather the nobles in one of the conference rooms and went to meet them.

On the way, Saifullah found her. Naeem-sahib went on as she stayed back to speak with her cousin.

"What's happening?" Saifullah asked. "What will you say to the nobles when they arrive? I assume you have a plan."

Durkhanai took a deep breath. "I do."

He waited for her to tell him, and she couldn't bring herself to say the words. She knew he would try and stop her, and she couldn't allow it. She was a queen, not a spoiled child, bending things to her whims. She would think of her people first, not herself.

"You won't tell me," Saifullah said, when she still did not speak.

"After," she said, voice weary. "Tell the other advisors, as well."

"Durkhanai—" he began, but she shook her head.

"After," she promised.

She took the slower route to the meeting room, and when she arrived, the other nobles were there, waiting for her. She did not detect animosity on any of them, just staunch belief.

"A trial is the best course of action, Your Excellency," one noble, an elder woman, said. "It will leave no room for doubt."

Durkhanai agreed. She wrote the terms of her trial, then signed it with each of them to witness. No matter the outcome, there would be no trouble, for her people believed in the trial, and would accept its outcome, whatever it would be. The matter was closed.

After all the nobles had left, Durkhanai stayed in the room, sitting in silence, staring at her own signature. She had expected her hands to shake when she'd signed, but they'd been perfectly still.

Even as she left the room, she felt a strange solace spread through her. She was confident in her decision—until Asfandyar found her and she saw the grief plain on his face.

It was the cruelest thing she could do to him.

"Durkhanai, what—what is this?" he asked, voice breaking. She pressed a hand to her heart and shook her head.

"I'm sorry," she said, tears welling in her eyes. "But it's the only way."

The only right way, at least.

"How could this be?" he asked, taking her hands in his, pulling her near. "I cannot risk losing you."

It was an awful thing to put him through. If she was guilty, she would be torn to shreds. She was not so removed from her own nightmares of his trial to imagine what that would feel like for him, especially after he had almost lost her in the Kebzu attack; especially after he had witnessed Naina's death.

After everything, they had finally found each other again, and this might be their end. She hated that.

"I must do this," she said. "It is what is right. It is what a good ruler would do."

"How?" he asked, incredulous. "How can this be right?"

"The nobles believe it! I could ignore them, retire or fire them all, make them silent, punish them—but to what end? It would not solve this, this haunting, this curse that might exist within me." She took a deep breath. "I must face it."

"Don't face it," he said, eyes mad. "Let's run. Let Zarmina and Rashid take over, and let's run."

For a moment, she considered it, but of course, she could not. She might be selfish, but she was not that selfish; she would not abandon her people thus. If she ran, she would be a coward, and she did not wish to be. If she ran, the question of whether she was cursed or not would continue to live inside of her, and it would inevitably affect Asfandyar. Maybe she should run on her own, away from them all, save them from herself—but what would be the use in a life like that? To be alone, far from her people, and her land, and her love.

No, she would rather face it now and know.

If she was guilty, she would accept her fate.

"I love you for saying it, but that won't solve anything," she told him. "I must do this."

"Are you crazy?" he cried. "I can't lose you, not again. Please, don't."

His voice broke on the words. Tears filled his eyes, and her heart shattered for causing him this pain. She pulled him into her arms, and he buried his face in her neck, holding her tight.

"I'm sorry," she whispered. "I'm so sorry, but I have to. I must."

It was bigger than her. Her people were superstitious, and so was she. Durkhanai knew this doubt within her would only grow and fester and become worse.

But they all believed in the trial. It would give them a conclusive answer and put this matter to rest, never be revisited again.

"You don't," he said. She shook her head.

"It isn't just Naeem-sahib and some villagers who think I am cursed," she said. "*I* believe it. If I am innocent in the trial, perhaps I can be free of this wretched feeling. If I am guilty, then perhaps the monster is what I deserve."

"No, please," he said. "Durkhanai, you aren't cursed, you are a blessing—the best blessing I have ever received. Don't take it away from me now."

Durkhanai was crying then, too, but she had to do it. She could not explain it further.

She had to do it, or she may never know peace.

She kissed him one last time, lips salty with tears, then pulled away and left him. It was the right decision, she knew it was.

It was what she reiterated to Saifullah, then again to Zarmina and Rashid, as each of them tried to intervene, tried to stop her.

"I must do this," she said, again and again. "I must."

Eventually, they understood. She would not be stopped.

By evening, Asfandyar had already gone away to the suite for the lady—or in this case, for the man. It was after he'd gone that Zarmina came to Durkhanai's room once more.

"Do not try to talk me out of it," Durkhanai warned, voice weary. "It is already done."

"That is not why I am here," Zarmina said, coming to sit with Durkhanai on the bed. "I know which door Asfandyar is behind. It's the—"

"Zarmina, no!" Durkhanai cried, covering her ears. She did not wish to know. "Let fate decide. I won't cheat again."

"But—" Zarmina began, crestfallen.

"No, please." Durkhanai's tone was final. "Let the trial run fair."

Zarmina sighed. "I will respect your wishes." She frowned. "Though I did go through all the trouble of finding out."

"Did Asfandyar tell you?" Durkhanai asked.

"No, he said to let you choose your own fate," she replied. "That he would not interfere."

He knew her so well. God, she loved him. She loved all of them.

"Thank you, anyways," Durkhanai said, pulling Zarmina into a hug. Zarmina pulled away quickly, not lingering.

"We won't say goodbye," Zarmina said, voice tight. "It'll be much too silly. Instead, I will see you tomorrow evening, where you will let me choose three of your prettiest dresses as recompense for putting us all through such a dreadful ordeal. Rashid would like a new sword made. And I'm sure we can find some boring books to appease Saiful-lah. As for Asfandyar, I am sure you know best how to please him." Zarmina wiggled her brows conspiratorially, and Durkhanai laughed.

"Done," she said, smiling through her tears. With a final squeeze of her hand, Zarmina stood and left. Durkhanai was alone, and she would stay alone.

If she saw anyone, she might lose her resolve, and she had to see this through. She needed an answer, or she would spend her whole life in unease.

Perhaps she was guilty, and justice needed to be served. She had committed so many wrongs, perhaps this would finally put her to rest. If she was innocent, then, she would know.

She could not be haunted any longer. She would not. Alone in her room, she was calm, on the brink of solace.

That night, she did not dream.

When she woke, it was time for her trial.

# CHAPTER THIRTY-FOUR

*T*he appointed hour arrived.

Durkhanai entered the arena, her heart beating like a roaring river in her ears. The crowds were silent as she walked forward under a pale white sky. A breeze carried through the air, and the people clutched their shawls and their children close.

As was custom, Durkhanai turned to look at the throne. It lay empty, but the surrounding area was filled. She saw the respected nobles and Saifullah. Her gaze traveled to Zarmina, who was clutching Rashid's arm.

Durkhanai knew that if it came to it, the pair would take care of her people.

Her beloved people.

She looked across the scores of people gathered in the arena, all of them standing, waiting with bated breath. Their eyes were wide with worry and anticipation.

She had never seen such a crowd.

It seemed every person from the mountain and valley had gathered. A spectacle to trump all spectacles: the queen herself on trial.

With a deep breath, Durkhanai faced the doors; those fateful and those fatal portals. She did not find them hideous anymore but natural. There was a beauty in that, too.

Durkhanai lifted her chin. She would not look back now. Her gaze was focused entirely on the doors. She regarded them carefully, waiting to feel pulled to one over the other, waiting for fate to nudge her forward with its hand.

If she was guilty, she would die.

She was afraid to die, as all people were. She did not wish to leave her loved ones behind. She did not wish to die like this, torn apart, limb by limb.

Being ripped to shreds by a lion was no easy death. But if it was what was written for her, she would bear it. It would not last long, besides, and then she knew her grandparents were waiting for her, as was the mother she had never known.

But if she was innocent, she would marry the great love of her life. Her life would stretch ahead of her, filled with peace and beauty and wonder.

Either way, she knew her people would be okay. That was the important thing. If she chose the door with the monster, she was cursed, and it was best for Zarmina and Rashid to rule.

If she chose the door with the man, she was blessed, and she would rule with Asfandyar by her side. She would spend her life atoning for her sins and doing better for her people, knowing it was not a futile effort.

Durkhanai was here to accept her fate.

She took a step closer to the doors, staying in between them, not yet choosing. Her heartbeat quickened until it deafened all else. She was afraid, in truth, but there was a solace spreading through her as well.

She closed her eyes, and in the darkness, she felt a nudge. She took a deep breath and chose.

The door opened.

# THE END

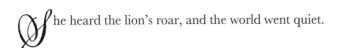

She heard the lion's roar, and the world went quiet.

# A DIFFERENT ENDING

*D*urkhanai couldn't see.

She sat on a pillow on the floor, looking at the pattern of mehndi on her hands. Beyond that, everything was covered by the veil that sat across her head, masking her from view. Across from her was a curtain of fresh flowers, and their scent filled the air.

Durkhanai's heartbeat was steady in her ears, and she bit back a smile as she searched the pattern of dark maroon swirls on her hands. The girl who had done her mehndi had hidden his name in there, as was custom, and again and again Durkhanai's gaze went to the shape of Asfandyar's name etched onto her hands.

She hoped the mehndi would never fade, but she knew even when it did, his name would never be gone from the lines of her palm. He was her ending, her beginning, her everything, and she sat here now to prove it.

He sat on the other side of the curtain of flowers, on an identical pillow. Beside him, the maulvi finished giving the wedding khutbah.

It was time.

Saifullah asked her. "Do you accept this marriage?"

"Qabool hai," she replied. "I do."

"Do you accept this marriage?"

"Qabool hai."

"Do you accept this marriage?"

"Qabool hai."

They asked Asfandyar next, and she heard his voice tight with tears when he said, "Qabool hai."

Thus, they were wed.

The hall erupted in the chaos of celebration. Around her, she heard the swish of fabrics and the tinkling of jewelry as people hugged, but still she could not properly see. She knew she was supposed to be demure like a proper bride, but she snuck glances through the thin fabric of her veil. Zarmina, Gulalai, and Shirin surrounded her, as well as her cousins and their children. On the other side, Saifullah and Rashid were hugging Asfandyar and each other, joining along in congratulating him and her other male family members.

Everyone wore shades of white, and the decor was similarly white and gold. It reminded her of when the world was covered in white from the first snow of the season, but it was no longer winter. It was May, and the landscape was in full bloom.

Finally, Asfandyar stood and approached the curtain of flowers which separated him. She looked down as he parted the flowers and approached.

"May I sit with my bride?" he asked politely, when Zarmina and Gulalai made no move to get up from their positions on either side of Durkhanai.

"You'll have to pay up first," said Gulalai, holding out her hand.

"Will this suffice?" Asfandyar asked, holding up a bag of coins.

Zarmina and Gulalai exchanged a glance. "Surely such a coveted seat is worth more to you than that," Gulalai said.

"Chalo, don't torment the poor guy," Saifullah said, doing sifarish on Asfandyar's behalf. "That's surely a good amount."

"I really don't think so," Zarmina said, getting comfier beside Durkhanai.

Durkhanai smiled as the girls extorted money from Asfandyar, going back and forth.

"Yaar, do something," Asfandyar said to Rashid. "Or I won't be saving you any money at your own wedding."

"Zarmina, meri jaan, take this and please let the poor man sit with his wife," Rashid said, procuring another bag of coins. Zarmina smiled, accepting it, then stood.

"Thank you for your business," Gulalai said, standing as well.

Asfandyar sat beside her. Durkhanai was trying desperately hard not to grin because her cheeks were already hurting, but she couldn't help it.

She was so happy.

She had felt at peace since the trial, but this joy was another thing altogether.

He sat beside her, and she pressed her leg against his, craving contact. However, she still did not look up.

Zarmina slid a mirror onto Durkhanai's lap, extending onto Asfandyar's knee, and that was how he got his first look. It was an old tradition, but for that moment, it was just them, gazing at one another in their shared reflection. She smiled, just for him.

It was just them two, and that was everything.

She saw there were tears in his eyes as he lifted her veil, and the world widened, and there was everyone else, celebrating, cheering. Durkhanai grinned, taking it all in.

Festivities had been going on for the past two weeks, during which she had barred him from seeing her, and while it had been hard, it was worth it now. She had missed him desperately, and now he was beside her, never to leave her side again.

Then food was served and through the chaos of the wedding event, of greeting people and accepting gifts and exchanging hugs and kisses, his knee pressed against hers, their sides aligned as if fused.

"Congratulations," Nazo Phuppo said. She slipped an anklet into Durkhanai's hand. "It was Ammi's."

"Thank you, Phuppo," Durkhanai said, smiling up at her aunt. Nazo, deciding to attempt recovery from her madness, was allowed brief respite from her jail cell in the palace's tower for the occasion, while heavily guarded of course.

While Durkhanai could not forgive Nazo for orchestrating her mother's death and the hand she played in her grandparents' deaths, it gave Durkhanai hope to see Nazo choose life rather than to waste away.

"Bohat mubarak ho," Naeem-sahib said, coming up next to congratulate them. Durkhanai smiled.

"Thank you," she replied.

When the trial had proven her innocent, she had been deemed divinely blessed, and Naeem-sahib had fallen back into line. She held no grudges against him, and once more, he was a valuable ally to the throne.

It was with his help that they also eventually ended the war against the Kebzu Kingdom. Everything else, too, was good in her zilla.

This was the best day of her life, and it was the first of many more to come, though not all were as extravagant.

There were the quiet mornings, the days working, the nights spent in each other's arms. Durkhanai no longer believed she was cursed, and thus, she opened the whole of her heart to Asfandyar and watched how their love expanded and filled her, more and more.

Every time she thought she had met the limit of her love, she surprised herself. The heart held such infinite capacities.

A few years after their marriage, she was blessed with a baby boy. He looked just like Asfandyar, and she was glad for it, for his beautiful dark curls and dimples. Their son had blue-green eyes, but rather than seeing Agha-Jaan or Wakdar in them, all Durkhanai saw was herself, and he was beautiful.

A few years later, she had a baby girl, who had Durkhanai's honey curls and little freckles across her cheeks that Asfandyar spent every free moment counting and kissing.

Just as he was doing now.

He stood out in the garden, which was covered in snow. It was so beautiful and bright, pure and perfect. After the trial, Durkhanai stopped seeing blood in the snow, stopped having nightmares about it, and now all she saw was the beautiful white.

Through the window, she saw their son was playing in the snow with Zarmina's son. Asfandyar held their baby girl, and around him, everyone she loved was there: Rashid and Zarmina; Saifullah; even Gulalai and Shirin were visiting. They were crowded around a bonfire, eating roasted mumphali and chilgozay.

"I want phali!" her son said, seeing Saifullah cracking the peanuts open. "I want phali! Where's Mama?"

"Yes, where is Mama?" Gulalai asked.

"She's coming," replied Asfandyar with a laugh. They were all waiting for her.

With a smile, she opened the door and went out to meet them.

# A PARTING RIDDLE

And so I leave it with all of you:

Which came out of the opened door—the man, or the monster?

# ACKNOWLEDGMENTS

*A*lhamdulillah. Everything I have and am is because of the grace of God.

Thank you to my family: my parents, my sister, my brothers, my grandparents, my aunts, and my uncles. My cousins: Noor, Mahum, Hamnah, and Umaymah. My best friends: Arusa, Isra, Sara, and Justine. My dear friends: Uroosa, Sadaf, Humnah, and Silke. My incredible agent, Emily Keyes. My brilliant editor, Bridget McFadden, and copyeditor, Elana Gibson.

Thank you to the publishing team at CamCat Books. To my friends from Twitter and all the book bloggers who boost my work. The people who sent me memes and fan art: Liya, Tajrean, Cossette, Humnah, and Aliyah. To everyone who has rated or reviewed my books or even just bought them and never read them. To all my friends, extended family, family-friends, and perfect strangers who have shown me so much love, excitement, support, and joy. I thank you from the bottom of my heart. There is warmth in my life because of you all.

Most importantly, I must thank the readers who came back for more of this story. I sincerely hope you enjoyed it and that I was able to do these characters justice.

Please pray for me.

# ABOUT THE AUTHOR

Aamna Qureshi is a Pakistani, Muslim American who adores words. She grew up on Long Island, New York, in a very loud household, surrounded by English (for school), Urdu (for conversation), and Punjabi (for emotion). Much of her childhood was spent being grounded for reading past her bed-time, writing stories in the backs of her notebooks, and being scolded by teachers for passing chapters under the tables. Through her writing, she wishes to inspire a love for the beautiful country and rich culture that informed much of her identity.

When she's not writing, she loves to travel to new places where she can explore different cultures or to Pakistan where she can revitalize her roots. She also loves baking complicated desserts, drinking fancy teas and coffees, watching sappy rom-coms, and going for walks about the estate (her backyard). She currently lives in New York. Look for her on IG @aamna_qureshi and Twitter @aamnaqureshi_.

If you've enjoyed

Aamna Qureshi's *The Man or the Monster,*

you'll enjoy

*Jester* by Brielle Porter.

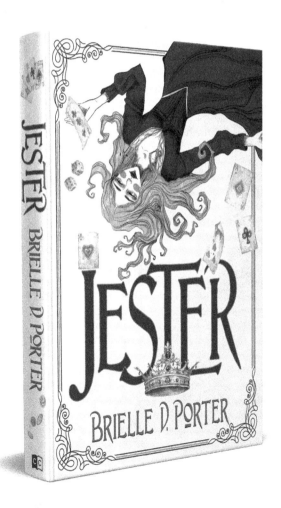

# CHAPTER ONE

*A* group of tourists has gathered to watch me throw knives at a shopboy. They've come here for magic; I've kept them here with misdirection and lies. Maybe it's not magic exactly, but it is undeniably entertaining watching my unwilling assistant flinch every time the knife point gets too close to his groin. I hold the knife steady, aiming, watching his limp hair flop as the wooden wheel he's strapped to slowly rotates.

Stefan lets out a whimper, and I toss him a smile. He was a lot braver in the shop where I'd found him, flirting as he bagged my books. It hadn't been hard to trick him into volunteering.

The crowd jeers.

"Aim lower!"

"Aim *higher*! Maim his ugly face!"

"Throw three at once!"

"Mirage, don't you dare!" Stefan shouts.

The nighttime crowd is always hungrier for violence.

I hold up my hands placatingly.

"Obviously, I can't throw three knives at once. That would be dangerous and highly irresponsible . . ."

There are a couple of groans, but my reputation must precede me, because there are a few whoops and chuckles thrown in as well. With a sweep, I pull my deadliest knife from my belt, the one with the wicked serrated edge, brandishing it for the crowd.

"But I think we can spice things up a bit!"

I stab the knife into a vat of oil, the shimmering liquid sliding down the tang of the blade. Then, with a flourish, I sweep it through a nearby torch. Flame devours the knife. The crowd roars its approval. Stefan pales.

The hilt burns in my hand, throwing off sparks, as I wonder if perhaps I've gone too far. I've only tried this a few times. And the jackrabbit I had caught to practice with wasn't even good to eat after, blackened to an inedible crisp.

Either way, I'll give them a show.

Even though the knife feels like it's blistering my palm, I take a moment to pan the audience. This is always my favorite part. The tension is a palpable thing, visible in held gasps, wide eyes, and awe.

Magic.

And that's when I see him. Expression carefully neutral, almost bored, one eyebrow raised, arms folded across a suit that costs more than my father made in a year. A seeker.

My heart pounds, as I realize more than Stefan's crotch is at stake here now. If I nail this, that pretentious clown in a suit has the power to get my act in front of the queen. I could be the next jester. It's the reason I've come here tonight, the same reason I've performed for thousands of crowds like this one.

Sucking in a breath, I hold the knife level. Stefan thrashes, but the binding's pinning him to the wheel like a dead butterfly hold. Right as I pull back to throw, there's a shout.

"Kingkiller!"

The knife slips in my grip, but it's too late. I watch, horrified, as the blade wobbles in the air, the trajectory off. It clatters to the ground a few feet away from Stefan, flames smothered in the dirt. There's a moment of shocked silence, as though the crowd is waiting for me to do something.

Make a joke. Throw another knife. *Something*. I can still save this. Even Stefan gawps at me as I stare unseeing at the crowd. But I don't do anything. I just stand there, the word pounding in my head, over and over.

*Kingkiller.*

Even real magic couldn't save me now. It couldn't save my father—traitor to the throne and murderer of the king. Not that I have magic anyway, as my father's magic died with him when they executed him for treason. Leaving my family disgraced, leaving me to peddle illusion in a cheap imitation of the real thing.

The seeker is gone. I watched him leave, head shaking as if disappointed, the crowd swallowing him up again. My one big shot, gone as quickly as the smoke from my act.

I gather up my knives, suddenly too exhausted to even finish the show. There are a few shouted threats, but I hardly notice through the fog of disappointment. I can't believe it's over. Seventeen months I've waited for the opportunity to impress a seeker, and with just one word, it's over. And I didn't even make enough gold dust to buy myself dinner.

I loosen Stefan's bindings, my fingers slipping as a loud gasp from the nearby crowd steals my attention. Stefan drops with a thud and a curse, but I hardly hear his complaints. Most of my audience has wandered off, inflating the already bloated numbers of the show next to mine. The entire stretch of street, known fondly to those in the business as the Noose, is filled with performers clamoring to be seen. Nowhere else in the kingdom of Terraca is there a place so glutted with magic: everything from the mundane enchantments like the ones used to keep the hotels refreshingly cool inside—even here in the desert—to the spectacular.

Sandwiched between the most impressive hotels in Oasis—including the impressive Crown Hotel—the Noose is one of the best spots to snag wealthy patrons with too much gold in their wallets and too much liquor in their blood.

A bolt of lightning so bright it leaves a streak in my vision cracks the pavement several feet away. Applause and gold nuggets are thrown at the magician, who bows.

Ignoring Stefan's shouts, I wander over to see what has the tourists so hot. I've seen most of the shows in the Noose multiple times; after all, I've got to maintain a healthy edge over my competitors. So, I'm not surprised when I recognize the performer instantly. His name rises in my throat like bile. Luc.

Long blond hair swept into a knot on top of his head and with a jawline that could cut glass, Luc is one of the most popular acts on the Noose, besides my own. Even with his face arranged in an arrogant sneer, he's still irritatingly handsome. A simple flourish of his long red coat sparks deafening applause. The crowds love him and he knows it. His gaze sweeps the crowd greedily, sucking in the cheers as though they physically sustain him.

I know the feeling well.

I jolt when his eyes land on me, pick me out in the crowd. I want to shrink, to disappear, the same caught feeling as a mouse in the gaze of a hawk.

"Can I have a volunteer, please?"

The hand of every eligible woman in the crowd shoots up. He grins, cocky, surveying the desperate volunteers. He raises an eyebrow at me, intention clear. I cross my arms, unwilling to give him the satisfaction of a reaction. With a disappointed shake of his head so slight I could've imagined it, he selects a different young woman.

Even from where I stand near the back of the crowd, it's obvious she is heartbreakingly lovely and fantastically wealthy. Luc's smile broadens as he helps her onstage. Flowing blonde hair, full lips, flushed cheeks, and a garnet necklace like a collar of blood against her pale throat. I roll my eyes. Luc definitely has a type.

He takes her hand gently and leans in to whisper something in her ear. She titters, cheeks rosy. She's clearly enraptured, unaware of the fate that awaits her, a butterfly in a web. Even if she did know, I doubt she'd care. Half the women in this audience have seen Luc's show before, and in spite of its macabre ending, they still keep coming in droves. He ignores her fluttering lashes, his eyes finding me again in the crowd.

A chill runs down my spine.

Without breaking eye contact, he stabs the girl onstage. And even though I've seen his show hundreds of times, know exactly how it ends, a gasp breaks free from my tight lips as she crumples to the ground. Blood stains the wood around her, a stage that has seen its fair share of death. Seeing my reaction, he actually has the nerve to smile as she bleeds out on the ground beside him.

He steps away from the blood before it can reach his expensive snakeskin boots, ignoring the paunchy man who clambers onstage with him, pawing frantically at the bloody maiden.

"Olivia! What have you done to her? Olivia, wake up!"

Olivia's father, I assume, if his age and resemblance to the girl are any indicator. Luc smiles down benevolently at the man, whose face is blotchy and panicked. Tears run down his cheek as he blubbers, and my gut clenches both in shame for him and pity.

"Who will pay the debt for this maiden?" Luc asks. He doesn't extend a hand to the man, who grasps at his trousers, unaware of the blood that stains his fine clothes.

"I will," the man cries, wiping the snot from his face. "Please, I'll do anything! Just bring back my daughter."

Luc has chosen wisely; it's obvious this man will pay anything for his jewel of a daughter. Luc eyes him as though weighing a handful of gold dust and then glances at the ropes of garnets choking the woman's fragile neck. The desperate father seizes upon his meaning, and with shaking fingers unclasps the heavy necklace and passes it to Luc. Holding it up for the crowd first, Luc pockets the jewels with a satisfied smile.

"The debt has been paid. Arise, fair maiden!"

For a moment nothing happens. Everyone's eyes are on the girl, whose lips have turned a faint blue. But my eyes are on Luc. I can see the strain as he tries to bring her back from Beyond. The sweat that runs, neglected, down his temple. The clenched fists. Watching for any kind of rise in her lungs. But they stay still.

I've only seen Luc fail once. That girl's family was desolate but could do nothing, because that's what these wealthy fools come here for. To be thrilled. To be entertained, no matter the cost. And Luc never fails to give them a show.

Heart pounding, I watch Luc cross the stage, jaw tight. To anyone else he looks collected, but I can see the way his teeth grind. *She's not coming back,* I think, and before I can register the thought, Luc lifts the dead girl up and kisses her passionately. The man, her father, I remember numbly, lets out a startled cluck like a chicken on a chopping block.

For a minute it's deathly silent.

Then the girl gasps for air, hands scrabbling at Luc's neck. I let out a gust of air, then feel my lungs inflate as hers do. Luc bows to riotous applause as gold nuggets rain on the stage. No one sees the girl, whose lips are still blue, whose lungs struggle to reset, her father crying into her hair. She'll likely suffer brain damage, being without oxygen for as long as she was. That's the price of magic, true magic. Luc's show is cruel but effective. There's a reason he's known on the Noose as the devil. Sell him your soul, and he'll give you a show. And although I'm loath to admit it, he's my biggest competition for the position of Jester.

Sure enough, not one, but two seekers have joined him onstage. I watch as they fight for his attention, eager to claim the commission that comes with finding a worthy act. As though he can feel my eyes on him, Luc lifts his gaze from the seekers. I can read the words on his lips as clearly as if he spoke:

"Kingkiller."

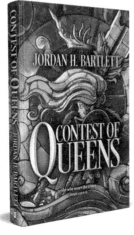

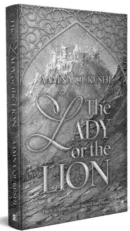

# CamCat
## Books

VISIT US ONLINE FOR MORE BOOKS TO LIVE IN:

CAMCATBOOKS.COM

CamCatBooks   @CamCatBooks   @CamCat_Books